THE LAST

—— OF THE ——

LUMBERMEN

THE LAST
——— OF THE ———
LUMBERMEN

A NOVEL BY
BRIAN FAWCETT

Cormorant Books

**Canada Council
for the Arts** **Conseil des Arts
du Canada**

 Canadian Patrimoine
Heritage canadien **Canadä**

The publisher gratefully acknowledges the support of the
Canada Council for the Arts and the Ontario Arts Council for its
publishing program. We acknowledge the financial support of the
Government of Canada through the Canada Book Fund (CBF) for our
publishing activities, and the Government of Ontario through the
Ontario Media Development Corporation, an agency of the Ontario
Ministry of Culture, and the Ontario Book Publishing Tax Credit Program.

Library and Archives Canada Cataloguing in Publication

Fawcett, Brian, 1944–, author
The last of the lumberman / Brian Fawcett.

Issued in print and electronic formats.
ISBN 978-1-77086-287-6 (pbk.). — ISBN 978-1-77086-289-0 (mobi).--
ISBN 978-1-77086-288-3 (epub)
1. Title.

PS8561.A94L38 2013   C813'.54   C2013-903666-0
                                               C2013-903667-9

Cover art and design: Angel Guerra / Archetype
Interior text design: Tannice Goddard, Soul Oasis Networking
Printer: Friesens

Printed and bound in Canada.

The interior of this book is printed on 100% post-consumer waste recycled paper.

CORMORANT BOOKS INC.
10 ST. MARY STREET, SUITE 615, TORONTO, ONTARIO, M4Y 1P9
www.cormorantbooks.com

For Gord Smetanuk, Jack Larkin, Alex Ritson, Ken Silver
my boyhood hockey heroes

Love is to reason as the eyes are to the mind.

LOUIS ZUKOFSKY, *On Shakespeare*, 1963, P. 266

PART ONE

ONE

L ET ME TELL YOU the story of my life.

First, I've got my head down. That makes me pretty much like an awful lot of people, so I'll be specific. I'm on a sheet of ice in a cold arena full of hockey fans and hockey players, and I've got my back to the other players with the puck on my stick just inside my own team's blueline, a step away from the boards.

I can hear things I can't see. This time it's a young kid a few rows into the stands above our bench. He's yelling at me in a high, reedy voice that's had the needle in me since the game began. No, wait a sec. This kid has been on me since the beginning of last season. Or maybe the beginning of time.

"Wake up before it's too late, Bathgate," he's screeching. "There's a hockey game going on."

For sure. I can also hear a stick banging the ice behind my left shoulder. That's going to be my winger, Gord. Last time I saw him he was near centre, but now he's come back to pick up the pass from me. Without looking I flick the puck between my legs along the blueline, a neat move that will allow him to deal the puck to my other wingman, Jack, who will be crossing centre ice.

Yeah, yeah. A blind pass in your own zone is hockey's equivalent of picking your nose in public. A house league move. But what's life without a little adventure? If the move works, Jack has a breakaway if Gord can make a pass as slick as mine. Or at least he will have until the Stingers run him down.

So, that's the plan. But in the real world, Gord is cruising toward centre like he ought to be, and my brilliant pass lands on the stick of the Stingers' right winger, who's too lazy to check Gord knowing how easily he can catch him. And when the puck lands on his stick, he slips it to the other Stinger winger, who's also screwing around at our blueline. He skates unmolested into the sweet part of the slot and rockets a shot at — not accidentally — our goalie's head. On cue, said goalie ducks, and the red light goes on behind him.

I'm not a witness to this, because the blind pass isn't my only mistake. I haven't heard the third Stinger forward coming in behind me. Just as I straighten up and begin to turn so I can watch my handiwork, he jackhammers me into the boards, and my stick jams against the bottom of them so the butt skewers me right above my solar plexus. A nanosecond later, my flimsy old Jofa helmet hits the glass, hard.

When the lights come up again, they carry a whole lot of soft pastels you're not supposed to see in a hockey arena. I can't get any air into my lungs, but damn, I hear birds. Robins sweetly twittering away about how tasty the worms are, but there's also a raven's squawk echoing in the hollow distance of a very dark forest. Then there's only the dark.

SO WHY IS THIS the story of my life? Well, first, that dark forest is a place I'm very familiar with. Second? I'm a guy who's seen a lot of plans that didn't work the way they should have. Sometimes it's been ignorant armies and falling trees; things got destroyed and money lost, and sometimes people got hurt or worse. Sometimes I've been on the business end, like now. Not that I'm complaining. It's how life is: a deep, looming thicket, and only temporary clearings.

Then there's hockey, which I've played since I can remember. Hockey has rules and it's played in the light. That makes it very different from life, which has no rules, and which asks you to spend all your energy and heart trying to invent ones that work or trying to elude the stupid ones other people are trying to plant on you. Hockey has been my clearing in the dark forest. It's preserved my sanity again and again, whatever it's done to my body.

And so I push my way through the darkness by sheer will and head for the clearing, thrashing my way through the coloured lights and the birdsong, and find myself where I'm supposed to be: the brightly lit ice surface of the Mantua Memorial Coliseum, Friday, January twenty-third, third period of a game between the Mantua Mohawks and the Wilson Lake Stingers.

The first thing I hear? It's the boobird in the stands.

"Niiice play, Bathgate, you old fart."

Better him than my teammates, who must be thinking the same thing.

Screw them all. It took me twenty-five years to perfect plays like this one. When you're a prematurely grey forty-something playing on a last-place team in a nowhere league just south of the North Pole some rules don't count. If my wingers had been playing as creatively dumb as I was, and the other team had been more cooperative, I would have looked like Wayne Gretzky, who also specialized in doing the unexpected. So he always knew where his wingers were. So what?

"So," Gord wants to know as we skate back to the bench. "What the hell was that all about?"

"I thought that was you calling for the puck," I say, opening the gate and letting him go first.

"Listen," he answers. "You know I don't call for a puck unless I can do something with it."

Gord is right. He isn't stupid, unless you count playing hockey at his age. I sit down heavily beside him — and instantly feel the darkness move in on me again. He has to grab my sweater to keep me from going backward over the bench.

"Who was that who nailed me? Was it that goddamned Bellado kid?"

Gord doesn't have to answer. Roddy Bellado, the Stingers' twenty-something centre, had been chasing me around all night, and we both know I'd been lucky to elude him as long as I did. "You going to be ready for another shift anytime soon?" Gord asks.

As a test, I straighten my spine. There's an odd pain somewhere between my shoulder blades that tells me tomorrow isn't going to be a barrel of fun. But then tomorrow is something I've never given much of a crap about. "Give me a sec here," I say. "Clear the cobwebs."

To Gord's right, I hear Jack guffaw. His standard line is that once I get on a sheet of arena ice, grey hair and cobwebs are the only grey matter I've got. I scowl, get to my feet, and bang the tips of my skates against the bench gate.

"I'm okay," I growl, making a show I don't feel. "Let's play some hockey."

That gets a laugh from the whole bench.

I DON'T MISS ANOTHER shift, but I might as well not be out there. A cloud of fog seems to be moving across the surface of the ice, and the lights keep dimming. And as the last minutes of the game wind down, the fog takes on the properties of thick, black bunker oil.

We score another goal, this one with Gord setting a pick on a Stinger defenceman like parking a semi in front of a Volkswagen. I have just enough of my wits left to see it coming. I take the puck into the corner and pass back to Bobby Bell, the one defenceman we have who can read an offensive play. He crosses the blueline behind me and puts the puck away, high and stickside, where it ought to go. As I come off the ice I use my remaining brain cell to point my stick at the kid up in the stands. I even make a little circle with the tip.

Nothing is going to impress this kid. "You're still dead on your feet," he screeches. It gets a laugh from the crowd, but I can't see the humour because I've gotten lost watching the way the fog pattern I made with my stick dissipates.

The Stingers score again too, but I'm not on the ice for it, and I don't really care. By the time I stumble onto the ice for my last shift, the sharp pain between my shoulder blades is gone, replaced by a numb feeling that has tentacles down into my fingertips and up into my skull. There are black cloudlets at the edges of whatever I focus on, and they seem to be on the move ...

A thud behind me brings me back. It's Bellado, the peckerhead, trying to finish me, and the only reason he doesn't succeed is that Gord has planted him halfway through the boards.

That's what they tell me later, anyway. I don't hear the final buzzer, and Gord has to steer me off the ice. The only things I recall after the game are the familiar scent of Je Reviens, a halo of red hair near my face, and fingers that don't seem to be mine undoing my skates. After that, warm water coursing over my shoulders and neck, snippets of conversation, some flashes of very electric colour in the air, and more fuzzy cloudlets. It's harder and harder to keep them at bay, but I'm damned if I'll let them win. I know what's waiting for me if they do. It isn't a hockey game.

I don't recall leaving the Coliseum, don't remember the drive home, or hitting the sack. I do have a glimmer out the window of a high-bed 4x4 as I fall, and a world that has just one colour in it. That, at least, makes sense. It is snowing.

TWO

SNOW IS BLANKETING THE ground outside the bedroom window the next morning, another thirty centimetres of it, and my brain is circling and recircling something Gord said to me a few days ago at practice. He was saying something philosophical about time — feeling it in his own bones, I guess. The two of us were standing along the boards, pretending, like we usually do, that the practice was for the other players. He was telling me he thought time operated like a freight train.

"And you don't care what train you're on, as long as it keeps rolling on?" I asked.

He leaned forward to flick a stray puck back to where Wendel and a few others were taking slapshots at Stan Lagace. "No," he answered. "This train stops for everything. Normal people toss their baggage into the boxcars and jump on. But in this town, most people just stand in the middle of the tracks and let the train run over them."

"I hate it when you talk politics," I said. "I never understand a word you're saying."

He brushed aside my try at laughing him off. "Sure you do. And I wasn't finished. I was going to say that you do something different from everyone."

I nodded my head as if I agreed *and* understood what he was talking about. "Different how?"

"You," he said, "keep your baggage hidden inside your head, and you don't go anywhere near the tracks."

I shrugged, but said nothing — hard to say what he was onto with this. He might have just been feeling foolish about playing a kid's game at his age and was taking it out on me, or he might have been up all night reading some philosophy book. Like I said, with him I'm never sure.

He fixed me with a stare that was just this side of a glare. "I was just thinking that the train must have given you one hell of a rough ride once upon a time. You act like a man who doesn't want a past or a future."

I decided he must be feeling *his* private freight train bearing down on him. But geez, did I have to get on it? "We have two games this weekend," I answered. "How's that for a future?"

He rolled his eyes and skated off to toy with a loose puck, and I skated after him. "So," I said. "Why do *you* keep on playing?"

He laughed out loud. "Because I can. And because" — he jerked the thumb of his glove at Jack, who was across the rink lecturing Junior about something — "somebody has to protect you two clowns."

I let that one go, no chippy remarks about the durability of dirigibles or the Michelin Man. I've learned to listen to Gord, and not just because he's the size of a freight train.

I SIT UP IN bed, cantilever my legs onto the floor. On the birdfeeder I put up outside the bedroom window, two whiskey jacks are arguing over something, stopping now and again to peck at the window so I'll get up and feed them: one of my smaller plans that's run amok.

I dress, find some bread to silence the birds, and I'm back at the Coliseum by ten. Except for a slight pinging in my right ear and an odd sensation between my shoulder blades, I seem to be a reasonable version of myself. My lower back has seized up, but it usually punishes me the morning after a game.

No one seems to think it's odd that I'm up and around this morning, acting more or less normal — not Esther at breakfast, not Gord when he arrives at the Coliseum. Hell, even our Newfoundland dog, Bozo, seemed to think I was okay when Esther sent her in to lie on my face to help me wake up.

I don't tell Esther how little I remember about the end of the game. If I went around declaring an emergency every time I get a bump on my backside, they'd have named a hospital ward after me a long time ago.

Gord you've met. He's my winger on the Mohawks, all two hundred sixty pounds of him, and my best friend. Esther you might be wondering about. The red hair and Je Reviens perfume in the dressing room last night was hers. She also drove me home in the 4x4 last night — her truck.

Esther did mention this morning over breakfast that she woke me several times during the night to make sure I wasn't slipping into a coma, but that's her standard practice whenever I get whacked hard during a game. Her training as a nurse kicks in, and she sets the alarm so she can flip my eyelids every hour or so. She does it without much to-do. In her mind, it's part of the deal. My eyeballs must have stayed where they were supposed to, because I woke up in my own bed. If she believes I'm okay, then I'd better act like it.

Except, really, I don't *feel* like it. While Esther and Gord yak, I wander over to look at the display of photographs in the Coliseum lobby. It's a display of the team photos of each team that won the old Mantua Cup, twenty years of them. I'm probably the first person to look at them for longer than a few seconds in the last ten years.

There are good reasons why nobody ever looks at these photographs. First off, there hasn't been a Mantua Cup tournament for twenty-one years. Second, no Mantua team ever won the Cup, and who wants to look at a bunch of scratchy-faced goons from somewhere else when your own town is full of them, live and in *living* colour.

And speaking of colour, the idiot who installed the display put tubes of fluorescent light right above the photos. You know what light does to colour photos? After two or three years every uniform turns the same limey yellow, and so do the faces. These photos make it look like Mantua hosted hockey tournaments for teams from outer space.

That's not far from the truth, actually. Everywhere I've been in the northern part of this country, the hockey arenas are the primary sites for local extraterrestrial activity. Mantua is no better or worse. Most days during the winter, the Coliseum is about as close a glimpse as you can get to alien life without having to be an astronaut. If space aliens walked into Mantua most citizens would simply assume the arena must be closed for the day. If it was a full-fledged UFO invasion, they'd assume there must be a hockey tournament about to start. Not worth stopping the pickup for a look-see either way.

Me? I'm Andrew William Bathgate, hockey player and minor industrial real estate magnate, a.k.a. hockey never-was and land-swapping sleazeball. I was born right here in Mantua. Then I left town for a long time, which might be why — not counting last night's whack on the noggin — I'm able to appreciate the other-worldly side of this place. I'm a homer and an alien at the same time, two men in one body in more ways than one. Gord says I've got a sixty-year-old head on a thirty-year-old body. He's talking about my grey hair, but he's right in other ways.

I'd better tell you about Mantua. It's a city of 80,000 people that a few decades ago was a much smaller town nestled around the junction of two rivers in Northern British Columbia. In the old days, Mantua had one industry — logging the forests and cutting them into spaghetti — and two kinds of recreation: making money and getting drunk. It isn't much different today, except that it has a lot fewer trees to be logged and cut up, along with a new form of recreation: worrying about where the jobs are all going. Or, for those few citizens with extra brain cells and some perspective, worrying about the town's future.

Then there's the Mantua Memorial Coliseum. Forget the grand name. It's really just an ordinary arena that holds two-thousand-or-so people if it's packed tight — which it never is. It got its fancy name when some local politician realized that Mantua was named after a city in Italy and decided that since Rome had a famous Coliseum, Mantua, Italy must have had one too — maybe a slightly less fabulous one, but a Coliseum either way. And since Mantua, B.C. is named after Mantua, Italy, it followed that *we* ought to have a Coliseum too.

The "Memorial" part is a bit more complicated. Some claim it's because it's the second Coliseum built here. The first one was built in 1963, a couple of years after the original hockey arena, the plain old Mantua Civic Arena, collapsed and burned after a big snow. The folks in charge didn't learn much from having the old arena collapse under a load of snow. The Coliseum they built to replace the Civic Arena survived just two winters before *its* roof collapsed after a snowstorm. Nothing very memorable took place in the two years the first Coliseum stood up to the elements, so damned if I can say what it is we're supposed to be remembering with the Memorial tag on the third arena. Maybe it's to remind the janitors to shovel the snow off the roof every once in a while.

And no, neither the Memorial Coliseum nor the one it replaced resembles the one in Rome. The first Mantua Coliseum was like hundreds of other hockey arenas across the country. The *Memorial* Coliseum is identical except for the two large sets of steel girders cantilevered across the outside to keep *its* roof from collapsing.

The steel girders were supposed to solve the snow problems, but they've been a mixed success. Every few years since the building opened there've been problems with the roof, including one time when a civic worker who was up there with a machine blowing the snow off fell through, machine and all, and broke both legs. I wasn't in town for that one, but things being what they are in Mantua it's even money he was up there with the Zamboni. Crazier things have happened.

I played scrub hockey in the old Civic Arena every Saturday morning until I was eleven. It was a great old building, built completely of wood thirty or forty years before, and its natural ice may explain why I'm almost as good a swimmer as a skater. With the climate around Mantua — we're either coming or going from a major blizzard or a major thaw — there were more than a few games where the skating rink looked more like a small lake.

I have a more pleasant memory of the old arena's steamy dressing rooms, with their pot-bellied wood stoves and unpainted benches, and of the scarred wooden walkways that led to the ice — when it was ice, that is. Except for the boards and a few signs, there wasn't a spot of paint anywhere in that building, so it was like being inside a giant cabin. Oh, yeah. There's one other memory I have of it: the day it collapsed.

It was a Saturday, and it had been snowing for what seemed like weeks. I was supposed to play that morning, and I set off unsupervised and happy through the unploughed streets with my skates hanging on my stick, dressed up in the Montreal Canadiens uniform that had me permanently in trouble with my Toronto Maple Leafs-outfitted friends. But when I arrived, I found a block-long pile of splintered timbers, with a giant bonfire blazing away in the exact spot where I'd been going to suit up for hockey.

The caretaker, I heard later, had just finished building a fire in the dressing room's stove when he heard the building rafters begin to creak and groan. He only had time, the story goes, to rip the photographs of the Mantua Cup champions off the lobby walls and run out into the street before the building came down.

As I stood there with my teammates watching the fire lick at the wreckage, it came to me that if the building had collapsed just an hour later I would have been one of about thirty-or-so seventy-five-pound potatoes roasting in the bonfire. The thought scared me so much I didn't play hockey for three years. By then, my parents' marriage had also collapsed, my mother had packed me up and moved south, and construction on the first Coliseum was nearly complete.

THIS MORNING ESTHER SEEMS to be finding whatever Gord has to say particularly fascinating, and it frees me to look over the photographs of the Mantua Cup champions. I half-hear the end of the conversation with Gord, but then I tune out again and miss him leaving for the dressing room and Jack's office. The next thing I know, Esther is standing behind me with her hand on my shoulder.

"What's up, Andy?" she asks. "Wondering who all those little green men were?"

"Nope, I know them all," I answer, more truthfully than she realizes. "Goofs like me. Only younger."

"You're only as old as you decide to be," she says.

"Today my backside is telling me I'm about two hundred years old," I tell her. "I guess that makes me old enough to be your great-great-grandfather, no?"

That makes her laugh. It's one of my biggest talents, actually, and an important one too, because Esther says she can't resist a man who can make her laugh. She's tall, red-haired — stacked, I guess you'd say if you were in a bar drinking beer and talking loose. For sure, she's shapely for a woman in her forties. But she also has an unusual sort of distance to her, an aloofness, "poise" I think the word is. It isn't the sort of thing guys around here are used to, and for her that's part luck of the draw, part design. Since she works as a sex therapist, the only one in Mantua, a certain degree of aloofness is fairly important.

Yeah, yeah, I know what you're thinking. No. She doesn't. She *talks* with her clients, usually couples, gives them advice and gets them to talk to one another with a bit of honesty. It's a tough job, because most of them secretly hope she's there to teach them how to have kinky sex.

More than a few of her clients around town probably suspect I know more about their sex lives than I should. They're correct. Esther happens to have a photographic memory, and she can repeat conversations she's had days ago, word for word.

"Andy," she's saying. "Earth calling Andrew Bathgate ..."

I shake myself loose from the cobwebs and turn to face her. "What?" I ask. "I was thinking about something."

"So tell me."

Here I have to lie to her. "I was thinking that you're the only woman I've ever run across who has freckles on her butt."

She goes for it. "Oh, really? And just how large is your sample?"

"Large enough," I say.

"There's a surprise," she answers, dryly. "Men who go around inspecting women's behinds for freckles usually don't get far — or live very long."

She *is*, for the record, the only woman I've ever seen with freckles on her butt. My lie was that this wasn't *exactly* what I was thinking about. You see, I was thinking about what she'd do if she knew that I first saw those freckles while she was still a post-teen working the concession booth at the the last Mantua Cup tournament. And I was imagining what she'd say if I told her I was looking at my own face in two of those greeny-yellow photographs inside the glass display cases. Mantua never won its own cup, but I played on two cup winners. The last two. And I'm the reason there hasn't been one since. For me, that's the darkest thicket in the forest.

THREE

WENDEL IS AT THE Coliseum's front doors. Wendel is Esther's son, and one of my teammates. He's twenty years old, tall, blond, and built like Superman. Whatever I may think of him personally, which is occasionally not very much, he's the best hockey player Mantua has ever produced, and he's pretty damned close to being the best player I've ever played with — or against.

Wendel doesn't have mixed feelings about me. It's hard to say what he likes least: having to play hockey on the same team as me, or me living with his mother. He bangs open the big steel-and-glass doors as if they're made of balsa wood and tramps toward us.

"Mom!" he hollers, as if he's seeing her for the first time in a month. "I was hoping I'd find you here!"

"What do you want?" she answers.

"I need to borrow the pickup."

"Sorry, but I need it to drive Andy to physio."

Now that I've been identified as the official obstruction, he officially notices me. "Oh, hi, Andy," he says. "Can't handle the heavy traffic anymore?"

"You saw Bellado bounce me off the boards last night," I answer.

Wendel is typically to-the-point. "Sure. Why don't you retire? You were playing like you already had most of last night."

Esther cuts him off. "Andy can't retire because your mother won't let him. So put that in your pipe and smoke it, Mr. Smartypants."

"I don't smoke," he snaps. His voice is prim.

Wendel *doesn't* smoke. He doesn't drink, either. He'll gladly explain to you that it's nothing personal, he just doesn't have the time for petty vices. He's the most serious young man I've ever run across, and that's part of our mutual problem. When he's not playing hockey, he's busy with his tree-planting business or attending some ecology seminar or petitioning the government — or trying to get the broken-down Jeep Cherokee he refuses to get rid of fixed, and not just because he's converted it to run on french fry oil he gets from a couple of the local restaurants.

If you've deduced that Wendel is a little, well, different, you're on. Around Mantua, it's close to unanimous that Wendel is cracked. No one minds the entrepreneur stuff, and they don't even mind his greenhead ideas. What gets them is that Wendel could be in New York playing for the Rangers, who drafted him in the first round eighteen months ago, and offered him a pile of money to sign.

Wendel doesn't *wish* to play in the NHL. He told them, and I quote, "I've got other priorities." Like playing with a bunch of boneheads and duffers for the Mantua Mohawks? That's right. He also wants to plant trees where nobody thinks they'll grow, and he's dedicated himself to driving every government in the country crazy with his demands and schemes. Not to mention his demands of me: leave my mother alone; stop skating like a porcupine; backcheck more; retire from hockey.

Right now he wants Esther's 4x4 to transport some panels of glass out to his greenhouses. He's the only tree planter in the area with his own greenhouses, of course. Shortly after he turned down the Rangers he decided that if the seedlings used for local reforestation were grown locally they'd be better acclimatized, and the survival rates would be higher than the current lousy rates. Along with that — and this part I agree with — it would create employment locally. Sound like a pipe dream to you?

It wasn't. Easier than most people could borrow fifty bucks from their best friend, Wendel finagled three hundred grand from the government so he could mess around with his theory, along with a permit from the public utilities commission that forces one of the pulp mills — at their expense — to pump excess steam from their power plant to heat the greenhouses.

The greenhouses are going up just fine. In fact, they'd be ahead of schedule except that the unemployed roofers he hired as builders suffer from perpetual hangovers, and keep dropping the glass they're supposed to be installing.

Wendel, here as with everything else, isn't letting up. "Christ, Mom," he whines, "Let the old fart take a cab or something. There's probably nothing wrong with his back anyway."

Esther glances in my direction, her hand on her hip. I shrug, and turn back to the photographs. "Rent a truck," she says, after a moment's consideration. "I need the pickup for later."

"Can't you go get his car?"

"It doesn't have four wheel drive." That's another of Esther's quirks. She doesn't like driving anything that doesn't have four wheel drive.

"Well, he can drive it, can't he?"

I see Esther's resolve start to waver, so I toss my keys to him. "If you bring my car over here you can take the pickup."

He catches them easily, grimaces while I tell him where it is — a few blocks away — then yanks the pickup keys from Esther's outstretched hand.

"Park it in the usual spot and stick the keys on the hook under the bumper, will you?" I say. "And see if you can manage not to put any dents in it on the way over here."

He waves the handful of keys at me as he kicks open the

Coliseum doors. "I'll try real hard," he answers, without looking back. "But there's a lot of fire hydrants around here."

JUST LIKE ESTHER DOESN'T know I saw her freckles all those years ago, no one in Mantua knows I'm in those team photographs in the lobby. It isn't that they've forgotten. They never knew. And no, it isn't because the photos are so distorted that I'm unrecognizable. If all that was hiding me was a green face, they have been able to read my name in the list of players beneath the photos, right? But that's the thing, see. I went by a different name then.

Let's start with Chilliwack and its Christian Lions.

Chilliwack is a town in southern B.C., in those days about the same size as Mantua. But where Mantua has always been loaded to the rafters with logging equipment, sawdust burners, and drunk loggers, Chilliwack was heavy on car dealerships, skating rinks with sturdy rooves, dairy farmers, and evangelical churches. While I lived there, there were so many Bibles being thumped on Sunday morning that it sounded like jungle drums. But since this is Canada, they also play hockey in Chilliwack, and one year someone got the idea that Chilliwack should send a team of nice Christian boys like me to win the Mantua Cup.

While we were winning our first Cup for Jesus a few of us slipped seriously south of the path of righteousness, doing our share of drinking, bar-fighting, and carrying on. When we returned home to Chilliwack, several ministers — friends of the Car Dealers Association that sponsored us — decided that too many native sons had come back with beer stains on their Bibles, and the next year they tried to stop us from going back.

If we hadn't had the argument that we needed to defend the Cup we'd won — and the commercial honour of Chilliwack's car dealers — the pious ministers might have had their way and the world — my world — would be quite different. As it was, each one of us had to make solemn promises not to drink or fight or chase around before they'd send us off to win a second championship for the Lord. We made the promises, but once again we didn't give Jesus anywhere near as much attention as we did hockey and Molson Canadian. And because of that, my name is Andy Bathgate and I live in Mantua.

Back then I was called Billy Menzies. A couple of years after my parents divorced and my mother and I left Mantua, my mother married a man named Fred Menzies, a good Chilliwack Bible-thumping car dealer and one of the Chilliwack Christian Lions' sponsors. Fred Menzies insisted on adopting me, and, under pressure from my mother to help her rebuild the family, I went along with it. According to her, my real father was spending his time and energy staring down the neck of an open whiskey bottle, and since he hadn't shown up to raise any objection to my being adopted, why should I? A little while after the adoption went through, Menzies insisted I use my second name, William. That got shortened to Billy, because you can't play hockey — even in Chilliwack — with a name like William.

I didn't much like old Fred, but at least he was there. And once I got over myself, I took to being Billy Menzies like a duck to water. Billy Menzies — at the beginning, anyway — was kind of admirable: quiet, self-confident, and even studious.

As a beginner in hockey, Andrew Bathgate had been a defenceman who didn't score much, took too many penalties, and made most of his stops by crunching other kids into the boards. But as Billy Menzies, comforted by the rock-solid arenas that never saw more than a dusting of snow, and after being sent off by Fred to Vancouver for power-skating lessons, my game improved. I was quick and smart, and the coaches said I was born with soft hands. I even grew a little pious.

As Billy Menzies I was good enough to be a star in Junior B when I was seventeen. Probably I didn't have the wheels to play higher than that — but I didn't have the ambition either. When I wasn't drafted, I let old Fred send me to Bible college in Oregon, which I didn't have much ambition for either. I skipped as many of the Bible classes and church services as I could get away with, got high marks in the business courses, played some baseball, and chased after the Bible college girls.

The girls were okay, I suppose, but they ran to type. They had names like Lynette and Tracy, and they all looked the same to me: thin, fine blond hair, pale complexions, and angular faces and flabby bodies that instinct told me would go to seed on them by the time they were halfway through their twenties. They were trailer-park princesses, no-brainers, Christian baby factories. If I didn't know much else, I knew better than to settle for that.

The other thing I knew was that I wasn't cut out for the life Fred Menzies had planned for me. Not for piousness, not for Christian princesses, not for the other Bible college nonsense. But I gave it a try, hanging in for almost two years trying my damnedest to please Fred because he was paying the shot, and trying to please my mother, who spent a lot of energy explaining to me that I didn't want to turn out like my real father.

I stopped trying when the college principal claimed I'd gotten one of his princesses pregnant. I wasn't guilty as charged, but someone had gotten her that way, and she decided I was the best catch in the school. So I cleared out about three seconds ahead of being kicked out, and went home to Chilliwack. Fred wasn't very happy about it, being a believer in how young men ought to keep their weapons holstered until marriage — I swear he really believed that — but he didn't say much.

I got an apartment of my own with a couple of other guys, went to work in a supermarket bagging groceries, and settled down to figure out what to do with my life. The figuring didn't go well, and before very long I slipped to about where Andy Bathgate had been headed — drinking too much beer, driving cars, and going to every party I could find. The part of me that remained Billy Menzies slipped into playing Senior hockey for the Chilliwack Christian Lions.

I'VE PLAYED ON A couple of Senior teams in my time that could have made pureed banana out of a lot of Junior A teams, and who on a good night might have given an NHL team a run. The Chilliwack Christian Lions, despite the goofy name, were one of the best. It wasn't religion that made us good, and it wasn't the coaching. We were all under twenty-five, and most of us had good skills. We hung out together outside of hockey, and we liked one another, and, despite the pious stage we were on, we spent a lot of time getting drunk together.

These days, most Senior leagues are filled with washouts from Juniors mixed in with a few older guys like me. The best players are what I call homers: local players who make their game — and the other parts of their lives — out of character and, more often than you'd think, brains. I've played with lots of guys in their thirties and early forties who are better players than they were at twenty. Sure, the legs may have died, and the grand ambitions are gone, but the love of the game is still there, trimmed down to a scale that fits. In a time when everyone and everything is trying to remake the world with levered debt, World Class pretense, and over-scale self-esteem, how many people do you know who can walk across the street in synch with their surroundings, and without wishing they were somewhere else? Well, Senior hockey has 'em. Not many, but enough.

Take Gord, for a perfect example. He's six-one and close to two hundred and sixty pounds. If you spotted him and his nineteen-inch neck on the street or in a bar, you'd swear he was a no-good down-and-dirty middle-aged trucker. The truth is that he needs that nineteen-inch neck to support his brain, which is big enough that he can't get a hockey helmet to fit around his skull. So what if he can't wheel because of an old back injury, can't turn to the left because the outside ligaments on his left knee are flapping with loose cartilage? So what if he's closer to fifty than to forty? You never hear him whining about what he could have been, because he doesn't want to be anywhere but exactly where he is. He's a medical doctor, not a truck driver, so he has real smarts. In fact, he's the district coroner.

Maybe, come to think of it, that's why he's always talking about time. He sees what's at the business end of it more times a week than most people do in a lifetime. Hell, he's probably seen a dozen people who've been run over by real freight trains.

Jack Lankin, my right winger, is another example. Jack's about my age, but he has even more damaged cartilage in his knees than Gord. Otherwise, he's Gord's opposite: five-seven, maybe one hundred and sixty pounds, and his neck wouldn't look out of place in a chicken coop. Gord calls Jack the flabmeister because he's never worked out a day in his life and lives on a diet of cheeseburgers and light beer. But he's got softer hands than I have, he's surprisingly quick, and he's a magician when he gets close to the net.

Jack's my tax accountant, and he's a magician at that too. He's also as gloomy as Gord is calm and cheerful. With the local economy what it is, sorting out people's finances, I guess, is more depressing than dealing with people's cadavers.

Oh yeah. Jack's also the general manager and playing coach of the Mantua Mohawks, and pretty much the man who keeps the North Central B.C. Senior Hockey League going. When Esther and I enter the dressing room, he and Gord are just sitting down to solve the league's latest crisis.

FOUR

ESTHER COMES INTO THE dressing room with me this morning just like she did last night to rescue me. She was wandering in and out of Mantua's hockey dressing rooms long before I became her main squeeze, so nobody thinks twice about it. She did it with Wendel before he went off to Regina to play Junior A, and I suspect she did it while her husband was playing. I'm pretty sure that if Wendel had decided to sign with the Rangers she'd be wandering in and out of NHL dressing rooms without anyone stopping her, too.

Having her around makes a certain subtle dress code necessary after games, along with a degree of verbal decorum, and I've got to admit I welcome both. I never did like the dressing room horseshit as much as most of the guys I've played with, not the rah-rah stuff and not the nastier stuff.

"So," I ask as I shed my coat and edge myself onto the leatherette training table. "What's today's doom and gloom?"

Jack and Gord are crammed into Jack's cubby hole of an office. Jack's behind the desk, Gord straddling one of the two rickety chairs. It isn't quite a confidential conversation we're busting in on, but then it really isn't an office they're in, either. There's no door, just the big oak general manager's desk Jack got in a furniture auction, a telephone, and the equipment lockup behind the desk. Jack has his elbows on the surface of the desk, hands over his ears. He doesn't look happy.

"It's the Roosters," Gord answers for him. "They don't want to play Sunday afternoon."

"What is it this time?" Esther asks.

With the Roosters, it's always something. They're from Camelot, the town one hundred klicks south of Mantua, and they're perpetually short of players. The reason is that the team is owned and run by Fritz Ratsloff, and he has seven of his own sons on the team, along with three or four of their cousins. You'd think having it all in the family would make it easier, but the Ratsloffs have their own unique style of hockey, and they expect anyone they bring in to play from outside the family to play their way. A Ratsloff is hard to emulate, and months go by when they only have the eleven Ratsloffs and their little goalie, Lenny Nakamoto. Lenny runs the old man's hotel bar for him and doesn't mind the way they play because he's wackier than any of them. He's a black belt karate expert, and the only goalie I've ever seen who can deliver a rabbit punch with a hockey blocker that can lay a man out cold. Not a lot of forwards care to crowd his crease.

Try to imagine a hockey team made up of eleven Hanson brothers and Bruce Lee, and you've got the Roosters. The Ratsloffs are all stark raving crazy, each, all, and in their own unique ways — except for the twins, who are crazy in the *same* way. When things get going, all of them are as likely to crunch a member of their own team they suspect of malingering as players on the opposing team. I can't remember when we last beat them, and it isn't because they've got better hockey skills. Excepting Gord, who they can't do much damage to, and Wendel, who's so fast they can't catch him, I think most of us let them win because we're afraid of what they'll do to us if we beat them.

They leave me alone too, sort of. Can't say exactly why, but I've been excused from the serious bone-crunching ever since I started playing in the league. I have a theory about why. Some-one, probably Jack, told them I'm the real Andy Bathgate, the one who played in the nhl back in the '50s and '60s. Only the Ratsloffs would be thick-headed enough not to realize I can't be the real Andy Bathgate. Or even if I were, I don't see why it would matter to them. But there it is. They give me a patch of ice free of blood and broken bones, and I take it.

"The twins got D & D'd last night after they beat the Bears up in Okenoke," Jack explains. "I guess they went to the bar, bit the heads off a dozen or so weasels, and then tried to bite the heads off a couple of the Bears who were goofy enough to think they could drink in the same bar. The cops've got 'em in the lockup, and won't let them out."

The twins are the youngest Ratsloffs, the babies of the family. Some babies. They're both six-foot-four, and nasty as wolverine snot. They're also dumb as wolverine snot. Jack's theory about the twins is that the angel in charge of brains didn't realize there were two of them in the tank and only tossed one in, which they damaged by squabbling over which one got to use it.

"I don't see why they can't play," Esther says. "That's only two players out."

"You're forgetting that you're dealing with the Ratsloffs," I say. "Not human beings. The rest of them won't leave Okenoke without the twins."

"I heard they spent all night driving their 4x4s up and down the street trying to run the locals down." Jack adds. "The RCMP detachment's thinking of declaring a state of emergency — or siege or whatever — but they're not sure how to do it."

"If they don't figure it out pretty quick," Gord says, "the bar's going to open and the Ratsloffs will really lose their minds."

"Well, what those animals do isn't your problem," Esther sniffs. "Let them default the game if they don't show up."

"Maybe we should send Andy up there to see if he can calm them down," Gord says. "They never behave like animals around him."

That gets a laugh from everyone but Esther, who pulls me down on the table and nudges me to turn over on my stomach. "You're not going anywhere," she announces. "Pull off your shirt and I'll see if I can get your back moving. Maybe I won't have to take you to the physiotherapist this afternoon."

I roll over onto my gut and instantly feel her strong fingers pushing at the snarly discs at the base of my spine.

MORE FACTS FOR YOU: the North Central British Columbia Senior Hockey League, known for short as the NSHL, has four teams: the Mantua Mohawks, the Roosters, the Okenoke Bears from the town just north of Mantua, and the Wilson Lake Stingers, the southernmost team. Over the years a few teams from farther away have joined the league, but sooner or later they pack it in. When I joined the league there were six teams, actually, but that only lasted the first year. It's been down to the basic quartet for the last four now.

It's really common sense that dictates the size of this league. Most players drive their own cars to the away games, and it better not take too long, because it's a league tradition for the players to load up on the way. With a three- or four-hour drive, sooner or later you're going to land up with an impaired driving charge, or in some ditch as a quad, or dead. Even when those distant teams made it to a game intact, it wasn't much fun watching the home team pound on a bunch of tired-out drunks.

Like I said, I'm in my seventh season with the Mohawks, all with the same linemates and most of the same players as when I started. Around the league they call us the Molasses Line, for reasons I don't need to go into. Still, we do our share of scoring, and we play smart. I don't think our defencemen are too fond of us, but, well, you know the answer to that one.

My nickname is *Weaver*. I can't remember who hung it on me, or exactly why. I picked it up in my twenties, and it stuck. People around here probably think it has something to do with the way I wander around an offensive zone, looking for open space — and trying to avoid contact with opposing defencemen. So I'm okay with it. I put things together. I suppose you could say that's what I do outside the rink, too, but slipping and sliding is a more common talent for people in real estate.

I'm a rangy six-two, one-eighty, and with a thick head of white hair I wear down to my shoulders. I guess I look pretty strange coming in on a defenceman. Outside of Wendel, I'm about the league's biggest draw. Who knows, maybe it's the Andy Bathgate thing. If the Ratsloffs will buy into that one, who's to say others haven't? The real Andy Bathgate is older than I am, even if the kid in the stands last night won't believe that's possible.

RIGHT NOW, WITH ESTHER's knuckle jammed into my left gluteus muscle, I'm having no luck at all trying to pretend my back doesn't hurt. It's excruciating, until her thumb connects with the spasming nerve and the needle goes off the register and I let out a howl in spite of myself.

Esther doesn't let up. She's done this enough times to know what'll happen next. The nerve connection overloads and severs, and I feel the muscles all across my back and down my left leg let go. Sensing it, she relaxes her thumb, and slaps my thigh.

"Congratulations," she says. "You've just given birth to one five-hundredth of the real thing."

Jack looks up from his desk. "What did you say?"

"Nothing," I answer. "She's just reminding me that only women know what pain is about."

He ignores me. "Oh. So you're saying Weaver will be able to play tomorrow afternoon."

Esther grimaces. "If he wants to."

"You're off the hook for practice today, anyway." Gord says.

"How come?" I ask.

"Nobody wanted one," Jack explains. "So we let the Juniors have the slot."

Now you know why we're in last place.

FIVE

THE COLISEUM IS USED pretty well around the clock on weekends, so Esther and I wander out to the stands to watch the minor hockey game that's on the ice. It's just past noon and the Peewees are playing, eleven- and twelve-year-olds. At this age, they can be fun to watch. They're fast and the no-hitting rules let their budding skills shine. They're not overdosed with hormones like they will be in a couple of years, so they don't miss the hitting, and they don't give a damn about fighting.

That's where the good stuff ends. Up in the stands, these kids have *parents*, and modern hockey parents are a separate species from the rest of us, one that gives up all traces of civilization the moment it opens an arena dressing room and pushes its offspring inside. I grew up before the kind of minor hockey played today was invented, so I can tell you what a great game hockey used to be. All you needed was a stick, a puck, weather cold enough to freeze a patch of ice, and some other kids. You could play for hours without seeing hide nor hair of your parents — or any other screaming adults — and you came home with a runny nose, not a bloody one. But somewhere along the line, somebody decided that it wasn't safe for children to play hockey without adults there to bullyrag them, and things went straight to Looneyville.

Esther has the right word for the people who did it. She calls them "Close Adults" — as in *Close Adult Supervision*. I don't think they're adults at all. They were invented by those job-sucking social workers who think the world would be better if everyone is strapped into safety devices or covered up to the ears with regulations. Close Adults believe there's a child molester hiding behind every clump of bushes, and a safety hazard everywhere else. You can tell the difference between them and the social workers who invented them because they're willing to ruin children's fun without being paid to do it. That's what they've done to minor hockey.

So let me correct myself. It isn't the game that's the problem. Minor hockey could be fun if they'd just kick the adults off the benches and out of the offices, and put the parents in straitjackets and stuff gags in their mouths while their kids are on the ice — and maybe for an hour or two afterward.

The parents in the stands this morning are jumping up and down and hollering at the referee, the coaches, and the opposition players as if they believe the fate of the world rests on how this mid-season game goes. They think that the big investment they've made on their kid's equipment entitles them to lose their minds over the slightest error, injustice, wavering will, or lapse in concentration on the part of anyone on or near the ice — the players, coaches, officials, — it doesn't seem to matter which. You might mistake these crazies for normally overprotective parents if you didn't see them screaming at their kids to play harder, smarten up, and kill every other parents' kid who keeps them from looking like the next Bobby Orr or Wayne Gretzky.

As Esther and I settle down into the seats, a two-hundred-pound mother in a pink parka and blue ski pants is clambering across the seats to yell from rinkside at her son, who has just been trapped up-ice on a breakaway.

"Skate, you little shithead!" she shrieks at his backside as he lopes up the ice after the play, hopelessly behind. The boy hears her, hesitates momentarily, and drifts sideways along his own blueline as the breakaway fails and the puck skitters back toward centre.

"Get on the puck!" the mother bellows, louder if possible, waving her arms like a windmill. "Move it, you lazy asshole! Move!"

Other parents farther up in the stands get caught up in her hysteria and add to the din, terrified that their sons will humiliate them the way this woman's son has. The boy glances toward the commotion, and, hesitating again, skates into a player from his own team who is rushing after the action. They both go down in a heap. A player from the other team retrieves the puck and pushes it ahead to his winger, who skates in on the net and scores easily.

I see the coach yanking at his necktie and muttering to himself as the teams line up for the face-off at centre. But as the puck is dropped, he turns toward the mother and makes a resigned "calm down" signal to her.

"That's nice," Esther says. "At least he's leaving the boy on the ice."

"He probably realizes it's the only place the poor little bugger will be safe from that Zeppelin."

Except that the coach is mistaken. The boy isn't safe. His mother waddles toward a spot near the bench, lifts one foot onto the top of the boards, and levers herself onto the glass so that nearly half her torso is looming over the ice. When her son picks up the puck behind the net and skates toward her along the boards, she leans over and takes a swing at him. He sees it coming, ducks, and a boy from the other team who's trying to check him from behind takes a thick forearm smash flush on his face-cage and crumples to the ice.

The parents from the other team, who are sitting on the other side of the rink — part of an unwritten rule that keeps opposing parents away from one another — get to their feet as one and begin leaping over the seats to get at their kid's assailant.

"Let's get out of here," Esther says. "I've seen this too many times before."

By the time we get up to the rotunda level the parents from both teams are flailing away at one another in the stands while the kids mill around aimlessly down on the ice, wondering if they'll get to finish a game that they alone seem to understand is supposed to be fun.

WENDEL PULLS UP IN my car as we reach the arena's front entrance. He sees us, and just to piss me off he floors it and jerks the wheel hard so the rear end spins around, spattering filthy snow and gravel across the just-cleaned plate glass that protects Esther and me. Then, as we watch, he pushes open the car door and leaps out in one motion, as if to tease me with his agility. Esther thinks he's funny, as always, and she's laughing out loud as he pushes the arena doors open, sticks his head in, and tosses my keys at me.

"Screw you, Weaver," he says, and is gone.

I'M FOND OF MY car. It's a five-year-old Lincoln Town Car, a four-door jet black number with leather seats, the only one in town. I got it in an auction three years ago from the City, which was conducting one of its phony austerity drives prior to the civic elections. Mantua's long-time mayor, Garvin Snell, extracts one of these cars from the city budget every two years, with the degree of slashing and chopping depending on how popular the candidate stupid enough to make an election run at him happens to be. Snell sobers himself up for a few months before elections, announces an austerity program, kisses a few babies, pulls a crowd-pleasing stunt like selling off the nearly new City limousine, and gets himself re-elected. Nobody seems to care that the manoeuvre always ends up costing the city more money than it saves, or that it enables Snell to run the city in his customary alcoholic daze for another term.

Since I'm the beneficiary of one of his stunts — I picked up the Lincoln for eight grand — I guess I shouldn't complain. It's just that the way people let themselves be suckered and deceived around here drives me crazy. If it isn't one thing it's another, and it's been going on since Alexander Mackenzie first came down the river and started screwing the native people out of their birthright.

You think I'm kidding about this? Let me tell you a few stories.

Back in the mid-1950s, a Swedish millionaire announced that he was going to build a monorail from here to Vancouver. The government promptly promised him timber rights all over the area along with the rights of way along his proposed route. A stampede was soon underway, with speculators — local ones included — buying up useless land and flipping it, and everyone generally overdosing on their own greedy adrenaline. Then, big surprise, nothing happened. Eventually a stretch of monorail was built in Seattle for the 1962 World's Fair, but when it proved to be expensive to build, dead slow, and unreliable, the lights still didn't go on. Anyone with an ounce of common sense could have figured out that monorails were too rinky-dink for hauling sawlogs, but so long as the real estate prices kept climbing nobody here had the common sense of a beagle. Anything connected to the real world was labeled "negativity," and negativity was treated as a form of communism.

In the '60s it got worse. There was the hydroelectric craze, and the same bunch of clowns who boostered the monorail got busy touting the government's plan to dam up the Peace River a couple hundred miles north of town. The government was in so much of a hurry divvying up fat contracts to their political allies that they didn't bother to log the valley floor or clear out the animals. When the lake was filled it drowned five thousand moose, and by the time they'd finished pulling out the carcasses and burning them it was time for the trees to start rocketing up from the lake bottom and killing boaters. Fifteen years later they were still hauling dead trees out of the water and burning them — a million board feet a day, I heard. The Americans got cheap power, and the government got a whopping project cost overrun we've been paying interest on ever since. The Indians got flown-in booze, junk food, and welfare cheques to live on instead of the fresh valley air and moose they'd begun with.

Mantua did get cheaper industrial power rates, it's true. That netted us multinational-owned pulp harvesters and supermills to slag the forests more efficiently than our own people could. More than five hundred of the six hundred small, locally owned mills Mantua started with closed down over the next ten years. The multinationals stunk up the valley with sulphur, polluted the rivers, tossed the mill-workers and most of the loggers out of their jobs, and shipped out the product and the profits. The eight-hundred-kilometre-long lake the power dams created, meanwhile, screwed up the ecology of the entire Western Subarctic. The weather patterns to the south changed too, with fog banks rolling down the Rocky Mountain Trench to carry the pulp-mill stench right into our beautiful downtown. It did put an end to the minus-fifty winters, but we'll probably pay for that in some horrible way too, eventually.

And listen, those are just *some* of the delusions. You ought to hear Wendel on the subject of how they're handling forestry today. He makes me sound like I'm the publicity agent for the Chamber of Commerce.

SIX

I EASE MYSELF BEHIND the wheel of the Lincoln, crank it up, and wait while Esther uses the rear-view to touch up her makeup. She knows I don't like her using the rear-view for that but she does it anyway, never mind that there's a mirror on the back of the passenger side visor, lighted.

This morning I watch her without a trace of irritation. In fact, today I'm finding it — and her — pretty fabulous. Her vanity isn't the same as a guy, say, combing his hair. Esther's vanity isn't tied up in her ego. Or if it is, it isn't going to start any wars or ignore what's around it. I can't say if it's essentially female, but it's Esther Simons.

I didn't always feel this way about her. The first time around, I wasn't capable of seeing much of anything in her except the opportunity to get laid. I don't think Esther had much of an essence yet, actually. Even now, her essence is the kind that sort of sneaks up on you. When I came back here seven years ago, it took more than a year for me to realize how terrific she is, even though she was right under my nose. And it wasn't until I saw her with her clothes off and saw the freckles that I realized she was the concession girl I slept with all those years before.

She was hanging around with Gord when our second go-round began, although I'm pretty sure she wasn't sleeping with him. They were friends, and she was still — not officially but in her own mind — mourning the death of her husband, Leo. According to what Gord told me about Leo Simons, he was a good husband and father, and a successful logging contractor until the day he decided to show one of his fallers how to clean up a big spruce the faller had dropped between two others. Leo got the chainsaw into one of the standing trees, and the vibrations loosened the hung-up tree, which slid along the trunk of the tree he was cutting. You can imagine the rest.

Leo left Esther comfortable enough financially. The house was paid for — the one she and I live in now — and she owns several large chunks of industrial land next to one of the pulp mills. One of them is the parcel Wendel uses to carry on his greenhouse ventures.

Esther doesn't need to work, and she generally takes the summers off unless a client is having really serious difficulties. I don't know for sure, but I think she and Jack tinker around with stocks and bonds the same way he and I do. I steer clear of that part of her life, she keeps her nose out of my business, and we both like it that way.

Like I said, it wasn't until I got her clothes off and saw the freckles that I realized who she was. I mean, really. There couldn't be another set of freckles like that anywhere. Blurting out that I'd already slept with her didn't seem like the sort of thing that would deepen the experience, so I kept my mouth shut. And since there was nothing I did (in bed or otherwise) that gave me away as the boy she'd had a late-night drunken grope with, she was none the wiser. I didn't seem to have made much of an impression on Esther while I was Billy Menzies anyway. Within a year or so she'd married Leo Simons and was pregnant with Wendel.

Trouble is, not telling her who I was saddled me with a permanently delicate problem. There doesn't seem to be any civilized way I can tell her much of anything about my past, either the part of it she'd been in or the rest of it. I don't want anyone to recognize me as an older Billy Menzies. Partly that's because I'm somebody else now, and I want to be judged as Andy Bathgate. But there's the practical side to it. I'm pretty sure there's there's still a warrant out for my arrest.

"ANDY," SHE SAYS. "WAKE up. You're making me think I should have taken you to the hospital last night."

"Why?"

"You've been acting like a zombie all morning."

"I've got some things on my mind, that's all. It's nothing."

"Like what have you got on your mind?"

"I dunno. Like why Wendel dislikes me, maybe."

"That's no big mystery," she says. "You're sleeping with his mother. It's an instinct. I've explained the Oedipus Complex to you. Stop taking it personally."

"Well, I do."

"Well, don't. Grow up. And if you really wanted to get along with Wendel, you could try harder yourself."

"What do you mean, 'try harder'? I do try. I just let him drive my car, didn't I?"

"Ooh, my," she answers, her voice dripping with sarcasm, "How generous of you. Why don't you start listening to what he says, instead of teasing him all the time. He'd like you better if you acted as a parent instead of a competitor."

"I'm not his parent," I say, "and he doesn't want me to be."

The moment it's out of my mouth I regret having said it. Esther's eyes flash, and she crosses her arms. "Let's get going," she says, her voice suddenly tight and hard. "We've got errands to do."

IN LATE JANUARY MANTUA doesn't remind anyone of April in Paris: mall parking lots filled with mud-splattered pickup trucks and the discarded furniture and green garbage bags people kick off the backs of those pickups late at night, after the City's privatized trucks don't pick it up in front of their houses. Huge, dirty snowbanks line the streets, riddled with winter debris — road sand, discarded milk cartons, cigarette packages, candy bar wrappers, more green garbage bags.

These days, there's a new kind of debris on the streets: surplus human beings. They're unemployed loggers, most of them. They hang around waiting for the industry to go back into a boom, which it does regularly, but without hiring anyone back who got boosted out in the last downturn. The loggers hang around town drinking off their unemployment insurance cheques and, when those run out, their welfare cheques. They aren't street people like you see in bigger cities to the south, but that's because anyone who tries to camp out in these streets will wind up as a human popsicle.

This kind of poverty makes people struggle and straggle on, selling off the RVs and Ski-Doos they bought during the gravy years, then their second cars, and, finally, their houses. Eventually most of the families break up, and the women and kids move elsewhere, usually south to Vancouver or the Okanagan Valley. Or, for the women whose husbands go crazy before they're dead broke and beaten, into shelters.

The men don't get off much easier. They end up living hand to mouth in the low-end hotels and rooming houses, lurching from drunken brawl to hangover and back to the bar, sucking up every omen that the old days are coming back. I don't know what to do about it, and neither does anyone else.

What I do know is that the answer the politicians keep coming up with — more logging — isn't an answer at all. If what Wendel and his cronies have been saying is halfway true there aren't enough trees left to continue at the present cutting rates, let alone enlarge the cut. Gord told me once that civilization is a place where people don't lie to one another in order to stay alive. If he's right, this isn't civilization anymore.

Once you get a few miles out of town — if you steer away from the huge clearcuts — this is the most beautiful landscape in the country. It's what brought me back here and now keeps me here — aside from Esther, of course. I mean, the climate isn't Hawaii, but there are compensations. Hawaii? I spent a week there once, and don't take me back, ever again. It's nothing but a giant outdoor hot tub lined with souvenir shops and wall-to-wall assholes. They don't play much hockey there, either.

ESTHER GIVES ME THE silent treatment while we do the grocery shopping. Eventually it sinks into my thick skull that I've seriously pissed her off, and I begin casting around for some way to get myself off the hook. It isn't easy to come up with anything. The truth is that I need her more than she needs me. I can't, as a matter of fact, see a single thing about me she absolutely has to have. I know she enjoys my company — most of the time — and I guess I make her laugh more than most men could. But I'm just a guy, and Mantua is full of guys. And today I haven't made her laugh at all.

Aside from the grocery shopping, for instance, our errands are all mine. I've got to go to Northern Sports to pick up a pair of hockey gloves they've put new palms into, and I need another half-dozen sticks — broke two on Friday night, so I've only got two left. Gord keeps trying to convert me to the new carbon sticks, but I've been hung up on Sher-Wood pmp 5030s since they started making them. The trouble is, I shave the shafts so thin they break all the time, and each one requires about twenty minutes of surgery before they're usable.

When we get to Northern Sports, Wally, the owner, informs me that the shipment of sticks hasn't come in, and he only has two left-side 5030s left, one of them with too much curve on the blade.

I'm a little cheezed off. "Jesus, Wally," I whine. "I told you I'd need more sticks three weeks ago. We've got a game with the Roosters tomorrow afternoon. You know you can't safely go into a game with those clowns with just two sticks."

"What I am supposed to do?" he hoots. "Mug a bunch of Old Age Pensioners and take theirs? You're lucky the factory is still producing these antiques. And anyway, what do you care about safe? You're just cheap. If you were really interested in safety you'd buy a proper helmet, and start using modern sticks. And you'd talk No Neck into wearing a helmet."

"You know damned well they don't make helmets big enough to fit his head," I answer, ignoring his crack about me being cheap. "And don't call Gord 'No Neck,' or I'll bring him in here and let him stuff your head down your neck and pull it out through your asshole like he keeps threatening to."

"Oh pulleeese, not again," Wally pleads, and then becomes serious. "Do you want me to phone around and see if anyone has 5030s?"

"Don't suckhole," I say. "I can always get them at Canadian Tire. I just shop here because I like you."

We drive over to Canadian Tire and pick up six 5030s — all they have. I'd prefer not to buy anything from the franchises, because I hate the idea that all the profits leave Mantua — I'd rather give up my bucks to a local business, even if it costs more and it's a smartass like Wally I'm paying. Besides, I've never seen a franchise in my life that gave a crap about service. They're there to merchandise products, and if they don't have what you want, then screw you. It's one of the few things Wendel and I agree on.

Esther gets out of the car when I do, but she doesn't come into Canadian Tire with me. As I'm about to enter, she veers off with out a word and whips out her cell. The moment she leaves the car, I get it: I've forgotten to cancel the physio appointment, and she's doing it for me. See what I mean about who needs who?

When I get back to the car with the sticks bundled under my

arm, she's already sitting inside tapping her fingers on the elbow rest, her eyes still cloudy with annoyance. The stew she's been simmering since we left the Coliseum is about ready to serve. I can't recall having seen her this annoyed at me, and I'm ready to do anything she demands. More than. I'll shave my head. Wear day-glo pink undershorts. I'll marry her and adopt Wendel. Anything.

She lets me have it the moment I get into the car. "You've really got to straighten things out with Wendel," she says.

"Okay," I answer, with perfect sincerity. "I will. How?"

"How the hell am I supposed to know that? You're a guy, and this is a guy thing. But if you want to go on living with me, you've got to get along with our son."

I shake my head. "What did you say?"

"I meant my son. You know what I meant. It just slipped out ..."

Her voice trails off, and, amazingly, she begins to cry. What the hell is going on here? If I didn't know better, I'd be tempted to say it was woman trouble — that time of the month. But it isn't, and besides, she isn't any different than usual around that time of the month. Esther Simons isn't a woman who cries unless there's a pretty damned good reason.

I reach over to comfort her, but she pushes me away. "Listen, Sweetie," I mumble, "It's okay. Why don't we go someplace and have a drink. Would that make you feel better?"

"Maybe," she says, and buries her face in the handkerchief she's pulled from her purse. I start the car and steer it slowly through the jumble of the parking lot.

SEVEN

W HEN ESTHER IS ON her game, watching her chase a mara-
schino cherry around a glass full of bourbon and grenadine
is one of my ideas of fun. But an hour in the bar and two Old
Fashioneds doesn't brighten her mood, and I don't learn anything
about what's gotten under her skin except that she's more upset
than pissed off, and that she's seriously upset about something she
can't — or won't — talk about.

So I sip my soda water and let the hour slip by clinking ice
cubes around the glass, staring out the window, and letting the
painful silences grow longer and more painful. I keep thinking
about one of Esther's pet theories — the Freudian Slip one, about
how nobody ever says anything they don't mean. Personally I
think that's going too far, but she takes it seriously. I know that
with all the things I'm hiding from her we're knee deep in banana
peels here, but damned if I can zero in on the one I've slipped on.

So I look to see if there are any banana trees: is this about her
wanting us to get married? Maybe. But why hasn't marriage come
up until now? If that's what this is about, I've got the answer: we'll
get married.

Does she want me to adopt Wendel? I'd go with that too even
if it doesn't make sense. Wendel is over nineteen, and adoption

probably isn't even legally possible at his age. And he'd never agree to it.

"Let's go home," she says, finally. "This isn't working. I think I need to be alone for a while."

"Okay. But I wish I could figure out what to say to make you feel better."

"This isn't your fault," she says, not quite meeting my eyes — and thus confirming that it most certainly damn well is my fault. "Just give me a couple of hours and I'll be fine."

It's a pointed hint that I should make myself scarce for a while, so I help her put away the groceries when we get home, watch a few minutes of the Hockey Night in Canada pre-game, and then announce that I'm going down to the Coliseum to work on the new sticks.

"How about I pick up some Chinese on the way home?"

"Fine," she says.

I press a small kiss on her forehead but don't put my arms around her. "See you about eight," I whisper.

She doesn't answer.

I WALK OUT OF the house without my car keys, and instead of going back inside to retrieve them — it seems important that I not appear to be a bigger nitwit than I already do — I get into the car and dig under the seat for the spare set I keep hidden under the mat. The keys are there, and so, surprise, is a wallet. I pull it out, dump it on the seat beside me, and flip it open. It's Wendel's youthful kisser staring up at me from behind the plastic driver's licence panel. I close it, and make a mental note to phone Esther from the Coliseum so she can let him know I have it — not that he's likely to miss it. Wendel never spends money, and he's too much like Jesus for the cops to pull him over.

By the time I arrive at the Coliseum Gord has left, but Jack is still there. He's on the phone with the dry cleaner, trying to get the team uniforms out before tomorrow's game. He isn't having much luck.

I wave to him as I enter and he waves back, distractedly. I plunk the new sticks down on the bench, place the first one in the set of wood clamps mounted on it, and poke through the toolbox for the wood rasps I keep there.

Jack slams the phone down. " Stupid idiot," he grumbles. "I told him we had two home games this weekend, but he never listens."

The dry cleaner is Korean, formal and polite the way all the Koreans around here are. I take my personal cleaning to him, he hasn't lost anything so far, and my clothes come back without being shredded by his machines. Most of the time, anyway.

"He listens okay," I point out. "He just doesn't understand everything you say to him. Be reasonable."

"Well," Jack grumbles. "I don't like his attitude."

"Who gives a damn about his attitude?" I laugh. "You're using him because his dry cleaning prices are thirty percent cheaper than anyone else's."

Jack sighs. "I know, I know," he says. "But Jesus H. Christ, can't anything ever go right around here?"

"It's the North," I say. "Everything is supposed to go wrong. Anyway, we can wear our away uniforms. We've done that before."

Jack takes this as an invitation to complain about the uniforms and the team name, both of which he hates. "You'd think they could have named the stupid team properly," he says. "Mantua Mohawks. What kind of a stupid name is that when there isn't a real Mohawk living this side of the Quebec border?"

I've sat through this rant dozens of times, but it's fun to see what variations he'll add to it. I also know the history. The name came from Jack's predecessor as GM, Wilf Cruikshank, a trendy-headed city alderman when the Memorial Coliseum was built.

"I mean, what's the name got to do with anything except alliteration?" he continues. "Might as well have been the Hopis, or the fucking Pueblos."

"Or the Apaches," I cut in. "At least they speak the same language root as the native people around here. And anyway, you know why we're called the Mohawks."

"Oh yeah, sure. So Cruikshank could put those chintzy Taiwanese Chief Wahoo crests on the jerseys."

Cruikshank owned a surplus clothing outfit, and it's a popular theory that he got our original uniforms, along with a two-hundred-year supply of Chief Wahoo crests, on the cheap. Still, I can't help myself. "Well," I say, "Maybe Cruikshank was a Cleveland Indians fan."

"I don't give a purple crap if he was Chiang Kai-Chek's long-lost brother," Jack roars, taking the bait. "We're not a bloody baseball team, and it's looked stupid from the beginning. I don't know what was wrong with calling us the Lumbermen like they used to."

We both know the answer to that one. The Lumbermen were the team that used to play in the old wooden arena before it fell down, and someone, probably Cruikshank — together with the same large minds who decided that the new arena ought to be a "Memorial Coliseum" — decided to come up with a new, catchy name for the city's hockey team.

"Didn't they change the name because the Lumbermen lost all the time?"

"Well, so do we," Jack snaps, "and we have to do it with Chief Wahoo plastered on the fronts of our stupid jerseys."

I don't take this as a personal affront the way Jack does, but I'm not going argue it with him. The uniforms are otherwise pretty much the same black, red, and white of the Chicago Blackhawks, and they're better looking than the former Soviet National team uniforms the Roosters are currently using — Ratsloff probably got those off one of his Russian relatives, who are sure to be the Russian version of the Canadian branch of the family. And they're a hell of a lot more attractive than the bright purple and white jobbies the Stingers have, or the baby blue and yellow of the

Bears, which Gord tells everyone they bought from the Ukrainian National Gay team.

It's time to change the subject before Jack blows a fuse. "So what's the juice on the Ratsloff twins?" I ask. "I take it they got out of jail, or you wouldn't be fussing over the uniforms."

Junior, our ducking goalie, walks in as I'm asking the question, and he answers for Jack.

"Yeah," he says. "The cops agreed to let the twins out and the Ratsloffs agreed not to burn the town."

"That's close," Jack concurs. "Who told you?"

"I been monitoring police band."

Junior, whose real name is Don Young, Jr. — hence the nickname — has come in to complain to Jack about his pads again. He does this about once a week, and rarely gets past the non-door of Jack's semi-office.

"You'd better come in here," Jack says to him, flashing a wink in my direction at the same time. "No doubt you've got something interesting to tell me."

Junior is a second-generation goalie, and he has his job because his father, Don Young, Sr., was the goalie for the old Mantua Lumbermen. I think there's a part of Junior that would rather skip playing hockey and spend his time pissing around with ham radio and running his father's appliance repair shop, but the old man won't let him. For Don Sr. hockey was a manhood thing, and he insists Junior play the game the same way he did — without a mask.

This is not without its problems for Junior. Like most people, he has a perfectly sane instinct to duck when small, rock-hard objects are directed at his head at high speeds. Naturally, everyone in the league knows this — they've known it for forty years, because Don Young, Sr. had the same instinct while he played. The difference is that Young Sr. played in the era before the slapshot was invented, and the game still had a few unwritten rules. In the old man's day, two or three pucks a game might stray above the goalie's shoulder in an average game. This being the era of cheat, lie, steal, fight with pipe wrench, every second shot taken at Junior is aimed at the bridge of his nose. He's just lucky most of the bozos in this league can't shoot straight. As it is, he's has taken eighty or ninety stitches in the head since I've been around.

The good side — there really isn't one, but we pretend there is — is that on shots along the ice Junior is decent. So what if Stan Lagace, his backup, is a better goalie? So what if there are better goalies playing Peewee and Midget on Saturday morning? After forty years the Youngs are a Mantua tradition. Besides which, Jack and Don Sr. are old friends.

This one-sided argument has been going between Junior and Jack for about two years now. Junior wants the team to pay for some new, lightweight pads — probably oversized, if I know Junior — and Jack is either too cheap to shell out for them, or he has a side deal with Don Sr. not to mess with the family equipment, all of which Junior inherited from his father when he retired — including the undersized brain.

JACK AND JUNIOR ARE in the office a long time. I hear them raise their voices several times but I don't really listen — I know which way this one is going to come out. Just as I'm finishing the third stick, over an hour later, Junior comes out with the predictable long face.

"Fucking cheapskate," he mumbles as he passes me.

"Why don't you ask him for a goalie mask," I suggest, "and then settle for new pads when he refuses?"

Junior stops and turns around. "Because the pervert probably would buy me a goalie mask," he answers. "Just to screw with me. And then," he turns again and heads through the doorways, "where would I be?"

"Just trying to helpful."

I see him wave his arms in the air as the door closes. "Sure,

Weaver," his voice drifts back from the hallway. "Go do yourself."

Jack doesn't come out of his office until I've finished shaving down the last stick. Judging from the look on his face talking to Junior made his pissy mood worse, so I let him be. He looks at me and glowers before he returns my courtesy. I bundle the sticks together with some black tape and put them in my locker, then climb onto the training table to do my stretching routine. My lower back still feels fairly loose, but the earlier tightness in my chest has worked its way from mild up to a solid medium. When I poke my finger along my breastbone above the heart there's another sensation. It isn't quite pain, but it ain't muscle stiffness either.

I start into a long-familiar routine: both knees up to the chest, hold that for thirty or forty seconds, then one knee at a time. Then I take a break — this is part of the routine, too — and stare at the bare light bulb above my head. This isn't just because I'm from the Satchel Paige school of exercise. I am, but this isn't to avoid doing the next stretch. I've done some of my best thinking lying on this table staring into the light bulb. And right now, I've got some items to think through.

One of them is how to get along better with Wendel. He really isn't such a bad kid — just a little righteous, that's all. He's probably like his father must have been, but smarter about it, or faster — at least on the ice.

How do I know that? Well, if I explain it, I have to explain a nightmare, and nobody can explain their nightmares. So let me put it together for you as a straight-up story, and we'll forget what it does to my head to remember it.

EIGHT

I WOULDN'T SAY I KNEW Wendel's father well. He was a guy I had couple of on-ice run-ins with. Leo Simons played defence for the then-newly minted Mantua Mohawks both years I came up with the Christian Lions. The first year, Mantua blew their first two games and we didn't get to play them. The second year, we drew Mantua in the first round. Early in the second period I cross-checked Leo head-first into the boards, and he came up swinging. We both got five minute majors for fighting, and I got an extra two for cross-checking. He was decent with his fists, but that was about it: he was slow, ugly with the puck, and he couldn't read a forward to save his soul. Wendel gets his talent from Esther's side of the family, I guess.

Leo didn't strike me as a speed demon off the ice, either. For sure he didn't have it to protect his girlfriend from a flash like me. But now that I think back on it, I thought everyone was slow-witted then, so who's to say what Leo Simons was really about. He turned out to be a pretty decent guy.

I know what you're thinking: I was the asshole, giant economy size. I was a twenty-year-old guy and when you're that age it isn't who or what you are that counts, it's what you do and what you get. I was Mr. Can Do. Can score, can stickhandle, can drink, can score with the concession girls at will. My undershorts weren't getting knotted up with a lot of deep thoughts in those days.

I did play some hockey in those tournaments. I potted eleven goals in the five games of that second tournament. Don't know why that statistic has stayed with me. I don't recall much of anything from the first tournament, but I must have scored a few in that one, too. They named me first all-star in the first tournament, though I only made second all-star in the second. Maybe the reason I can't remember anything about the first tournament is that I was either drunk, asleep, hungover, or on the ice the whole time I was there. Not one second reading the Bible or thinking deep thoughts. The second tournament, as you know, I got a few other things done.

The way they selected the all-stars for the second tourney was probably a message to us not to come back, because though we creamed every team we played I was the only Lion named to an all-star team. And when they presented us with the trophy and the two thousand dollars in prize money after the final game, they made a bigger to-do of calling the all-stars down onto the ice than they did of presenting us with the Cup. The player who beat me out for first all-star centre was a sorry-looking kid from Northern Alberta whose team we knocked out in the semis. I scored two goals in that game, and the player we had checking the kid flattened him every time he crossed our blueline. I'd have been surprised to hear he'd gotten a shot on goal in that game, unless he shot it from behind his own net.

After the trophy presentation, we — my two closest friends on the team, Neil DeBerk and a Metis kid named Mikey Davidson — pulled our share of the trophy cash, cadged more from the other players, and caught a taxi out to the local bootlegger's place. We drove through a snowstorm for half an hour, filled the taxi's trunk and most of the back seat with beer, skidded the thing back to the Coliseum, and unloaded the contents through the emergency door of the bus. Then we told Mantua and its snow banks what they could do with one another, and headed south.

By the time we were three hundred klicks down the highway the snow had turned to sleet, and everyone was loaded — including the coach, who'd been drinking all weekend anyway, even during the games. By the time we reached the junction where the roads divide off to the Okanagan Valley or through the Fraser Canyon to Chilliwack and the coast, it was fifteen degrees warmer and raining.

The bus driver pulled in at the junction's Greyhound depot so we could empty our tanks. In a fog, I remember everyone piling out of the bus, shouting and banging on the hoods of parked cars as we navigated our way through the muddy lot to the depot. As I left the bus myself I noticed the coach was passed out in his seat, not stirring a muscle. I thought about waking him up, saw his silver mickey in his lap, and decided he'd appreciate sleep more than a piss-call. That was the first of the big mistakes I made.

I guess because I'd been the instigator of the beer buy and the coach was in dreamland I got the perfectly lousy idea that I was now responsible for keeping things together. As I watched my teammates stumble and trip over one another as they wended their way across the parking lot to the washrooms, I saw the bus driver — a mean-eyed middle-aged French Canadian I'd run into at every bar I drank in while we were in Mantua — wending pretty erratically himself.

Bad sign. I crawled back into the bus and checked the map compartment to the left of the driver's seat. There were a couple of mickeys of rye in it, both empty. Now WHAT? I remember thinking.

I had the answer: I would have to take charge. I paused to take my leak behind the bus, then counted out my teammates as, one by one, they staggered back onto the bus. Everyone present and accounted for — except the driver.

I staggered into the depot, where I found him in one of the washroom cubicles, passed out on the toilet seat. I crawled over the top of the cubicle and made a half-hearted try at slapping him awake — half-hearted because he was plainly far too hammered to wake up, let alone drive. So I pulled him across my shoulders and carried him back to the bus, where I somehow dropped him into an empty seat. When he slid to the floor like the bundle of irresponsible crap he was, I let him lie there. That way, at least, he'd puke on the floor and not all over the equipment bag on the seat beside him.

If I'd been in my right mind, I would have realized that my blood alcohol was as topped up as everyone else's. But wasn't I Billy Menzies, the Bull Goose Loony of the Chilliwack Christian Lions, tournament all-star, Bedpost Diver Supreme, and All-Round Ace? I was in charge, and the power surge it gave me convinced me I was sober. And because I was sober and in charge, wasn't I the one to drive the goddamn bus? What could be more logical?

Never mind that I'd never driven a bus before, that I wasn't licensed to drive anything more complicated than a pickup truck, that by getting behind the wheel I was voiding any insurance the team held, and that the bus was an old, rickety International Harvester school bus with a two-speed stick shift that'd been giving the Frenchman trouble. I was Mr. Can Do, Captain of the Mantua Cup Champions, the captain of the ship, driver of the bus.

I took charge. To sober up my teammates I yanked down every window on the bus that would open. It had warmed up enough that they weren't going to freeze to death, and even if they could, alcohol doesn't freeze. A few of them, including Neil and Mikey, simply went to sleep with their heads hanging out the open window, and a couple more nodded off face up on the seats with their legs sticking out. And then, though I can't quite remember this, I must have settled behind the wheel and started the motor. I remember the gears grinding as I slipped the old bus into gear, and eventually I had us lurching through the parking lot and onto the highway.

THAT'S THE LAST THING I remember clearly. The rest I've had to piece together. It seems I got twenty klicks down that highway before I let the bus veer across the centre line on a curve that was sharper than it looked. I must have been thinking about something else, maybe the rhythm of the windshield wipers or a goal I'd scored during the tournament, or the red-headed girl I'd bopped. Or maybe I wasn't thinking or seeing anything at all.

That didn't matter. What did was the semi-trailer, headlights on high beam, horn blasting, bearing down on me in the same lane. I remember that it didn't seem to be bearing down on me very fast, and that I seemed to have time on my hands. I remember trying to wrench the bus out of the semi's path, but nothing happening.

The semi and the bus brushed one another, coming together just behind where I sat, and I heard the sickening sound of metal shrieking and grinding and tearing away, and inside that sound there was another, utterly distinct one, a sound that was far more strange and sickening, and one that I couldn't possibly have heard.

I did hear it. I couldn't have seen what I saw next either, but I saw that as absolutely as I heard that sickening sound-within-a-sound. In the split second after impact, I looked up to the rear-view mirror that had to have been ripped off by the initial impact and I saw human body parts tumbling through the illuminated air between the torn side of the bus and the jagged and receding metal of the semi. Three heads, an arm, part of a leg. Each one of the heads hit the tarmac as I watched, and then, I swear, bounced back up as high as the windows.

Then they were gone, and the bus was cartwheeling across the road into a field of sagebrush.

I WOKE UP IN a Kamloops hospital, a nice old building overlooking the city. From the windows I could see the North Thompson River stretching out to the northeast, languid and serene, and the huge weeping willows of Riverside Park where the North and equally languid South Thompson conjoined. The instant I woke up I knew Mikey was dead, because his had been one of the heads bouncing along the pavement. I found out later that Neil was dead too, along with two others, one of whom lost both legs from just below the knees. I had a third degree concussion, and a lot of bruises from bouncing around the bus after it flipped, but otherwise I was unhurt. Aside from the bus driver, who must have been wedged between the seats and the coach, I was the only person on the bus without broken bones.

The hospital nurses were decent enough, given what I'd done. Everyone around the hospital seemed to know the whole story: I'd been driving the bus, and blood tests had revealed how far I'd been into the impaired zone. One nurse told me I'd been interviewed by the highway patrol while I was still half-conscious, and I guess I confessed to everything in lurid detail, including what I'd seen in the bus mirror. So everyone knew. And everyone, including most of the nurses, was giving me the cold stare.

Before I was discharged from hospital the police charged me with impaired driving and vehicular manslaughter. Then, as if they'd decided that my goose was properly trussed and ready for cooking, they eased up and released me into the custody of my mother and stepfather on five thousand dollars' bail. Neither Fred nor my mother said a word to me during the four-hour drive from Kamloops to Chilliwack. That was fine with me. I didn't have anything to say, no excuses to make.

For a week I stayed in the house while my bruises healed. I tried to read, watched a lot of television, some of it religious, and I stared at the wall. Before too long, I realized that while my body was going to heal there were some other parts of me no one could put a bandage on. I thought about killing myself or making a break for it, but I wasn't capable of either. I'd take my lumps, do my time in jail, accept whatever anyone wanted to dish out to me.

Fred Menzies didn't see it the way I did. He sat me down the

Sunday afternoon after the accident while my mother was out at a church auxiliary.

"You know," he said quietly, "that your life here is over."

Warily, I nodded agreement. "I guess," I answered. "What's going to happen?"

"If you're convicted, you'll spend time in jail. And believe me, you'll be convicted." He began rummaging around in his jacket pocket, and stopped. "But that isn't what I mean."

He looked at me long and hard. I let the silence hang between us without trying to excuse myself or apologize. I had a lot of things coming to me, and this lecture was the least of them. Fred had his right to it — he'd bailed me out of jail, and since then he'd somehow kept everyone away from me.

But the lecture didn't start, and I found myself looking back at him the way he was gazing at me. I really hadn't realized that he gave a damn about me, but it was there in his hard face — along with the more easily recognized emotions. Finally, I couldn't stand his pain any longer.

"So, what do you mean, Fred?" I asked.

His answer, after another long silence, was a single question: "What's your name?"

"What are you asking?" I answered. "I'm Billy Menzies."

"That isn't your name from here on in," he said with a dark, simple patience in his voice. "As of right now, your name is Andrew Bathgate."

He slapped what he'd been rummaging in his pockets for onto the table in front of me. It was a folded sheet of paper, and an envelope. I opened the piece of paper first. It was my original birth certificate, and it named me Andrew William Bathgate. In the envelope was two thousand dollars in hundreds and fifties.

I looked up into Fred's face for the explanation.

"I want you out of here," he said, "before your mother comes back."

NINE

GORD PUSHES HIS WAY into the dressing room carrying three huge bundles of freshly dry-cleaned uniforms. He drops one into my lap.

"Christ, Weaver," he says, leaving the uniforms atop me and moving away to slam open the metal door to his locker. "You looked so peaceful there I was tempted to put the tubes in and drain you."

Aside from being my closest friend, and the district coroner, Gord is a trained mortician. He stopped practising long before I knew him, but the mortician's sense of humour has stayed with him. I've seen him and Jack put perfectly sober people on the floor laughing with their Undertaker routine from the WWF, and he and I have a running joke about what morticians do with the gold teeth from cadavers.

Gord got tired, as he puts it, of the makeup business, and went to medical school. But there's a part of him that doesn't forget what he's seen and done, and he doesn't give up trade secrets, even to his close friends.

And there are secrets, you know. Ever heard of anyone who's asked what becomes of the gold from their loved one's teeth after cremation? Well, neither have I, but the gold must be going somewhere. I figure there's a lucrative underground trade in cadaver gold that goes on between morticians and dental mechanics, but I'll be damned if I can get Gord to confirm it. He just laughs at me, and claims the gold is vapourized by the heat.

"I don't think I'm quite ready for what you have in mind," I laugh, pushing the bundle off me and onto the floor without sitting up. "Where have you been all afternoon?"

He sighs. "Some kid drove his car off the road about forty kilometres south last night. No one knew they were missing until his girlfriend crawled back up to the road this morning.

"Dead?"

"Yeah," he says. "You don't want to know about it."

"What about the girl?"

"She'll be okay," he answers, then adds, "someday."

"How old was the kid?"

"About Wendel's age. But not very much like Wendel."

"No one is." I'm momentarily grateful for Wendel's virtues, one of which is the kind of common sense that most males around here don't have until they're in their mid-thirties. If ever.

"I feel sorry for most of them," Gord says. "They're just smart enough to see they've got no future. Their parents weren't any smarter, but at least they had a shot at making a decent living. These kids are…"

He falls silent, then shifts up a gear.

"The Juniors are coming off the ice in few minutes," he says. "Why don't we suit up and burn off some lactic acid. Toss the puck around a little."

A glance at my wrist watch tells me I've got a little over an hour before I'm supposed to be home. Why not?

THE JUNIORS COME FLOODING into the far end of the dressing room as we're lacing up our skates. They're pushing and shoving one another, high as kites on the combo of testosterone and adrenaline kids run on at that age. It makes me wonder, as I tramp the runway to the ice behind Gord's massive back and thick neck, what guys like us are using for fuel. It ain't testosterone anymore. But the moment we step on the ice, I remember why I'm still playing. Then I take my second step, on the left leg. A jolt runs up it into my spine, and I forget. The first turn around the ice, that's how it goes: remember, forget, remember, forget, remember, forget.

By the time we've circled the rink ten or fifteen times my left lumbar has loosened, and there are several more things I remember: the sound of steel against ice, the peculiar colour and crispness of the air over a hockey rink, the here and now of hockey, with everything else at bay in the world outside. There's a zone of quiet inside me that matches it.

Gord bangs his stick on the ice and a puck whistles by my head, just close enough to make me wince. "Man, but you *are* in Dreamland today," he says. "You'd better not play like this tomorrow afternoon."

While I'm trying to think of something smart to say I hear a shout from the far end of the rink, and Junior crashes onto the ice, full gear, carrying a bucket of pucks.

"Take some shots," he hollers. "Look at what I've got."

Gord and I turn around to look, and it's impossible not to see what he's got. Even from this distance they look bigger than the old pads, probably because they're white. From this distance, they make him look like a hospital nurse with elephant legs.

"You finally talked Jack into new pads?" Gord asks as Junior skates toward us. "I don't believe it."

"Oh, to hell with Jack," Junior answers. "I gave up. Bought 'em myself. What's money when you're in search of excellence."

Aha! I've seen Junior reading those business wanker books in the dressing room recently and now I know why.

"This isn't going to bankrupt me. I'll write it off as a business expense."

Junior empties the bucket of pucks in front of us, tosses the bucket over the boards, and glides backward into the net. From just outside the blueline, Gord and I start punching pucks at his new pads.

"These pads are a little more bouncy than the old ones," I holler, as a rebound skitters back close to where I'm standing.

"After all those years the old ones were like dead cushions on a pool table," Junior yells back, doing a double take as Gord rings a shot off the post and in behind him. "It'll keep the rebounds from dropping in front of me. Should cut a goal a game off my average right there."

"If you cut ten inches off your waistline," Gord says, "you'd be able to see the puck when it's in front of you."

"Screw off," Junior sneers, gaily. "Now I won't have to, will I?"

Just for fun, I whistle a shot close to his head. On cue, he drops to the ice.

"I see new pads haven't improved that part of your game."

"Just shoot the fucking puck and keep it down," Junior growls. "Either that or pay my dentist bills."

We pepper him with low shots for close to twenty minutes before he tires of it and retreats happily to the dressing room, taking the bucket and pucks with him. It's quarter past seven, and there's enough time for a couple more turns around the ice before Alpo Numinen, the Zamboni driver, will want us off so he can flood the rink for public skating.

AS LOCAL CHARACTERS GO, Alpo is unique: to him, everything and everyone is intrinsically despicable. It doesn't matter to him whether it's his job, or hockey, old players, young players, recreation skaters, his Zamboni. As far as Alpo is concerned, life is a crapbag filled with clowns and villains, all of them out to disturb his peace or steal his dignity and sanity. Alpo's only virtue is that he can bring up a different lump of crap out of the bag for everything.

He hates his job because he gets razzed by the crowds, who regularly drone "Aaal-Pooooo, Aaaaal-Poooooo" at him while he's flooding the ice between periods. He believes they're mocking him, and he's right — life can be rough when you have the same first name as a popular brand of dog food. He despises hockey because it's too violent; he despises the older players because they know from experience what a sour goof he is; he despises the young players because they're too stupid to pretend that they're intimidated by his antics. That isn't all. He despises recreational skaters because they're (in his words) paying money to slide around on a sheet of ice, and he despises his Zamboni because it breaks down on him while he's trying to flood the ice, making him the object of further taunts.

Alpo saves the biggest, smelliest lump of bile to smear across the memory of his own son, Artie, who was until Wendel the only local kid to make it beyond Junior A hockey in Mantua. Artie got to the NHL about ten years ago for a cup of coffee, and as far as anyone knows, it was his final cup of coffee. He was last seen stumbling out of a bar on Long Island dead drunk, fine Mantua product that he is.

Alpo hasn't seen his kid since he left town for the NHL, but he'll curse him out in front of anyone who'll listen. And to give credit where credit's due, he has his twisted reasons. As soon as Artie left town to go to Junior A in Peterborough, he changed his first name from Arno to Arthur, and his last name to Newman so no one would think he was one of those pansy Europeans. As far as Alpo was concerned, Artie was betraying his Finnish heritage.

Alpo is exaggerating here a little, since he didn't exactly arrive here straight from a smorgasbord himself. He's a third-generation cheeseburger like most everyone else around here. The only thing about him that's Finnish is his name and maybe his sour temperament — although lately I've heard him mouthing things in some bjarny-bjarny language to impress the Juniors. Since the most consistent thing about Alpo — aside from his bad temper

— is his laziness, he probably got his knowledge of Finnish from IKEA commercials on television.

I've never met Artie, but Gord says he was a decent kid, although — like his old man — chronically lazy. That probably explains why he didn't stay in the NHL, together with the fact that he'd had his appetite for climbing into the piss-tank since he was fifteen. That's hardly unique around here.

I don't get people like Alpo, to tell the truth. Life kicks everyone, but that's no excuse to whine about it all day and all night. Alpo's job is really a pretty decent one. A City maintenance supervisor's wages get him a new pickup every two or three years, and he really doesn't need to take all the crap he gets. Fact is, he chooses to run the Zamboni at all the big events because it gives him something to bitch about. If I had his job, I'd use the facilities every chance I got. Alpo? He hasn't been on skates for years, just out of sheer perversity.

Look at it this way: life is reasonably sweet provided you don't stick the air pump into your miseries, which everyone has. So we don't live in Los Angeles, and we're not all rich movie producers. We're not exactly in Mogadishu shaking empty milk jugs at the United Nations, either. If you live in Los Angeles, you make money, go to film premieres, and keep a loaded gun under your pillow. Fine with me. Even in Mogadishu there's the beach. And if you find yourself driving a Zamboni at the Mantua Memorial Coliseum, for crying out loud, go skating once in a while.

THE GATES AT THE Coliseum's far end swing open, and I hear Alpo shouting at us.

"Alright, you jerk-offs, get off my ice before I come and run you down."

I look at my watch. It's past seven-thirty, and Gord and I have been skating, side by side, for almost ten minutes without a word exchanged.

TEN

I'M NOT A TOTAL ditz. As soon as I have my skates off, I call the Lotus Inn from the phone in Jack's office. I have a standard order for them: mu shu pork, beef with black bean and garlic sauce, and their special chow mein with shredded duck. Neither Esther nor I are what you'd call hearty eaters, but Bozo makes up for us. If she had her way, she'd go off dog food permanently and live on chow mein. So we usually order more food than we'll need, eat what we like, and let her have the rest. Most of the time, that means she gets nearly all the chow mein.

The girl on the phone recognizes my voice — or maybe it's just the beginning of the order.

"This Mr. Weaver, right?" she says, and reels off the rest of it.

I admit that she's got me, and she says, "You come in fifteen minutes. We very busy tonight, but you are special."

I thank her without feeling special. The chef at the Lotus knows what he's doing, and that makes him a civic asset. My kind, anyway. Towns like Mantua are generally a hell of a lot less notable for the quality of their Chinese restaurants than for the number of drunken after-hours diners who barf up their dinners in the restaurant parking lots on their way to their pickups. At the other Chinese food restaurants in Mantua, parking lot puke can get a foot thick by this time of winter. The parking lot outside the Lotus stays pretty clean — maybe because it's the only Chinese restaurant in Mantua whose chef knows what black bean sauce is and cooks dishes like mu shu pork.

Gord and I change in silence, another habit we've gotten into. If there's nothing to say Gord doesn't talk, and I've learned to respect that.

Tonight, neither of us bothers to shower — the leisurely skate cooled us down to no-stink temperatures. I park my gear in my locker, flip the padlock shut, and twirl the dial.

Gord is standing at the door waiting. "I'll walk out with you," he says.

I nod without saying anything, and we walk to the front doors and look out. It's snowing again, the relentlessly calm kind of snowfall I've never quite seen anywhere else but Mantua. It might add another twenty centimetres to the snowpack before morning but not a single flake of it will drift. You move through this kind of snowfall or you move it out of your way, but it never comes looking for you the way it does in the East.

"Pretty out there," Gord says, gesturing at the snow. "It might give you some problems getting up the hill."

"I always seem to make it up somehow," I answer. "See you around noon."

"Have a fine evening," he says.

I squeeze out a laugh I don't much feel. "I should be so lucky."

Gord glances at me, sees that I don't want to explain why, and lets it go. He opens the door, waves at me without looking, and wanders off into the snow to the rear of the Coliseum and his truck. As I watch him go it occurs to me that he's off to do the autopsy on that kid who was killed last night.

I'm already late, but I pause for a moment by the case that holds the team photo of the 1972 Chilliwack Christian Lions. There's Mikey's handsome, dark face smiling through the veil of lime green, and Neil with his more serious expression. For a brief second I can't find Billy Menzies, but no, there I am, second row centre, with one hand on the Mantua Cup, and a wide grin on my face.

I'D PARKED THE LINCOLN in the VIP spot next to the front door, so I don't have as far to walk as Gord. I park the car illegally all the time, actually. Not just here, but all over town. The police and metermen tolerate it because the car still has the old City Hall Limousine sticker on the windshield — and I keep telling them I bought the privilege with the car. They know better, but what the hell.

I make my own exit from the building, and by the time I've reached the car my shoulders are spotting with white. As I'm dusting off the car with my elbows, I spot Wendel's wallet lying on the passenger seat. Dumb. I left the car unlocked.

At least it's still there. Another of the advantages of small town life, although this particular advantage isn't quite so automatic in Mantua as it once was. I'm lucky, really. Not a fabulous piece of luck, but I'll take it.

While the Lincoln warms up, I turn on the dash light and flip open the wallet to inspect its contents. It contains the usual: the driver's licence in the window pocket, and behind that two bank cards, one of them a Visa. In the pocket across from those, hidden, is a plastic-covered birth certificate, and a couple of business cards from Wendel's suppliers. Inside the billfold is twenty-nine dollars — a twenty, a five, and two twos — all fairly crisp. Behind them, folded several times and half-concealed by a flap, is a piece of paper.

I pull the piece of paper out — what the hell, I've gotten this far — and unfold it beneath the dash light. It's another birth certificate, and from the look of it, the original: name, Wendel Alan Simons, born, Mantua, December 13, date of registration, February

17 the following year. I refold the document and put it back where it was, open the glove compartment, and push the wallet inside.

I'm a couple of blocks away from the Coliseum when it hits me: The dates on Wendel's birth certificate make him twenty-one, not twenty. He's a year older than he's supposed to be. I slam on the brakes, pull the Lincoln over to the curb, and reopen the glove compartment. I check the birth certificate again: same data. Then, on a hunch, I check it against the plasticized one. That one reads December 13 too, but a year later. Wendel was born nine months after the last Mantua tournament.

By the time I pull up in front of the Lotus Inn, my heart feels like it's trying to crawl out of my throat. Who am I kidding? Now I understand the Freudian Slip: possible, hell. It's probable, and from there the complications stick out like quills from a porcupine's backside. Every time I try to get my mind around the probability, I get a muzzleful. They sting, each one, and the more I paw at them, the more certain it is.

"Sonofabitch," I say aloud. No, that's exactly wrong. The "bitch" involved isn't a bitch, she's Esther. And her son is my son. This afternoon's upset takes on an entire new dimension — and so do my chippy remarks about Wendel.

I pick up and pay for the Chinese food with two twenty-dollar bills, by now completely distracted. I'm two blocks down the street before I realize I gave the cashier a seventeen-dollar tip. No wonder she knows me by name.

ESTHER AND I LIVE near the top of Cranberry Ridge, just west of the city. It's a good place to live, barely developed until recently, with fine farmland further west and deep, rich soils. The ridge is one-hundred-and-fifty-or-so metres above the river, and a little colder than down below, with more snow. And this winter, the drive up there has been more of an adventure than it usually is.

The reason getting up Cranberry Ridge is an adventure is the same reason it's good farmland. It, and the entire plateau that runs twenty miles to the west of town, is composed of fine, soft clay up to two hundred metres down, alluvial fan laid down ten thousand years ago when the glaciers receded. Left undisturbed, Cranberry Ridge looks much like any other piece of real estate in the North, except that its deeper soil supports deciduous trees, mostly poplar and birch. But if you mess with this kind of soil it turns into quagmire, and if it's disturbed, it will slide down-hill. Because of this, the original road up Cranberry Ridge was built carefully and at small scale, and it was steep. Even then it had its share of problems — shifting grades and the occasional mudslide.

That changed a couple of years ago after the City conned the government into building a university in Mantua. Since every-one involved, locally or otherwise, was a certified idiot with delusions of grandeur, they set out to make appropriately grand, idiotic decisions. The first one — and the biggest piece of idiocy — was to choose the least stable building site within a hun-dred-kilometre radius. They chose the top of Cranberry Ridge instead of the derelict downtown where everyone with half a deck knew it should have been. The result is what aesthetes without common sense usually deliver: a nice viewpoint for visiting dignitaries to see how bad Mantua's air pollution is, and a flood of cost overruns.

The fun started when the government's contractors tried to build a four-lane highway up the side of the Ridge. The Ridge didn't co-operate. The road-bed slipped, so the government con-tractors licked their lips and rebuilt, gouging deeper into the clay, which slipped again. Since then it's been the Chinese fire drill: underground springs opening up, new creeks emerging, the Ridge slipping more, and so on. The site where they're trying to build the university buildings is nearly as unstable. Let's just say that the announcement that a university was coming to town may turn out to be unintentionally prophetic.

All this would be amusing as hell if the road hadn't already cost fifteen-million dollars they could have used to rebuild the downtown, and — not incidentally — if it weren't making getting home a royal pain in the ass for Esther and me. I've had to take the long way around more often than I'd care to count since they started, and that entails almost forty klicks of gravel road — mushy, muddy gravel when it's been raining. When spring breakup comes this April, after the latest round of construction, the long way around is likely to be the only route we'll have.

Tonight, though, the road isn't too bad — at least until I'm closing in on the hairpin curve near the top. Right there, an overconfident moron in a Ford Explorer loses control in the curve and does a one-eighty-degree four-wheel drift in front of me. A second or two elongates into an eternity, and I actually close my eyes because there's no way to predict which direction the Explorer will go. Okay, I think, fine, this is it, I'm toast.

My life doesn't pass before my eyes like it's supposed to. I merely understand that in a second or so I'm likely going to be dead. There'll be the pain of impact, the Ford Explorer stuck in my gullet, and a mess of Chinese food splattered all over me like puke in a parking lot.

But there's no impact, and when I open my eyes I catch a glimpse of a frightened man's face whizzing past, and I see the Explorer straighten itself on the road — only backward. In the rear-view mirror I watch it brake, spin a second one-eighty, and skid to a stop.

I don't stop to console the driver. I'd like to do it with a tire iron, but I've got — and suddenly I'm recalling that Robert Frost poem Esther likes — miles to go before I sleep. Even if I didn't, it isn't a good idea to stop a car on Cranberry Ridge to recite poetry.

IT'S FIVE AFTER EIGHT when I pull into the driveway and turn off the ignition, still bathed in that strange, resigned calm I felt when the Explorer was about to do me. It's a relief to see Bozo, looking like a black bear, sitting on the front steps waiting for me and for her dinner. Esther must have whispered the magic words in her ear, because this time of day she'd normally be on one of her nightly romps with her pal Sweetie, the neighbour's Newfoundland. Until two years ago last fall there was a third Newfie in the neighbourhood, Camille, but an American hunter decided she was a black bear, and shot her in her owner's front yard. Since then, Bozo and Sweetie have spent hunting season with the word "DOG" painted across both sides of them in day-glo pink. So far, so good.

I know, I know. Anything but dealing with the matter at hand, right? Well, here's what I'm going to do: I'm going to walk into the house without a plan, just like I've done all my life whenever the crap gets close enough to the fan that I can smell it. That seems right. There are times in a life when the world moves too fast for even the illusion of control. I got lucky with the Explorer, so maybe I'll get lucky again.

I click off the car lights, slip Wendel's wallet into the inside pocket of my jacket, gather up the bag of rapidly cooling Chinese food, and slip out of the car. As I close the door and take my first step toward the house, Bozo greets me with a flying tackle, and I find myself lying in a snow bank with one hundred and twenty-five pounds of black Newfie slobbering in my face.

At least she wasn't going for the Chinese food. And she isn't a Ford Explorer.

ELEVEN

L YING IN A SNOWBANK forever with Bozo isn't an option, tempting as it is. For sure, she'd be happy about it, provided I gave her the chow mein. But Esther's dinner is getting cold, and if I let Bozo sit on my chest like this much longer I'll drown in dog drool. I place the food bag as far from me as I can, push Bozo off the other way, and climb out of the snow bank. When I'm almost clear, she grabs the tail of my coat and pulls me back in.

"Cut it out, you stupid slobber-bag."

These are words she's heard before, but she knows they don't always mean the same thing. She cocks her head as I glare at her, picks up the signal that that I'm serious, and sinks back in the snow, disappointed.

"It's okay," I say, softening my voice. "Just let me get the bag here, and we'll go inside and have dinner."

Dinner is a word she understands perfectly, whatever tones come with it. Along with *romp*, it's her favourite part of human language, and she leaps out of the snowbank in one graceful bound to stand, attentive and still salivating, in front of me, ready to follow me respectfully anywhere in the universe I — and the chow mein I'm packing — care to lead her. As she hopes, I lead her into the house where her food dish is.

Inside she sits patiently as I remove my coat and boots, and she doesn't fuss when I wipe her jowls with one of the towels Esther keeps by the front and back doors. I also retrieve Wendel's wallet from my coat before I hang it up. Bozo follows me into the kitchen with her snout pressed devoutly against the bag, sucking in the fumes.

Esther has two places set at the table, but there's no sign of her. I take the food out of the bag, turn on the oven, and put the covered aluminum containers inside to reheat. Bozo lies down to wait beside the table with her snout between her paws.

Esther is sleeping. Her ability to fall asleep anywhere, anytime, is only a little less remarkable than how oblivious her slumber is, and how swiftly she can pull herself out of it to complete alertness. Being able to sleep deeply in an unlocked house is partly Bozo's gift, of course. Short of a grizzly, nothing and no one she doesn't know can enter this house without Esther's or my consent.

Bozo isn't exactly a normal guard dog. She doesn't bark when strangers come around, and she doesn't bare her fangs if they approach the house. What she does do is sprawl in the doorway and grab their ankle or their pant leg in her jaws if and when they try to get past her, after which she holds on until one of us tells her to let go. Last summer, a mail courier spent three hours on the front porch after he tried to slip past Bozo to place a package between the screen and front doors. By the time I returned home, the courier and Bozo were best pals, but Bozo hadn't let go of his ankle.

As I lean over to plant a kiss on Esther's cheek, her eyes open. "Ah," she says. "You're back. What time is it?"

"Just after eight. Are you hungry?"

She ignores the question, pulls herself upright, and stretches languidly.

"I've been out for almost three hours," she says. "I didn't think I was *that* tired."

"I could run you a bath," I offer. "That might cheer you up."

"Who says I need cheering up?" She's fully awake now, and we're right back to the impasse we were at when I dropped her off.

"Well," I say, "Come into the kitchen, and let's eat."

WE EAT QUIETLY, WITH bursts of small talk that quickly trail off into silence. I'm about to feed the chow mein to Bozo when she drops her bomb.

"I think you should know," she says, "that Leo Simons wasn't Wendel's father."

There it is. She's confirmed the probability that has been cooking in my brain since I saw the dates on Wendel's two birth certificates. And I'm hearing much more than she believes she's telling me. I know more than she does now. And that's bad.

First, there's danger in my knowing more than she thinks I do. Yeah, most people play the game of letting on they know less than they do, and the worst thing I might find out in the next few minutes is that she doesn't much like Billy Menzies — something I've lived with for years. That's not the danger. This is about us, and the reciprocal trust we've built up. Aside from the Billy Menzies stuff and what I do with my money, I've kept very little from Esther. About as much as it now turns out she's kept from me. But now she's dropped a major secret. Why tonight, and for what reasons, I'm not clear.

If you've ever lived in a place like Mantua, you'll understand why reciprocity makes sense. You rely on the people around you for things city people either don't need, or that they get from the big, anonymous systems that rule their lives. Around here, a lot of those systems don't exist, and when they do, they don't work all the time.

So not lying about important stuff is common sense. It keeps you from giving into all those lowest common denominators that are always inviting you to screw up or lie to yourself about how low the denominator is. More than once in the last few years that small rule has kept me from chasing around. It's also earned me the one close friend I've ever really had as an adult: Gord.

Gord says that if you lie to people about important things it damages their ability to decide what's true or false right across the board, and makes it impossible for them to care about you accurately. Point is, Esther knows nearly everything about Andy Bathgate, and *everything* about Weaver Bathgate. But if my early life comes up, I say I don't remember much, and that isn't a lie. The fact is I remember only four or five of Billy's days with any detail, and those are the ones I can't tell her about.

But now those four or five days are smack at the centre of what she's revealing, and unless I can think of something fast, our system of telling the truth to one another is about to come apart.

"As a matter of fact, I was wondering about that in the last hour," I say, truthfully.

Esther's eyes narrow. "What do you mean by that?"

I pull Wendel's wallet from my pocket and plunk it on the table in front of her. "Wendel has two birth certificates in here. One says he's twenty, the other says he was born a year earlier. He left his wallet in the car, and I ..."

For a split second there's anger in her eyes. There's no point accusing me of going through Wendel's wallet, because I've already confessed to it. She doesn't, and the flash point fades. "I wanted to protect him from it while he was young," she says. "And Leo agreed. We weren't exactly expecting his father to show up and claim him."

That one makes me wince. "How long has Wendel known?"

"He doesn't. Oh, I had to tell him about the age business when the Rangers drafted him. He was born in December, so I just told him I didn't want him starting school at five. Sooner or later it would have come out, and I didn't want him to be unprepared. But he doesn't know Leo wasn't his father."

She turns her back to me and stares out the kitchen window into the darkness. "Look, I was going to tell you everything — not that there's very much to tell. There was a boy from one of the teams at the last Mantua Cup. You know how things like that go. I was drunk, and so was he. It just happened. I was going with Leo at the time, but we weren't ... you know. When I turned up pregnant, I told him. I had to. I was supposed to enter nursing that September, but by late June I was already starting to show."

Bozo is nuzzling my leg, wanting her chow mein. I push her away, but she's insistent. She grabs my sleeve in her mouth and nearly drags me off the chair. Esther turns from the window to watch, distractedly. I gesture at the nearly full platter of food. "Do you want any of this?"

"No," she says absently. "Give it to her."

I slide the platter in front of Bozo and she greedily buries her face in it.

"We left town in July. Eloped. Leo worked while I had the baby."

"That was a generous thing for him to do," I say.

"Leo was a generous man." She seems troubled by that thought for a moment. "Anyway," she continues, "the next fall I went to Simon Fraser instead and took a B.Sc. in psychology. I went there because I could take classes year round. It only took three years. Then I went to UBC and started an MA in social work."

"What was Leo doing all this time?"

"Working for a logging supply company. And being supportive, whenever he was around. We lived at the university residences, so there was daycare and all that. It wasn't so bad."

"You didn't come back here at all?"

"Not until Wendel was three-and-a-half. By then nobody asked questions. Why would they? He was small for his age. Anyway, when I was a year into the MA Leo's father died, and we moved back here so Leo could take over the company. You know most of the rest of it."

The crisis point has come, and, despite my good intentions, I embark on a deception, if not quite an outright lie. "What about ..."

She cuts me off. "His biological father? He disappeared, the poor bastard." There's neither malice nor resentment in her voice. While I listen to her version of who I was and what I did the night after I helped her conceive Wendel, I feel a strange kind of elation. She does something I've never quite been able to do: she forgives me, all the way to saying that it wasn't my fault. She knows the basic details of the bus accident, right down to the drunken bus driver and the fact that two of the dead were my closest friends. She's also aware that I flew the coop before the vehicular homicide charges reached the court. It's another bizarre moment. She actually tries to excuse me:

"Really, what else could he have done? Such a waste."

TWELVE

WENDEL OPENS THE BACK door and barges into the kitchen, oblivious to everything but what's sizzling in his private frying pan. For once, I'm grateful.

"What's with you guys?" he asks, stopping in his tracks as a flicker of recognition alters what began as a greeting into a real question. He isn't used to seeing his mother in tears.

"Oh, silly stuff," Esther answers, wiping her nose with the back of her hand. I reach up and pull a Kleenex from the box on top of the fridge and hand it to her.

Wendel glares at me — this must be my fault, he's thinking — while Bozo happily shuffles around his legs, demanding attention. Wendel leans well over her so he can scratch her ears without getting a face-full. With a Newfoundland, position is an important tactical consideration unless you're wearing snorkeling gear.

"Well," Wendel says without looking up, willing to be satisfied with Esther's bland explanation and with me as the source of all domestic evils, "I've got some news. The government's going to cut the annual harvest by forty percent. The Coalition finally got to the Minister."

"How'd you hear this?" I ask, suppressing any trace of scepticism. I've heard these rumours before, usually via other Coalition members — the college professors, local industry screwees, and the one or two union members I know who aren't so terrified of losing their jobs that they're more pro-cut than the multinationals. When it comes to forestry, Wendel is always willing to talk, even with me. "You know the routine, Weaver," he says, sitting down at the table beside his mother. "Everyone in Mantua who isn't on a respirator knows the multinationals have been overcutting the forests for thirty years."

I nod, hiding my skepticism.

"Course," he says, "now the multinationals are going to put on a big show about being upset about the cuts. And you know what bullshit that is."

I shrug. "That's their way of stoking up everyone who's dependent on the industry. What do you expect? They're out to whip up whoever thinks the forests are the only gravypot in the universe. If you threaten to downsize the industry, you're threatening their livelihoods or their pickup trucks or whatever."

"It's so stupid," Wendel complains. He goes on to explain what he thinks is going to happen, though it's murky: someone sent him a fax outlining a still-secret Cabinet document that will recommend sharply reducing the annual cut, and so forth. Normally I'd be teasing him for sucking on his own wishbone, supposing that a government is capable of planning further ahead than the next election. But not tonight.

"What's the difference between this and all the other times cutbacks were supposed to happen?" I ask, trying to sound neutral.

All he's got on that is his optimism. "Well, this time it's going to happen, for one."

"Then what?"

"Hopefully the bastards will pull out, and leave us to do our own logging."

I've heard this before, too. It's an idea that is teasing the brains of a lot of people around here, and not just the greenheads. But tonight I want to hear his version. "Explain how that will work."

He looks at me to see if I'm setting him up, decides he doesn't care, and launches into it. "The theory behind it is pretty simple, once you accept that we don't have to do exactly what our predecessors have done for the last two hundred years," he says. "First, you stop clearcutting the forests."

"Stop? How do you stop it?"

"It's easier than it sounds. For one, you won't *have* to kick out the multinationals. Once clearcutting has been banned they'll close down on their own, because the equipment they use won't be efficient and neither the harvest nor their profits will be fat enough. Having them leave won't involve the huge loss in jobs most people think, because the harvest technologies they're using have become so labour-efficient they don't provide that many jobs.

"There's something else about multinationals nobody pays any attention to. In the twenty-or-so years since the takeover of the forests began here, the profits have completely stopped going through Mantua. The resource simply gets harvested and exported" — he pauses here for effect — "and so do the profits. The multinationals don't just take the profits out of the region, either, they ship them out of the country. What we're doing right now is letting our future be shipped to Hong Kong, Tokyo, and New York without any compensation. And with stumpage fees as low as they are, and with all the raw log exports, it's a complete giveaway."

"So what you're telling me is that since nobody around here is getting anything out of the harvest the logical thing to do is to close down the industry? Okay. But how does the alternative work? You can't just do nothing."

"We start small," Wendel answers. "We wedge the locals into what's left of the forests to harvest trees on a selective basis. But to make this practical there has to be a local co-operative to scale and sell the logs to the highest bidder — hopefully someone in Mantua who can do some local added-value manufacturing and create more jobs. The result? More jobs locally, and whatever profits are produced stay in the community. It's called Equivalent Community Value."

"What does that mean?"

"It's a political idea. It means that a community has a right to a fair share of the profits that come from the use of the natural resources around it."

"Okay," I say, sitting down across from him. "But what are you going to do about practical reality?"

"Practical reality?" he hoots. "You call what's been going on practical? It's totally nuts."

"Nobody ever said practical means sane. The multinationals have got a billion-or-so dollars of capital investment invested here. They aren't going to leave willingly. They've also got their dicks stuck in the government and the big unions up to the hilt, and whenever people like you try to shake them loose with common sense they hump harder, and what's already loony gets worse."

"It takes a leap of faith," Wendel says, sounding a little lame. "We're all going to get fucked if we're as cynical as you are."

"I didn't say I don't agree with you. I think you're right about this stuff. But what have you got so far? Some grunting by a few powerless Cabinet committees, and the usual horseshit promises that the interests of the community are, har, har, foremost in the minds of the experts?"

He doesn't buckle. "That's just more cyncism," he says. "What if you turn it inside out? There isn't any alternative to what we're proposing. Not in the long term. The locals have to get off their asses."

I don't know what the hell Wendel was doing at school while he was in Junior hockey, but he's got his head further around this than I have. My cynicism and my twenty-some years of experience seeing little guys being worked over by bigger guys haven't taught me anything. I stand up. "Okay, kid. I think you're onto something here, if you can get around all the ifs."

"Geez, thanks for telling me," he answers, his voice dripping sarcasm.

He *is* onto something. And he's not about to listen to any advice. Being twenty — twenty-one — he doesn't see how powerful those ifs are. Life may have gotten nastier around here than it used to be, but it's like everything else about living in a fat, wealthy country: relative. There's a point where getting screwed forces people to smarten up, but we haven't reached it around here. There's still beer in the bars, money and perks to buy off local politicians, and now there's fifty channels to keep us in front of our TVs.

"Where's your truck?" I ask, hoping to distract him from further sermonizing.

"Still in the garage. They want to replace the queen pins, or whatever."

Wendel's grasp of auto maintenance is a touch lighter than his grasp of forestry. "They're king pins," I say. "I hope those clowns haven't been messing around with you again."

"Whatever," he answers. "Queen pins, king pins. Who cares? It'll be ready Monday night, so ..."

"You can keep the pickup until then," Esther interrupts, freeing him of having to ask. "I'm not going anywhere Andy can't drive me to."

With that settled, Wendel cheerfully shifts his focus from us to the refrigerator, which was his original motive for coming over. He hasn't lived with us since he returned to Mantua from Regina and Juniors, but he hasn't exactly been a stranger, either. He comes over five or six times a week to hoover the fridge. Esther hoped he'd find a steady girl and settle in with her — or maybe that was me, hoping to cut the grocery bills. I can't quite remember, all of a sudden.

Whatever we wished, it didn't happen, and not because Wendel has been short of girlfriends. There was a steady one for a while, but they didn't move in together. He just brought her with him to help apply the vacuum to the food supply.

"There's nothing in here," he complains from inside the fridge door.

"We ate Chinese tonight," Esther says by way of explanation.

"Aren't there some chicken pies in there somewhere?"

I can't stop myself. "If you'd gotten here half an hour ago you could have fought Bozo for the chow mein."

Wendel ignores us both, and pulls out a loaf of bread, a jar of mayonnaise, and a block of cheddar, and moves to the counter to fix himself some sandwiches.

WHILE HE'S BUSY WITH this I have a good look at him — a parental look. It's hard to see how I missed our physical similarities. He's built the same way as I am, larger and a little more spectacularly muscled, sure, but he has the same square shoulders and long waist.

When he turns and I see him in profile the resemblance isn't so strong. His jawline is stronger than mine, the forehead broader. Hard to say about his nose, since mine's been broken enough times that its impossible to say what it would look like if I'd grown up to be a toe-tapping banker or violinist.

He has Esther's features — and her strength of character. When he turns to ask if we've got another half gallon of milk in the basement fridge, I see that his eyes are hers too: large, deepset, and the same luminous green.

Without me realizing it, he's helped me to make a decision. I'm not going to drop the truth on Esther until I can establish a few more solid links between Wendel and I. He's going to be a tough nut to crack, though.

Esther gathers the dishes and, elbowing Wendel aside, begins to load the dishwasher while I crumple the empty Chinese food containers and put them in the garbage. Our talk, apparently, is over.

Well, not quite. Wendel quits his sandwich-building at six, slices the pile into halves, and sits down at the table with the plate in front of him.

"I saw you looking at all those stupid team photos this morning in the lobby," he says, eyeing me with a strange friendliness. "They used to have tournaments here every spring, didn't they? How come those stopped?"

Esther answers the question for me. "There was a bus accident after the last tournament," she says. "Five players from the team that won got killed."

"Four," I say, without thinking. "Only four players were killed."

Esther glances at me, and just as quickly looks away. "How come you know about that?"

"Gord told me the story. You know I've got a memory for details."

It's Wendel's turn. "Since when?"

"Hey. There's a lot of things about me you don't know, kiddo." I'm veering dangerously close to the truth here.

"I was thinking," he says, "we should start up the tournament again."

"What in God's name for?" Esther and I say, as one.

"Why not?"

"I just told you why not," Esther answers. "The last time we had a tournament four people died."

"That was a long time ago," Wendel scoffs. "Who cares about that now?"

"Who'd want to sponsor a tournament?" I ask, as if it's a rhetorical question.

Wendel doesn't blink. "The City. Why wouldn't Snell go for something like that?"

"Because it would bring in ten or fifteen teams full of crazy shitheads to wreck the town," I say. "He wouldn't want the policing problems. It's bad enough around here when just the Roosters are in town."

Wendel starts to argue his case, speculating that the independent loggers might sponsor it, and rattling on about the prestige a good tournament would bring.

I decide that it's better to let him harangue his mother about this. She isn't as likely to put her foot in it as I am. I get up from the table and pull my leathertops and snowshoes from the kitchen closet.

"I think I'll take Bozo out."

THIRTEEN

"**Y**OU'RE GOING OUT WITH her now?" Esther says, eyeing my snowshoes. "There's close to a metre of new snow out there."

I reach into the closet again, this time for my wool pants and mitts.

"It'll be okay. We won't go far. And anyway, I rebroke the trails on Thursday. Back in half an hour or so."

The instant Bozo catches sight of the snowshoes, she begins to bounce up and down. Wisely, Esther and Wendel clear out of the kitchen and leave me and the dog to our preparations.

Bozo splatters a mouthful of saliva across the kitchen wall, and she's ready. She prances up and down while I look for my wool shirt, which isn't where it ought to be. After a moment's cursing and fumbling around I find it underneath a nearly full fifty-pound bag of dog chow, with the pockets full of kibble. I shake the bits out onto the floor and Bozo sucks them up.

By the time I'm ready to leave, mother and son have settled down in the living room to watch the video Wendel has brought with him. I lean in just long enough to watch the credits. It's one of his Sierra Club videos, with one of those depressing, bearded yo-yos talking about the end of the world in the same bland enthusiasm as a television announcer announcing this week's bargains at Canadian Tire. They don't stir when I jam a toque over my skull, open the door for Bozo, and follow her outside with a snowshoe tucked under each arm.

"Don't be too long," I hear Esther call as I release the storm door. It shuts before I can answer.

THE SNOW HAS STOPPED falling, and with the skies already cleared by a southward-bound cold front the temperature is plummeting. No matter. The east side of the heavens are star-filled, only slightly dimmed by the pink glow of neon from Mantua. The moon is rising in the southwest, the direction we're going, and it is bathing the poplar meadows in brilliant silver light. To the north, there's the faintest traces of the Northern Lights — Aurora Borealis. It's a pretty sight, and the snow muffles every sound. The new snow has settled a little, and beneath it is a full metre of compacted snow with a slight crust on it from last week's thaw.

The moment we clear the backyard both of us abandon the trail and head out in our own directions. Bozo proceeds with great pouncing leaps that leave her, each time, shoulder deep in snow. If I used her method of locomotion I'd be done in a hundred metres, but I've seen her keep this up for hours. Even with the snowshoes it isn't easy going for me, and my brain begins to empty with the effort. With each snowshoe I plant, there is a swish-crunch as the powder billows away and the snowshoe's wood and webbing cracks the lower crust and sinks another few inches. I listen, and the rhythm empties me.

By the time our half hour is up, the dog and I are a kilometre from the house, still outward bound. I'm as much working my way into the tangle of new facts in my life as into this winter landscape, but Bozo is in paradise. My track is straight, meandering only to catch the easiest topography and stay out of the dense stands of poplars, human in the respect that, even here, it's *going someplace*. Bozo's trail is a zigzag that intersects sociably every hundred metres or so with mine as she checks in. I can feel the cold against my face, making my cheeks feel thicker than they are, but there's no threat in this kind of cold, no hidden bite, no life-sucking chill. It's simply there, a precise and inviting cold, and I accept its invitation.

I LEFT THE HOUSE to escape, really. It wasn't just the talk of the tournament, it's the whole spooky package looming over me — the past pressing in, the present doing the same, right down to tommorow's game with the Roosters. I need this emptiness so I can find some sort of balance.

No, I'm not a very Zen kind of guy. Despite the perfect conditions, finding that balance is a battle. While I'm breaking trail it slips toward it, but after a hundred or two metres that pinging in my chest returns. So I flip-flop, following the the easier trail I made days ago, then back to breaking trail. The irritable conversation with myself goes on and on.

And what's the conversation about? Not what you'd expect. I recall what started me snowshoeing several years ago, not long after I moved into this house with Esther. I'd lived by myself for years, and for a time being around one person every day crowded me. With Esther being who and what she is I didn't feel crowded for long, but I've kept up the snowshoeing. The dog loves it and it keeps me from having to buy a snowmobile, or *ever* having to go skiing.

Well, I'm sorry. I *don't* like snowmobiles, and I don't ski. Why? Too much hot-dogging and high speed. I know, hockey has both of those. Maybe I get enough there. But snowshoeing, that's the opposite end of the universe. When your shoes are a metre and a half long, looking like a clown is easy. But it won't turn you into an asshole. You're on your own, the technology is minimal, there's no judges to mark form and there are no safety supervisors reminding you to stay inside their boundaries. You're nose to nose with the elements, you have to pay attention to what's in front of you and what you've got inside of you — meaning you have to respect your limits and nature's signals. If you're not up to that you'll pack in your snowshoes in fifteen minutes, because the payoffs are subtle. When conditions are good and your head is in the right space, you bond with winter, almost. I say "almost" because if you do bond fully, you're a popsicle — just like if you bond with summer you're a skin cancer patient. I prefer winter. It's the only season in which you can go everywhere, and the colder it gets, the heavier the snowpack, the better. A forest you couldn't struggle your way through during summer without a chainsaw and a gallon of mosquito dope becomes a stroll through the park when the snow is two metres deep.

I snowshoe alone, always, except for Bozo. Esther isn't much for the great outdoors. She never misses a hockey game, but she leaves me to nature. She knows I'm not going to get my head smashed against a sheet of plexiglass, and she's learned I'm not one for getting myself lost. And of course, it counts for something that while I'm out snowshoeing she knows I'm not hanging around bars getting drunk and watching the strippers, which is what most guys my age do for recreation.

With tonight's bright moonlight I alternate, going on- and off-trail, letting the inner talk return for a while on the easier going, then pushing it back out by breaking trail. When the trail I made days ago runs out, I keep going until, at the top of a long, upward slope, I stop and squat down on my shoes, nearly emptied of thought — and feel the conversation restart. Ah well. I've got things I ought to be talking to myself about.

Out here though, it's hard to fuss — except about Bozo, who has gotten nearly two hundred metres directly ahead, chasing a rabbit she's flushed. I reach into my pocket and pull out the dog whistle. A single, inaudible-to-me burst brings her to a halt. Reluctantly, she lets the rabbit disappear into the trees and, lying down in the snow, waits for me to come to her. It's her way of complying without quite obeying.

We tramp across the wide bowl of an open meadow side by side, and at the next hilltop find ourselves looking to the south along a gentle slope of mixed poplar and pine as pretty as a Christmas card. At the bottom of it, a half kilometre away, is the construction site of the university campus. We've come more than four kilometres.

Under the blanket of new-fallen snow, the site looks like a Christmas card too. But the reality — I feel a mental hiccup as the conversation kicks to life again — is the usual pipe dream. I remind myself that beneath this particular Christmas card lies Mantua's current version of the monorail and the power dams, and, except for the smaller scale, this one is as big a fiasco as the others. When the campaign to get it built began, the project boosters blew it up like it would make Christmas every day for Mantua: business as usual in the North.

Stillness, stillness is what you came for. Stillness is all. And inside it I see the pattern of things: light and dark, mud and snow, brainlessness and graceful beauty. Where am I in this?

I'm at home, one of the idiots. I'm cut from the same cheap cloth as everyone here. But there's something else, as of today. I'm now implicated in this mess as much as it's possible to be: not just a procurer and producer but a father, like my father before me — wherever the poor drunken sonofabitch may be.

I'd like to stay here on this hilltop and enjoy these airy thoughts, but this isn't a country that lets you have those kinds of luxuries for very long. A whiff of sulphur from the pulp mills, carried southwest on the cold front, reminds me of where it is I live. So does the cold beginning to penetrate the wool that protects me. My nose is running, and Bozo is snuffling impatiently at my mitts, wanting to get on with it. She doesn't care which way we go, but she thinks it's time to move.

On the way back the moonlight is at my back, and the winter-whitened trunks of the poplars are a ghostlier silver than I can remember, etched with ebony where the young boughs have withered and broken off. Prettier than a Christmas card, even if doesn't smell anything like Christmas. Maybe that's what I came here to figure out: that I can't stand still.

It's after midnight by the time we arrive back at the house. Esther and Wendel are sitting at the kitchen table with pads of foolscap, furiously making lists. Esther looks up at me as I enter and smiles. She's unperturbed by my long absence, her mind evidently — thankfully — on other things. I hope it isn't a hockey tournament. But if it is, I can imagine worse things.

Just barely.

FOURTEEN

THE THREE OF US sat up until after two AM talking about the tournament.

We talked about it, sure, but agreed? Not bloody likely. By the time I got back to the house Esther had bought into Wendel's enthusiasm, and I was outnumbered and outgunned. So they brainstormed about how to reinvent the Mantua Cup tournament — already real in their minds — and I offered them arguments why what they were suggesting was impractical, ill-advised, and goofy. When that didn't deflate their enthusiasm, I went to impossible, suicidal, and deranged.

Nothing I said deterred them. It was like discussing how to soft-boil eggs with a steamroller — in this case, two steamrollers. Esther and Wendel rolled over whatever dish I served up, crunch, crunch, crunch.

The next morning, I can hear Wendel snoring on the couch while I make some scrambled eggs. He's inherited a version of his mother's gift for sound sleep, except that his sound sleep could drown out a band saw. Bozo is outside somewhere on dog business, having wolfed down her breakfast and splashed most of the contents of her water dish across the kitchen floor.

I'm not expecting Esther in the kitchen. She likes to be

awakened Sunday morning by breakfast in bed, and I rarely get a word out of her before her stomach has fully communed with a steaming cup of black coffee.

When the eggs are ready I shut off Wendel's sawmill imitation by putting my hand over his open mouth. On cue, his eyes pop open. "Breakfast, chum," I tell him. "Serve yourself."

He staggers into the kitchen behind me to watch me load a tray with orange juice, black coffee, and a second plate of eggs for Esther. She snaps awake the moment I sit down on the bed next to her, smiles, and sits up. I prop a couple of pillows behind her back while she settles the tray in front of her, sips a first and second draught of coffee, then samples the eggs, all without a word. Talked herself out last night, I guess.

Okay by me. I return to the kitchen, where I shovel the remainder of the scrambled eggs onto a plate, top up my coffee, and sit down across from Wendel, who is emptying a nearly full bottle of ketchup across his eggs. He's as silent as his mother, but without the smile.

Game time is one-thirty, so there's no need to hurry. It's almost ten before Esther wanders out and orders me into the bedroom.

"What for?" I ask, mainly for Wendel's benefit.

"Your back, silly. I'm not letting you out of here until I've worked out those kinks I found yesterday."

Wendel ignores us, too busy shoveling mouthfuls of a second batch of ketchup and eggs he's made for himself into his mouth.

It's amazing the way normality asserts itself. Every and any crisis we go through — short of actually dying — attaches itself to whatever live normalities it grows from, and weaves itself into the fabric. Yesterday's revelations — Esther's confession and my accidental discovery about Wendel — are *already* normal. This morning and its specific priorities — breakfast, preparation for the game — don't leave enough room for the crisis to go on clamouring for attention. The real world has ordered it into the back seat and told it to shut up unless spoken to. It's as if the past is the child of the present, not its parent. Life is going to go on. Sometime in the near future I'll have to figure out how to make a clean breast of things, but not right now. Maybe, like this morning, the three of us will eat scrambled eggs together when that secret is gone. I sure as hell hope so. This morning, anything seems possible.

ESTHER DROPS ME OFF at the arena around noon, and wanders off on some errand of her own. She'll be back at the Coliseum by game time even though she's long since stop watching the warm-ups. Too many chilly early mornings years ago helping Wendel lace up his skates, I guess.

Wendel, never one to hang around in the morning, left the house while Esther was still working over my back. By the time I get to the Coliseum dressing room he's there, suited up, and he's lacing on his skates all by himself. Gord and most of the other players have arrived and are in various states of readiness.

Jack breezes in from the direction of the ice, still in his civvies, frowning. "Gonna be a rough one today," he says. "The Roosters stayed out of the bars last night."

This is not good news. The Roosters are much easier to play when they're hung over. They're not any nicer or any less owly, but they're slower. Chances are the Old Man lowered the boom on them after what happened in Okenoke Friday night.

"They'll take it out on us," Bobby Bell whines from across the room.

"Maybe you should practise your diving instead of doing your normal warm-up," Gord answers.

He doesn't mean this entirely as a joke. We're neither the biggest nor the bravest team in the NSHL. On a good night we'll hold our own against the Bears or the Stingers, but the Roosters, like I said, are different. They have a nasty habit of skating with their sticks at jugular height while they're not carrying the puck, and more than one player on our team has found himself spitting out his own teeth after forgetting it. So that's what we're thinking about in the dressing room: getting slashed, cross-checked, crushed, splattered, splayed, beaten up. Except Gord, who has this dreamy look in his eyes, like he's thinking something serene and Buddhist. With him, you *never* know.

THE PRE-GAME WARM-UP IS uneventful, meaning that none of the Roosters crosses the red line to beat on us. As I line up for the opening face-off, Godin, the referee, delivers a speech to Neil Ratsloff and I that makes it sound like we're about to begin one of those twelve-man over-the-ropes wrestling matches, not a hockey game. Or maybe it's boxing he's thinking of, probably because Neil is standing across the circle giving me the old Sonny Liston stare-down. I wait for Godin to finish.

"I don't know why you're telling me this," I grin at him. "Tell that crazy sonofabitch. I'm just here to play hockey."

Godin rolls his eyes and drops the puck. I swipe it backward to my left and step aside as Ratsloff rolls through the spot I've just vacated. Bobby Bell takes the puck, pulls it toward his body momentarily, then, from just beyond our blueline, flicks it ahead to Jack, who is skating, not very fast, toward the Rooster blueline. Jack plays the puck off his skate onto his stick and crosses the blueline without looking up. Then he does something very uncharacteristic: he veers toward the slot, still holding the puck.

Jack doesn't see JoMo Ratsloff coming at him until the last second. When he tries to deke left to avoid a collision, JoMo, the oldest and dirtiest of the Roosters, splays his big knees wide and pumps forward, catching Jack's right knee flush. Jack goes down, sliding though the left face-off circle in a heap, with the puck underneath him.

It's no dive. He's hurt. I spin around, looking for Godin,

but his back is turned, and, interestingly, his head is down. He's examining his whistle as if he thinks the pea has dropped out. Gord doesn't wait for Godin. He drops his right glove as he crosses the blueline, skates a couple of steps and plants his bare fist in the middle of JoMo's grin as he comes out of the spin-around. The punch connects with a "whup" that sounds like someone kicking an empty cardboard box, and down goes JoMo on his backside. He doesn't move except for the blood spurting from his ruined nose.

A few seconds later I'm waltzing around the ice with Neil Ratsloff, who is doing all the usual dance steps, along with one I haven't seen before. He keeps lifting me off the ice and shaking me like a wolf would a rabbit. It's annoying, but he could just as easily be pounding my skull against the ice. Jimmy Ratsloff makes a half-hearted lunge at Gord, but Gord catches his arm as he comes in, spins, and flings him toward the net. Everyone else is dancing too, except the goalies. The moment Gord clobbered JoMo, Lenny Nakamoto went kiyiing down the ice to pair up with Junior. Junior, as usual, isn't having any of it, and is playing peekaboo with Lenny around our net. JoMo is still out cold, and Old Man Ratsloff is soft-shoeing across the ice toward him with a towel and a bucket of ice.

"I don't know why the fuck I have to play against you," Neil is grumbling, looking very much like he'd rather make a run at Gord, who is now bending solicitously over Jack.

"Why don't you go for it?" I suggest. "Die young."

This time Neil does take a swing at me, but I duck the punch and lean on him, Muhammad Ali-style. I'm lucky enough to get hold of both his burly arms, and I bury my face in his sweater and try to push him toward the boards. Just as I'm about to lose my grip I hear Old Man Ratsloff yell his name, and Neil stops flailing at me.

"Let's cut this shit," I say. "Jack is hurt."

Neil lets go of me without a word and grabs Dickie Pollard, one of our defencemen who normally just heads for the bench the moment there's a fight. Gord is motioning for Geezo Williams, our trainer, to come onto the ice, but Geezo is standing on the bench, motioning Fred Milgenberger out of the stands. Fred is a doctor, and I see him begin to move across the benches to the walkway.

The look on Jack's face alone convinces me. He's as white as a sheet, grimacing, and pawing at his right knee. "Jesus, Jesus," he groans, and gazes up into Gord's concerned face. "That's it for me. I'm gone for the season, done."

"You'll be fine," Gord says, not sounding very convincing. "You took one hell of a whack on your knee there. Maybe you can skate it off."

Jack struggles to get up, but Gord recognizes that it's too painful and plants his big fist in the middle of Jack's chest to keep him down.

Jack closes his eyes, lets out a wail, and opens one eye. This time he's looking at me, knowing I have a glass head. I shrug and turn away. I heard the ligaments go, and I can't hide it as well as Gord can.

Geezo and Milgenberger take over, and Gord and I skate to the corner to confer.

"It's bad," I say.

Gord nods. "You wanna coach, or do I have to?"

"You do it. We'll double-shift Wendel, keep it simple. I'll help."

Godin skates by Jack to take a look, then stops in front of us, arms folded. In spite of the referee posture, he's got a guilty look on his face. "Five minutes," he says to Gord.

"Did you call five on JoMo's hit?" Gord demands. "That was a deliberate attempt to injure."

Godin looks away, and repeats himself. "Five minutes. For fighting. Now get off the ice before I give you two more for instigating."

Gord skates after Godin. "You're not calling a deliberate on

JoMo?" he hisses, herding Godin into a corner and standing over him. "We've got a man lying on the ice with torn knee ligaments and you're not calling it?"

"I didn't see it," Godin answers, weakly. "I'm calling five minutes on you for fighting, and I could charge you for attempted murder. So get your ass over to the penalty box before I call a misconduct."

Gord doesn't back off. "Listen, you cowardly prick," he snarls, managing to crowd Godin against the boards without actually touching him. "If you don't make the calls, I'll pull your fucking arms out of their sockets and jam them up your ass, whistle and all. You got that?"

"That's enough for a misconduct," Godin snaps, and tries to skate away.

Gord circles around him and stops in his path. "Where's the misconduct?" he says, reasonably. "I'm going to wait until after the game and do you in the parking lot. You drive that red Ford 250, right?"

It's a stand-off, but Gord has apparently made his point: Godin, when he skates shakily over to the timekeeper, doesn't call instigating on him, or a misconduct, and JoMo gets five minutes, too.

I skate over to the bench to explain what's happening to the rest of the players. I can see they'd like to come off the bench for a brawl, but wiser heads — probably Wendel's, since we're not exactly deep in wise men — prevail.

"We'll just play the game," I say. "Wendel, you can double-shift our line and we'll see how it goes."

Indeed we will. We've still got fifty-nine more minutes of this horseshit to get through.

FIFTEEN

I<small>T TAKES TEN MINUTES</small> for the Roosters to scrape JoMo off the ice and cart him into the dressing room, and at least ten more for us to stretcher Jack off the ice and into the same ambulance they've got JoMo in. After that, the first period is pretty routine. When the buzzer sounds, we're down three to one.

The Roosters are banging on us like they usually do, and they're shooting high on Junior, who is ducking like he usually does. His new white pads don't help much — all three Rooster goals go in over his shoulder. Wendel scores our goal on a breakaway, sent in alone by a neat flip pass from Gord. I'm not being checked very hard, but it doesn't seem to matter. After years of playing with two slow players, I can't quite connect with Wendel. Every time I look, he's two or three steps ahead of where I think he's going to be.

During the intermission I notice that Junior is looking more spooked than usual, and I suggest to Gord that we sub in Stan Lagace, who's only played about thirty minutes all year. Gord looks at me like I've just crapped on the floor. "Junior's our goalie," he says.

I understand what he's saying. It's a variation on his working premise about everything: loyal and local. Junior's our goalie because his father was the goalie before him. If Junior's seven-year-old son wanted to play goalie, he'd be the backup if Gord had anything to say about it. Stan knows all about this, but he's such a glue-sniffer I don't think he cares. He gets his minutes playing commercial league at three AM, and he sits on our bench game after game, waiting for his chance like a pilgrim waiting for the return of Jesus.

Whether we win or lose doesn't mean very much to Gord. He'd prefer to lose a hockey game the right way than win the wrong way. He gets his wish, too. Half of it, anyway: we lose and we lose.

Who's going to object? Not Jack. He believes that so long as we have that stupid Chief Wahoo crest on our jerseys we deserve to lose. I see Wendel get irritated with losing once in a while, but nobody listens to him anyway, and most of the rest of the players are so used to getting thumped by the Roosters they wouldn't know what to do if we did win. Me? I like playing with Gord better than anyone I've ever played with, so doing things his way is fine with me. Hockey is supposed to be a *game*, remember?

THE SECOND PERIOD BEGINS with a bang — literally. Neil Ratsloff gets away from me right off the face-off, skates across the blue line, winds up like he's Brett Hull, and lets a slapshot go. It's high, naturally, but he's so close to the net that Junior doesn't have time to duck. The puck catches him on the side of his forehead, spins high into the crowd, and Junior crumples to the ice with blood spilling from a nasty gash.

He comes to faster than JoMo Ratsloff did, but when he does he doesn't have a clue where he is or what he's supposed to be doing. While Geezo tries to staunch the flow of blood — Milgenberger is still at the hospital with Jack and JoMo — Junior wanders up and down the ice, throwing his stick and gloves into the stands and trying, as far as I can figure out, to execute some quite complicated figure skating moves. The crowd thinks this is pretty funny, but the players — the Roosters included — understand it better.

It's one thing to get your bell rung, but the way Junior is acting that shot may have cracked it.

We have to dragoon him off the ice and into the dressing room, where Gord and I help Geezo immobilize him so the cut can be worked on. That's easier said than done because Junior won't lie still, and even Gord has trouble holding him down. We lose another ten minutes trying to settle him enough that Geezo can patch him up, and by the time Gord and I return to the ice the crowd is getting bitchy.

The same little bugger who was riding me Friday night is in his usual seat, leading the pack. As I skate back to the bench I catch his eye and motion him down. He surprises me and does what I ask. By the time I get there, he's jumped up on the ledge and is leaning over the glass.

"What's your name, kid?" I growl.

Again he surprises me, this time by answering politely. "James, sir."

"James what?"

He delivers surprise number three: "James Bathgate, sir."

Is this kid hosing me? I whack my stick against the sideboards for effect. "So just exactly where are your parents, kid?"

"At home, sir. They don't approve of hockey."

"Well," I say, pulling off my gloves and flexing my knuckles under his nose. "Listen up. If I hear any more out of you tonight I'm going to squeeze your head until your brains come squirting out of your ears."

"Yes sir."

"And stop calling me 'sir'!"

As he retreats back into the stands I hear his high, unmistakable voice. "Yes sir, you asshole, sir!"

I'm laughing out loud when I sit back down, and so is everyone else on the bench. Even Wendel. The kid is good.

OUR PLAY IN THE second period is looser, but it doesn't seem to help. We're in our end for most of it, and I still can't locate Wendel. Twelve minutes in, they're up on us five-two. But we're lucky in one way. If Junior had been in the nets the Roosters would have had a dozen goals, because they keep shooting high. That doesn't bother Stan Lagace in the least, even when one glances off his mask. It isn't that his glove hand is quicker than Junior's, just that he doesn't flinch and duck.

As the period begins to wane I find myself sitting on the bench next to Wendel. He looks right at me. "Speed it up a little, Weaver," he says. You're playing me like I'm in the next time zone."

My first impulse is to tell him to screw off. Then I remember I'm his father, and try to hear what he's telling me. "What do you mean?" I ask.

Wendel is visibly surprised. But after a hard look to ensure that I'm not setting him up for some gag, he gives it a try. "Well," he says, "Gord isn't having any trouble adjusting. He's seeing me where I am. But I see you looking behind me, expecting me to be where your clock puts Jack and Gord. Turn your time switch up a little bit, and see what's there. Think of it as daylight saving."

He isn't grinning when he tells me this, so he's not just jiving me about being old and slow. He's talking on terms that I understand. Gord and I have talked a lot about what allows us to play with players who are much faster than we are.

I slap him on the shoulder as we're clambering over the boards for our next shift. "I think I know what you're talking about," I tell him. "I'll see if I can adjust."

About halfway into the shift, with only a minute or two left in the period, I find myself mucking along the boards for the puck. I hear a stick slap the ice; without looking, I know *exactly* where Wendel is, and what he's going to do. I push away the Rooster who's checking me, and backhand the puck hard through the air across centre. I duck an elbow, and up-ice I see Wendel folding himself behind the puck on a clean breakaway. He swoops in on

Lenny Nakamoto and dekes left as Lenny sprawls across the crease. Lenny's too late and too slow. It's an easy, pretty goal.

WENDEL AND I IGNORE one another during the intermission, both of us wary of acknowledging that we co-operated on something that was actually quite beautiful. I've got other fish to fry, anyway. Milgenberger is on the blower from the hospital telling us that Jack has probably torn every ligament in his right knee. It takes a while to get the medical explanation because Milgenberger is so upset about it. The stupid dork keeps using the expression "shredded."

"It's bad, eh?" I commiserate, simultaneously shaking my head at Gord.

"Real bad," Milgenberger confirms. "Shredded. He's going to have trouble walking on this one after it's healed, never mind playing hockey. I'd say his playing days are over."

"Well, don't tell him that," I say. "Let me and Gord break the news to him."

Milgenberger cheerfully agrees to that, and listens while I explain Junior's antics to him. Junior, meanwhile, is still in Lulu-land, bouncing up and down on the table like a chimpanzee.

"Have Geezo put an icebag on the swelling," Milgenberger says, serious again. "There's an outside chance of a subdural haematoma, and maybe a skull fracture. I'll send an ambulance over to get him." He explains that he's still got to put JoMo's nose back together, but that he'll keep a sharp eye on Junior once he gets to the hospital. We hang up.

As we troop back to the ice from the dressing room, I catch Wendel's eye. He actually smiles at me.

THE THIRD PERIOD IS a blast. I'm not just able to tune in on Wendel's tempo, my own game jumps up a gear to follow it. A couple of minutes in, Gord straight-arms one of the Ratsloff twins and Godin calls him off for elbowing. As he skates to the penalty box, I tell him that Wendel and I will kill the penalty.

"You?" he asks. "You don't kill penalties."

"Why the hell not?" I say. "Can't be an old man all my life."

"Suit yourself," he answers, and, shaking his head, clambers into the box.

Wendel scores two shorthanded goals in the first forty seconds. Both times I hit his stick with blind passes while he's in full flight, one of them after using a fake stumble move to sucker the Roosters' defenceman into committing to me. The game is tied, and I feel like I could play the rest of the game without coming off the ice.

I don't, but on the next shift I catch Neil Ratsloff cruising over our blueline, veering toward the slot with his head down, believing that he's invulnerable. I decide to go for it. I put my hip into his thigh and suddenly two hundred and fifteen pounds of beef sausage is flying over my head. I haven't laid a hit like that on anyone in ten years, and to tell the truth it feels kind of good: even though I caught Neil in the same spot JoMo caught Jack, I did it within the rules. Godin was leaning against the glass at the blueline when I did it, and he didn't even blink.

Even Neil recognizes that it was clean. As he gets to his feet he points a finger at me and grins. I'm going to have to keep my head up around him for a couple of games because, no matter what protection I may have been under before, I just gave him a licence, and we both know it.

I don't have to wait long, either. He catches me in the corner on the next shift and gives me the crunch. I'm back on my feet before he's five feet away, and except for one quick, sharp pang in the middle of my chest, I'm none the worse for it.

ABOUT MIDWAY THROUGH THE third, Wendel scores again, this one all on his own, and two or three shifts later Gord sends the two of us in on a two-on-one. I get to bury this one in the upper right corner, after an Alphonse and Gaston routine that has the Rooster defenceman's head spinning.

The final score is seven-six for us. Wendel has five goals and an assist, and I've got a goal and four. Not bad for a game that started off looking as if we were going to get eaten.

As we're headed off the ice I have a sudden generous instinct, no doubt brought on by having won the game. I spin around on my skates and gaze up into the departing crowd to see if the kid is still there.

He is, sitting by himself as if waiting for someone. I wave my stick at him again. This time he hesitates, as if he thinks maybe this is it, that now I'm going to make his brains squirt out of his ears. I grin to assure him it's okay, and he leaps across the benches to stand atop the boards as before.

"Hey, kid," I say, making it up as I go along. "You come to all the games, right?"

"Yes," he answers. "Every one." There's no smartass "sir" tagged onto it.

"How'd you like to be our stickboy? You'd get to see the games for free, and you'd have the best seat in the place." And, I say to myself, it might get you off my case.

For a second, his eyes light up. Then I see a calculating look cross them.

"Can I practise with the players?"

"Why not? Sure. You keep the sticks in good order, pack some equipment around for us, and you can do whatever you want. Be here Tuesday night at five."

For a moment I think he's going to leap over the boards into my arms.

SIXTEEN

YOU'D HAVE THOUGHT WE'D just won the Stanley Cup the way the guys whoop it up in the dressing room. The beer box empties in thirty seconds, and, while they're not pretending it's champagne and squirting it over one another's heads or talking about going off to Disneyland, the joy is palpable. When I look around and see that every player under thirty-five — Wendel included — has a Molson's stuck down his throat, it's simple to predict what's next: Chinese food and a major league parking lot puke-o-rama. Stan Lagace, with his first Senior win, is so high he's bouncing off the ceiling.

I'm pretty pleased myself, and so is Gord. But we've got Jack and Junior in the hospital, and that comes before any celebrating. As the players start to stream out, I grab Bobby Bell by the collar and jerk him into Jack's office.

"Keep your eye on Stan, will you?" I say. "He's underage, and we don't want him getting mouthy and having someone beat the shit out him. We've got two games next weekend, and from the way Junior was looking we're probably going to need him for a while."

Bobby reluctantly agrees to chaperone Stan, and off he goes with the little goalie in tow. I call the hospital to tell them we're on our way, and as I'm leaving the office I see Wendel still walking around the dressing room, half-dressed.

"Aren't you going with them?" I ask. "We don't beat the Roosters every day."

"Nah, I've won hockey games before, you know?" he explains. "Besides, I'm pretty bagged. Mind if I come up to the hospital with you guys?"

"Suit yourself," I answer, more pleased than I let on.

Esther comes in as the last players leave. "You guys were something else tonight," she says, cheerfully.

"Weren't we?" I agree. "We haven't beaten those suckers in a coon's age."

"Ready to get out of here?"

I've still got my equipment to clean up, and since Jack isn't here it'll be up to me or Gord to help Geezo bag the uniforms so they can go to the cleaners. I decide to do it myself — Gord will have other matters to attend to, like making sure we've got our share of the gate receipts.

Esther helps me stuff the uniforms into the big transparent plastic bags, chattering away at me as she does. I only half listen, because as I lean over one of the benches to pick up a sweater something grabs me around the ribs and squeezes. At first I think it's Gord fooling around, but he doesn't let go, and it isn't him. Then it changes again. This time three or four hot steel rods are being rammed into my chest. I try to take a breath but can't.

I'm having a goddamned heart attack. It's an unbelievable thing to think, so I don't. Then the rods go deeper, and I change my mind. Oh, shit, I think. No. Not me.

I lift one knee up onto a bench, lean on it, and try not to move, hoping it'll go away. My brain continues to insist that nothing is happening, but my body doesn't believe it. I still haven't gotten a breath, but I'm determined to not let anybody see it. If I'm going to kick the bucket, I'm going to hold the pose until I keel over. No writhing around on the floor or whining for divine intervention. I may not have lived my life with enough dignity, but I damned well want to die with a little.

It occurs to me that my life is supposed to be passing before my eyes, but it isn't. The only visuals I'm getting are of the concrete floor in front of me, and there's no soundtrack at all. Maybe I'm too busy fuming about the lousy timing: this is wrong, the wrong moment to be dying. I've just found out I have a son, and instead of dying in front of his mother I ought to be getting married to her, and now, goddamn it to hell, I'm not going to be able to ...

As abruptly as it appeared — whatever "it" is — it lets up. The vise gripping my chest lets go enough to let me get a breath, the hot steel rods pull back. I suck in some air and release it. I can literally taste the oxygen.

There's another, more tactile sensation. Esther's hand is on my shoulder. "Are you okay?"

I straighten up and shrug. "Fine. My back just gave me a little twinge there."

She's eyeing me. "Really?"

"Really," I insist. "Let's go see Jack."

WE TAKE THE LINCOLN, and using the sore back excuse I ask Esther to drive. Gord and Wendel climb into the rear seats.

"I love this car," Gord says. "It's damn near the only kind left I can sit in the back seat of without it feeling like it's going to flip over on top of me."

"Yeah," Wendel agrees, "and if you were any bigger I'd have to sit on your knee."

"Well," Gord laughs, "it wouldn't be the first time."

In the front passenger seat, I'm having a hard time listening. Bubbling from the memory of those steel rods — despite my efforts to stay in control — is panic, and a weird sort of shame. I've always been one of those people who sails through injury and pain as if it's nothing special — broken bones, sprained joints, that sort of thing. But this isn't an *injury*, and, worse, I can't see it because it's inside me. If it was a heart attack, it could have just been a warning shot across the bow, a minor tremor. The real one, the big one that's going to do me, might arrive any second.

Esther keeps on glancing at me suspiciously as she drives. I'm thankful that the already-fading light isn't giving her much. I keep my face averted, looking out the window, until we reach the parking lot outside the hospital emergency ward. At least we're in the right place if the big cranker comes.

Comforted by that thought, I pull myself together as Esther glides the Lincoln into a parking spot. It isn't a huge effort to get myself out of the car, and that's comforting too. Maybe I'll be okay.

I keep up, barely, as the four of us hustle to the emergency ward's entrance. We all know the nurse on the desk by name — the emergency staff are used to seeing Mohawk players in here after games — and since she's expecting us she waves us in the direction of one of the cubicles, without bothering with any chit-chat.

Jack is composed and still, so drugged that even speaking is tricky. Now that the hockey game is over Gord is willing to be a doctor again, and he doesn't have time for small talk. He busies himself with the X-rays Milgenberger left for him on the bedside trolley and leaves the bedside comforting to me.

Jack's damaged knee is raised slightly above the bed in a traction sling. It doesn't look shredded from the outside, just bloated. It occurs to me that my heart might have the same appearance.

"You don't look so bad," I say, dousing that last thought and giving the bed a small test nudge. "I was expecting a corpse."

"Check inside my knee, there," he mumbles.

"I'll leave the autopsy to Gord. Where did they put Junior?"

"Couple of stalls down," Jack answers, ignoring the attempt at play. "Pretty noisy when they brought him in. And stop pushing on the bed, you nitwit. It moves fine, but my knee is strapped to the ceiling."

He closes his eyes, and Gord elbows me out of the way. "I'll go check on Junior," I say, and slip through the curtain.

I find Junior three stalls away, his forehead swathed in bandages, the eye beneath it puffed and starting to discolour. He's stopped babbling and jumping around, but he's still a few sandwiches short of a picnic. He's also a lot uglier than Jack, but it's hard to get a bead on how hurt he really is.

While I'm questioning him, or trying to, a nurse slips into the cubicle, checks his eyes, and makes small talk. Junior tries to paw her aside, wanting — now that he realizes it's me in the cubicle with him — to know how the game went.

"We won," I tell him, carefully nonchalant. "Seven-six. We got some lucky goals."

"How did Lagace do?"

"He did fine," I say, holding the pose. "He made a few saves, but he didn't really have much to do."

Junior recognizes that I'm lying to him. "Don't you try to shit me, Weaver," he says. "If they only scored two goals in two periods, that little horse's ass must have been doing cartwheels."

"Stan's just a dumb kid," I answer, cutting through the bullshit to his real question. "You're our goalie."

Gord and Wendel slip into the cubicle, and Wendel promptly sticks his foot in it.

"It isn't that Stan's so great," he says. "It's that you're so lousy."

Gord clears his throat to stifle what looks suspiciously to me like laughter. "What he's saying is that if you wore a mask you'd be a better goalie than Stan is."

Wendel jams the other foot in. "Right," he says. "Why don't you wear a goddamned mask? If you did, you wouldn't be here and we wouldn't be telling you this."

"It's a tradition," Junior answers. "I can't break that."

"Being stupid is a tradition?" Wendel hoots. "Since when?"

I can't help myself. "Around here? Since about 1792. We have a God-given right to be stupid and ignorant."

Gord gives me a dirty look. "Well, you know how it goes, Junior," he says. "Traditions are supposed to make your life better and deeper. If they don't, it seems to me that you're free to get rid of them. When your old man started playing hockey, there was no such thing as goalie masks. Now there is. You wouldn't be any less a man if you used one. Just a better goalie."

Junior's eyes glaze over. "My old man would never let me live it down."

Gord isn't having any of it. "Screw your old man. He would have been a better goalie if he'd started using a mask. And he might have lasted longer, too."

Junior is starting to whine. "What about you? You don't wear headgear."

Gord laughs. "They don't make helmets big enough. I can't help it if the manufacturers think hockey players are all pinheads. I'd love to be able to wear one. I'd probably wear a visor if I could."

"I dunno if *that's* such a good idea," I interject. "If you had a visor you'd stop murdering those jerks who come at you with their sticks up. What would become of the rest of us?"

"Maybe you're right," Gord admits. "Someone has to take care of you pussies."

Esther, who has been listening through the curtain without entering, leans in. "Hey, you guys," she says, "the Ratsloffs just arrived. Maybe you ought to stay inside the curtain there until they've gone."

"I guess I really ought to apologize to JoMo," Gord says, and slips out. The truth is, the Ratsloffs aren't too bad off the ice unless they've been drinking. I follow Gord over to the cubicle, where they're crowding around JoMo, laughing and joking.

JoMo, when I catch sight of him, does look pretty funny. He's got a tin snozzle over his ruined nose, held there by twin stripes of thick white tape that end at his jowls and his hairline. A pair of spectacular shiners are blooming around his eyes. In a few days, they'll be glorious. From each of his nostrils hang fuses of cotton batting, there to hold the cartilage in place from the inside. Good thing snot isn't flammable. Even his own kin would have trouble keeping themselves from putting a match to those fuses and blowing up JoMo's remaining brains.

It's hard to tell if JoMo is pissed off or not. He isn't talking — he's had his nose broken before, and knows that one word from him will have his relatives honking and huffing in imitation. He and Gord simply nod to one another.

"Sorry I caught you on the beak," Gord says.

In answer, JoMo shakes his head once and shrugs. Part of the game, he's saying. A couple of the Ratsloffs nod to me as I stop to pay my respects to JoMo. I don't have much to say to him except "Tough break," which he accepts with an expression that could be a smile. None of the Ratsloffs ask about Jack. That's part of the game too, as far as they're concerned.

ON THE WAY OUT I mention to Jack that I appointed the kid stickboy, and he goes through the roof.

"You can't do that without an insurance release," he scolds when he calms down. "If the little bugger gets nailed by a puck on the bench his parents would end up owning half the city."

Sounds reasonable to me, but there's a simple solution. "Where are you hiding the release forms?"

Maybe it's because we're talking about money and printed forms, but Jack is suddenly very coherent. "They don't exist. You have to make one up."

"What does it have to say?"

"I dunno. The kid's name and address at the very least, and a couple of sentences about how he's there at his own risk and with his parents' consent. And you have to get one of his parents to sign it."

"I've got his name. No address, though."

"What is that kid's name, anyway?" Jack asks. "He's been at every game in the last two years. I always see him there, but there never seems to be anyone with him."

"His last name is the same as mine: Bathgate. Wonder if we're related."

"Well," Jack answers, his head sinking back on the pillow, "he's got one hell of a mouth on him, so I wouldn't be surprised."

I feel someone's hand on my elbow. It's Esther, waving the car keys at me. "Time we got out of here," she says. "I'll stop by and see you tomorrow, dear."

"Come and see me at my apartment," Jack answers. "I'm not letting them hold me in here overnight. People die in hospitals. Ask Gord."

Esther stops me in the lobby. "Are you sure you're all right?"

I insist that I am. She puts her palm to my forehead, and frowns.

"You're too pale for my liking," she says. "I'll drive."

I don't argue.

SEVENTEEN

GORD STAYS AT THE hospital with Jack — probably all night, knowing him — so Esther and I have only Wendel for a passenger on the way back to the Coliseum.

We say our goodbyes — I'm half-convinced they'll be last goodbyes — and let him out near the arena's already-darkened front doors.

"Are we in any hurry?" I say as we watch Wendel make his way to Esther's truck.

She flips the limo into drive. "No, not really. You have something in mind?"

"Let's take the scenic route," I say.

She can't help herself. "What scenic route?"

I laugh despite myself, because she's right. Less than twenty-four hours after the snowstorm ended, the usual combination of fly-ash from the sawmill burners and airborne sulphur from the pulp mills has fouled everything. Downtown Mantua already looks like someone pissed on it.

She pushes the gearshift back to park, pumps the gas pedal, and waits. "Well?"

"Turn off the car," I tell her. "Let's go inside for a moment."

"You don't have a key," she objects, sensibly not wanting to walk around to the back doors where the commercial leaguers come and go.

"I've got Jack's keys. There's something in the lobby I have to show you."

"*Have to?*" she asks.

"Want to," I say, then amend it again. "Need to. You need to know this."

We walk to the door, and I slide Jack's key into the lock. The genius who set up the photo display all those years ago thoughtfully rigged it so that the fluorescents inside the display cases are wired to the main door, and as the bolt swings back inside the key door the cases light up. Maybe he thought illuminating those immortals would help their custodians to remember to lock the door. Tonight, his small invention is going to help us perform a more serious act of memory.

I enter the lobby and stop. Esther steps toward the bank of light switches on the wall.

"No," I say. "We don't need any more light than we've got."

I guide her, my hand on her elbow, toward the display case nearest the doors, the one that has the team photo of the first Chilliwack Christian Lions champions in it. As we near it I feel her hesitate, but she doesn't pull back. It takes me only a second to key in on Billy Menzies, even through the lime green, but as I catch sight of myself the way I was twenty-one years ago an already-familiar tightness grabs at my chest. I'd better get this out quickly. I may not have time to spare.

I press my right index figure against the glass over Billy Menzies. "Do you know who that man is?"

She begins to speak the name, but then hesitates again, stops. After a moment she clears her voice and speaks. "That's Wendel's father. His name is ..."

"His name is Billy Menzies." One of the hot steel bolts slams through my lungs as I speak the name. "Now look at his face," I wince, squeezing the words out as a second bolt rockets through me. "And then look at mine."

She doesn't do what I ask. Instead, she looks into my eyes and sees the pain there, and loses all interest in what I'm trying to show her. As a third bolt sears through my chest cavity I double over, my face against her chest. I hear a sharp cry of distress escape her, feel her arms folding around me, and then, from everywhere, there is darkness coming at me, swift and aggressive. My last two thoughts are that it hurts like hell, and that I don't want to go.

BUT I WAKE UP, and things are pretty much where they were when I blinked out — the important things, anyway. Esther's face about eighteen inches from mine. She's pale and concerned, but oddly I can't read any fear in her face. Nor, for that matter, any evidence to suggest that she's figured out what I was trying to tell her before I keeled over.

Beyond her, though, the scenery has changed completely. I'm lying on a hospital gurney, and white-clothed men and women are scurrying around the periphery of my vision. I recognize the hospital emergency room, and on my chest, as I look down, are a series of electrodes, taped down in an asymmetrical array. They disappear behind my head, where I assume there is a machine. There's an IV stuck in my arm, also taped down, and around my waist a canvas restraining belt.

"That was interesting," I say, trying to sound cheerful.

"I can think of several better ways to describe it," Esther answers, dryly. "You scared the sweet Jesus out of me."

"What happened?"

She gestures at the equipment behind me. "That's what they're trying to find out."

"How long?"

"What do you mean, 'how long'?" A familiar twinkle alters

her concerned expression. "You've always told me it was nine inches."

I try to repress my own laughter, can't, and am surprised that it doesn't hurt. "No, I mean how long was I out?"

She shrugs. "About an hour. Maybe more. You've been doing some very silly things since you got here."

A nurse enters, looking very stern, and motions Esther out of the way. The nurse fiddles at the electrodes, pulls a printout from the machine behind my head, and presses a button. I hear the machine whirring. She takes my pulse, frowning while she does it, then pulls the second printout from the machine.

"Try to be still," she says to me. To Esther she adds, "Try to keep him from moving around. The doctor will be here in a minute."

Esther moves back to my side, picks up my hand, and squeezes it gently. I try to think of something to say that will comfort her, but all that's coming to mind is that I'd die for her. It's true that I would, but judging from the way she's looking at me — fondly — it isn't what she has in mind.

"I think it might have been a heart attack," I admit. I don't tell her about the one earlier, in the dressing room.

"That's what I thought, too," she replies, after a moment.

"What do they think?"

"You know how doctors and nurses are. They don't think anything. They just run tests and write things on pieces of paper."

If she understands what I was trying to tell her about myself before I conked out, I can't read it in her face, just like I can't tell if she knows more about my condition than she's letting on. She's the picture of poker-playing calm, as usual.

"I've got something I need to say to you, in case ..."

She cuts me off. "Not now. It can wait until you're stabilized. I want you to calm down" — here she hesitates — "and stop acting like a baby." She leans against the bed and rests the side of her face against my forearm. "Gord is going to be here in a minute, and he'll get to the bottom of this."

"Don't they know what it was?"

"Apparently not," she answers, peering back to examine the script coming off the machines behind my head. "Your EKGs are normal."

At least I did one thing properly. I had a will done last year, without telling Esther. It makes her my sole beneficiary, so if I kick she'll get everything. That's a comfort. And Wendel will get the use of my assets eventually, I suppose.

I blurt it out. "Esther. I'm Billy Menzies."

"I know," she says. She doesn't move her head to look at me, and her voice is flat when she goes on. "I've known all along."

I feel a surge of emotion, somewhere between anger and disappointment. "Why didn't you tell me?"

"I was waiting for you to tell *me*. I don't know. I didn't want you to feel burdened. Not by me or by Wendel."

"Don't be crazy."

"I'm not," she says with a hint of irritation in her voice. "Look at it from my point of view. At first it seemed wrong to drop it all in your lap. I mean, I didn't know what kind of person you really were, and I didn't know where you'd been. After that, I wasn't sure if I loved you or even wanted to stay with you. So things dragged on. I got caught, that's all. People don't see every-thing, you know. And you kept your cards up pretty damned high."

I'm dumbfounded. "You know how I feel about you," I say. It sounds lame, and she doesn't go for it.

"I know you love me. But I also know you keep secrets."

"I had to. Or at least I thought I had to. Doesn't everyone?"

"Yes," she answers. There is a long silence that's more empty than tense. "Everyone keeps secrets. Maybe," she adds, "that's what's wrong with all of us."

We don't get time to talk about it. Gord comes in, moving like a cross between a wrecking ball and a whirling dervish, ordering people out of the room, including Esther, and demanding to see test results. It's as if it's not me lying on the table but a medical abstraction, a crisis, maybe an opportunity. I can't read him at all, but I've rarely seen him this stressed out.

"Not used to dealing with people who aren't dead, I guess?"

"You shut up," he answers curtly. "For all we know you might be dead any second."

As I watch him peruse the data sheets the nurse gave him, I see his concern shifting to puzzlement. "Describe your symptoms to me," he says. "And no jackassing around."

I give him the basics, but it doesn't satisfy him. "Earlier," he snaps. "What about yesterday, the day before?"

I don't want to tell him how fucked up I was after the Friday game, because he'll be pissed. Then I remember Esther's remark about keeping secrets. This doesn't seem to me like much of a secret, and I'm certain it isn't connected, but I tell him anyway.

He interrupts me in the middle of it. "You silly shit," he says, then hollers for the nurse, who is standing behind him. "I want X-rays on this man's skull, upper back, and sternum. STAT!"

He turns to me. "This *might* not be as serious as it looks," he says. "But I'm going to give you something for the pain."

"There isn't any pain," I say.

"There will be if you don't button it and do what you're told," he says. I watch him turn to the nurse and say something I don't catch. She leaves the room.

She returns seconds later with a small syringe, and hands it to Gord. "This," he says with a grin, "will make you relax."

I flinch as he punches the needle into my biceps. "Does this mean I'm not going to die?"

"Who knows?" he answers. "If you are, I'll try to let you know before your eyeballs roll up for the big plunge."

EIGHTEEN

PALE WINTER SUNLIGHT IS streaming through the windows when I resurface from whatever it was Gord squirted into my arm. The twenty-four-hour wall clock claims that it's seven in the morning, the sunlight and the unfamiliar windows tell me I'm in one of the wards, but it isn't until I roll over that I discover why I'm awake. Gord is standing beside my bed, staring at me. I don't think he's been there all night, but somehow I'm not surprised to see him. The irritation is gone from his face, but he looks tired, and that reminds me that I'm not the only patient on his caseload.

I don't recall much after the sedative — bits and pieces of a gurney ride to X-ray, and later a moment when Gord pressed his big fingers into my chest around my breastbone. Even the load of painkiller he gave me couldn't suppress the pain of that. But otherwise, there's nothing. Not even dreams, good or bad.

"I'm afraid," he says, answering my question before I can ask it, "you're going to live."

"What does that mean?" I want to know, still feeling groggy. "For how long?"

"There's absolutely nothing wrong with your heart, except that it's as black and evil as it ever was," he answers. "What you were experiencing were esophageal spasms brought on by a severely cracked sternum. Probably a present from Mr. Bellado on Friday night."

"Bastard," I mumble.

"Well, there's another explanation, actually. None of these festivities would have been necessary if you'd admitted you were hurt on Friday night. We also uncovered," he adds, "a reasonably serious concussion. You might have mentioned that as well."

"You know how it goes," I say. "I had a few other things on my mind."

"So I understand," he says, coolly. "Esther and I had a long talk after I figured out what your medical problem was. How does it feel to have that cat out of its bag after all these years?"

It seems appropriate to play this with caution. "Which cat are you talking about?"

Gord throws up his hands — a dangerous gesture in these cramped quarters — and sighs. "I've known as long as Esther has."

I can't quite integrate this piece of information, so I change the subject. "Where is she?"

"Here within the hour, I'd imagine. She didn't leave until nearly four, but I can't see her staying away much more than a few hours. I think," and here his expression lightens, "she's quite fond of you."

"Right now I don't feel as if I deserve it."

"Maybe it's time to start earning it a little more. Make some changes."

Before I can think of an answer — there isn't one, really, and we both know it — he shifts topic.

"Speaking of changes, I've got a few temporary ones you're going to have to make."

"No more hockey, right?"

He nods his head. "That's one of them."

"For how long?"

"Not as long as you deserve. A few weeks, maybe more. But

that's fine, because we're going to need a coach. And a GM, until Jack is back on his feet."

"How is he?"

Gord shakes his head. "If I let Milgenberger operate on Jack he might never walk again."

"Is Milgenberger that much of quack? I always thought he was okay."

"He is okay, for a GP. It's Jack's knee that isn't okay. I'm having him flown to the coast."

"What about Junior?"

"Oh, he'll be okay. Nasty scar is about all. It isn't like there was a whole lot of grey matter to damage in the first place. But he's gone for a week, maybe two. Hard to tell with a concussion."

"We're going to need players," I say.

"Yes indeed. I think that's what a general manager is for."

WHILE I WAIT FOR Esther, I go over the list of things I've kept from her. It isn't as long as it is fundamental: my identity, my finances, and, tied to my identity, where and what I did after I left Chilliwack.

I'll put them together for you. After I left Chilliwack I slingshotted across the continent to the Florida Keys, and sat on the beach staring at the ocean for a few months. Around the time the money began to run out, I realized my blood was too thick for tropical climates or for loafing around, and I headed north along the east coast. I stopped in New Brunswick, wangled a new social insurance card as Andrew Bathgate, and picked up work driving cab.

I let the first winter go by without hockey, but in the end I couldn't live without it. By the time hockey season rolled around I was playing in a semi-pro league that spanned the border. Things being what they were in those days — the end of the Vietnam War — I jumped to an American team in the loop halfway through the season, got myself a green card, and went to work for a development company in Maine while I worked on getting my realtor's licence.

After that I worked my way west through New York State, Ohio, and into Michigan and Wisconsin. It was pretty slow progress, maybe because the scars inside my head didn't heal on their own. I felt like a leper, and my only real insight then was that I ought to keep to myself and steer clear of entanglements. Things started to come around in Wisconsin five or six years after I left Chilliwack. I went out and got myself an "A" licence and spent a winter doing exactly what frightened me most: I drove other human beings — school children, actually — in a school bus exactly like the one I drove that night. I'm sure you get the picture.

After that I went back to land assembly and development, mostly in small towns or in the suburbs of bigger cities in the Midwest. The money was good, the risks minor, and there was nobody interesting enough to get tangled up with. I took a few college courses, too. Some urban planning and architecture to help me at work, but also a little philosophy, and some psychology and history. Those ones kept me from thinking that the world is as narrow and stupid as real estate makes it look.

My only other requirement — not hard to fill — was a decent amateur or semi-pro team to play hockey for. By the time I left the States I had an easily transferable realtor's licence, and a quarter million bucks to invest. The success with real estate isn't as impressive as it may sound. In the markets of the late '70s and early '80s a chimpanzee could have amassed that kind of grubstake, and the industry was full of people who couldn't outwit a chimp.

Back across the border I skipped from Winnipeg to Saskatoon, then northeast to Edmonton, and I started to recognize my final destination. I wasn't sure why but I was going home, to Mantua. I highballed for two-and-a-half years in Edmonton's quiet market, brought my grubstake beyond a half million, and I was ready.

I arrived in Mantua at exactly the right moment. The local

economy was in trouble, but the province was being flooded with offshore money from the Japanese and the Hong Kong Chinese. While I was qualifying for local accreditation (a process that amounted to learning how not to look *like* a monkey) I put together several parcels of industrial land north of the city and then flipped them to a Japanese consortium for double what I'd paid. Two years later the consortium noticed the dark clouds forming over Mantua, and I reclaimed both parcels under my original cost. After that I sold one to a Korean chopsticks manufacturer who went broke four months after his plant started up, and the other to a panicky Hong Kong doctor who gave it back to me with a two-hundred-grand profit when he decided that the Red Chinese were turning soft pink and weren't going to execute all the capitalist lackeys who remained in the Protectorate after they took it back from the British.

After that I quit, and invested my ill-gotten gains in T-Bills. Right now I don't even have an office, and only my bank manager and Jack have any idea what I'm worth. The taxman comes around once in a while, but Canadian tax law being what it is all I have to do is scratch myself in front of the auditors, unloosen a few flakes, and off they go.

Does that make sense? To me, it does and it doesn't. I made a life, I made money, I played hockey. That makes sense because the alternative — doing nothing — hasn't ever appealed to me. But the system I worked with doesn't make any sense to me at all. The only real work I've done in the twenty years since I became Weaver Bathgate, the only work that actually helped anyone, was the winter I spent driving the school bus in Wisconsin. And outside of a couple stints driving taxi early on, that job was the most poorly paid I've had.

As far as I can see, there was just one thing that separated me from a thousand other clowns who lost their shirts in real estate. I made it because I had just enough brains not to show around. I didn't buy any Mercedes 450 SLs after I made deals, I didn't wear silk suits, and, most of all, I didn't party. Very little booze, no dope, no nose candy. I don't want to sound puritanical, but I think that bus accident sobered me up about a lot of things.

After I killed those four people, including my two closest friends, I couldn't get drunk. For a while I tried — mostly in Florida right after it happened — but the only things booze released in me were waking nightmares about what I'd done. Sooner or later I'd find myself reliving the sight of Mikey Davidson's head bouncing on the pavement.

Sure, I'll have a beer once in a while, or open a bottle of decent wine with dinner. But since the day I ran that bus off the road I haven't gotten loaded on anything. Not alcohol, not women, not money or real estate. I figure I owe it to the world to be able to see what's coming down the road. Or, at the very least, to be playing with a full deck when it comes at me.

Maybe seeing people die because of what I did gave me perspective, I dunno. Like I said, I'm not one of those Safety Nazis who do everything by the rules, and I'm not what you'd call a total-philosophy-of-life kind of person the way Gord is.

One thing I've figured out is that covering ourselves with all these private rights to protect ourselves from the government and all these corporations who are trying to turn us into dopes and slaves and automatons doesn't work. I mean, things have gotten pretty nutty lately, with everyone thinking their ancestors are more real than their neighbours and bullying other people over things that happened two hundred years ago, or people wanting equal pay and equal access to this or that, public rights to private property, and private rights to shoot the public when they trespass. It just gets us fighting amongst ourselves. You end up calling everybody "Your Honour" in public, and thinking of everybody as "motherfucker" in private. And meanwhile, the rich get richer.

Basically, we need just two rights. One of them is the right to be treated decently, by everyone and everything. People will fight like hell over what decency involves, but so long as we don't divide ourselves up into gangs and tribes those kinds of arguments are what life is about.

The other right we need to have is the right to make smartass remarks. If we have that right guaranteed — and if we practise it — all the other personal freedoms we're whining about are guaranteed, and so is democracy. You know that because that's the right that all those authoritarians want to take away, whether they're in a corporation's boardroom, or down on the street corner trying to prevent you from getting on a bicycle without putting on a combat helmet and body armour. Check it out if you don't believe me.

I guess the other thing is that we ought to wake up and realize that nothing is black and white. Life's like a rainbow, for Christ's sake. It's always over there — until you get over there and discover it's over here, and you just walked through it and missed everything.

ESTHER ARRIVES AT EIGHT on the dot, carrying a fresh change of clothes. Before Gord left he gave me a fat bottle of muscle relaxants to control the esophageal spasms, which, he says, aren't likely to return unless I decide to take up gymnastics or weightlifting — or hockey. He also told me to be checked out by nine.

It's an awkward moment. We have a thousand things to talk about, a hundred decisions to make, but no obvious place to start. So we start simple. She smiles at me, I grin back. I feel shy, almost. I thought I was hiding a stranger from her, and now I have to deal with the idea that the only stranger she had to put up with was the one she lived with every day — the one who didn't open himself and his past up to her. The metaphysics of that one make my head spin.

"Get dressed," she says, "and we'll go home."

This tells me one thing I badly need to know. I still have a home to go to.

PART TWO

NINETEEN

A S WE CLIMB CRANBERRY Hill in the crisp winter dawn, it comes to me that it was less than twenty-four hours ago that I had that hair-raiser with the Explorer, and that, despite the two near-deaths, the mayhem and the revelations, the world is better now. My nervous system, no doubt helped by the muscle relaxants Gord gave me, lets loose a flood of endorphins, and an insight.

It's this: it'll be the familiarities, and maybe the practicalities that have built up over the last six years that will carry things — if it doesn't send them wheeling into the cosmic ditch. It's not just the sunlight and the drugs, either. Subtly, Esther is letting me see that she's prepared to go on with our life together.

How do I detect this? First off, she's talking about the day we're about to launch into as if it will actually happen: she has appointments with several clients, Gord has asked her to go over to Jack's apartment to pack a bag for him and get rid of the perishables. She's already picked up Fang, his Jack Russell terrier. The other news is that Wendel has gotten word that the Cabinet report on the northern harvest cuts is going to be released at one o'clock, and he's organizing a press conference with the Coalition — at one-forty-five.

But the truest signal is that, as we cross the first intersection outside the hospital, she slips her right hand across the seat and onto my thigh. So there it is. Not just that she does it, but the *way* she does it. Esther touches in two distinct ways. When she's pissed with me, she touches me with her fingers, like she's handling a dead fish. When things are good, she touches me with the palm of her hand, a firm, comfortable touch that is both possessive and intimate. The touch of her hand on my thigh this morning is the palm-touch, so warm and electric that I can feel the emotional glue it exudes. I'm so grateful for it that I have to turn my head to the window to hide the tears.

To distract myself, and her, I offer to take on the job of packing Jack's bag.

"That'll help a lot," she admits. "I've got my first appointment at nine-thirty, and I'd have had to scoot over between then and eleven-thirty. The plane leaves at one, so you'll have to deliver the bag to the hospital. You up to that?"

"Sure. Who's taking him to the airport?"

"Gord will be taking him out there, but his knee will have to be immobilized, so they'll probably take him out in an ambulance. Not sure how they'll handle that on the plane."

"Don't they normally wait a couple of weeks before they do this kind of operation? To let the swelling go down?"

"Gord wants Jack out of town before Milgenberger gets a chance to convince him that the injury isn't serious, and that he can do the job here. You know Gord. He doesn't pull strings gently. When he wants something done his way, he wraps the strings around everyone's throat so they have to do what he wants. He had the specialist in Vancouver lined up by the time I got to the hospital this morning."

"Nice guy to have around when there's trouble."

"Yes indeed," she agrees. "If it weren't for him, you'd likely be in intensive care with electrodes stuck in both ears, with some idiot planning to open you up for an exploratory surgery."

WE HAVE JUST FIFTEEN minutes at the house before we have to leave — time to put Bozo outside for the day, and Fang out for a quick pee. Being what he is, Fang wants to spend the day pretending he's a Newfoundland. He tries to follow Bozo through the snow, but since the recent snowfall is still powder he simply goes submarine and I have to dig him out of the tunnel he digs, grousing and nipping. If Bozo had Fang's personality and ambition, we'd have to put her in a steel cage to keep her from eating the neighbourhood.

As I try to settle Fang down, who has by now decided that my pantleg is a raccoon, I replay last night's telephone messages. The one that interests me is from Wendel, left while Esther was at the hospital picking me up, saying that the Coalition is meeting at one at the Alexander Mackenzie coffee bar to discuss the government's announcement.

I've never been to a Coalition meeting. People who think they're right have a way of being righteous about it, which in my mind isn't quite the same thing as being right. It's usually the opposite of knowing the right thing to do. Righteousness is what a few too many Coalition members run on, and like Wendel they can be a real pain in the ass when that's all they've got.

But since Wendel is my pain in the ass, I'm going to drop in on the meeting to see if there's anything I can do to nudge him and his friends toward the real world. Gotta start somewhere with being his father, and if I'm going to start laying a parental hand on him it best have some practical application.

Esther is standing in the hallway. "Ready to hit the road?"

"One sec. Do you know where my briefcase is?"

I see her eyebrows rise slightly. "It's probably in the spare room with your other junk."

"Right." She's surprised because I almost never use the damned thing, preferring to carry whatever I need either in my pockets or in my head. But in the briefcase is one of the few organized things I've been working on recently. It's a handmade analysis of forestry employment records and job multipliers I've been fiddling with over the last few months. What my research shows is that forestry employment has been dropping steadily since 1979, and that under current industry values there *aren't* any employment multipliers. This might prove useful to Wendel.

I busy myself scattering papers and books across the spare room without finding the briefcase, and then remember that it's in the trunk of the Lincoln. I spin around, and there's Esther leaning against the doorjamb. She's laughing at me. She's seen this routine before, and there's no contempt in her laughter. She told Gord one time that I don't clean up or do housework, I fight chaos. Or spread it.

I DROP HER OFF at her office and drive over to Jack's apartment, which is over a second-hand store in the nearly derelict downtown. Jack's business would do better if he moved out to one of the shopping centres, but he's like Gord that way: he has his loyalties. He lives and works where he does because he believes his job is to do services for the community, not just "do better" for himself. So he stays in the old downtown because that's where Mantua is — for better or worse. The malls could be anywhere in North America, and what goes on in them is pretty much the opposite of what he means by community. His office is at one end of the building overlooking the street, and his living quarters at the back. He owns the building.

He's lived in the apartment since he broke up with his wife, who got the house as her part of the settlement. That was about twelve years ago, before I knew him. In my time I've seen women come and go from his life, much as they've come and gone from Gord's. Jack will tell you he's still looking for the right woman, and then laugh and say she doesn't seem to be looking very hard for him.

I retrieve my briefcase from the trunk, and use the keys Esther gave me to let myself into Jack's place. It doesn't take long to find his flight bag in one of the closets, spread out the bag on the bed, and begin to put together what he'll need. I find his shaving kit in the bathroom, toss in his toothpaste and a new toothbrush still in its plastic case, and a bottle of shampoo. There are five vials of pills in the medicine cabinet, and, not sure which he needs, I take them all and return to the bedroom.

Let's see. Pyjamas, bathrobe, check. Three pairs of undershorts — no, five — a half-dozen pairs of black socks, some T-shirts, three shirts, a couple of pairs of cotton trousers, a pair of casual shoes, and a suit, which I hang over the door with a clean shirt and tie. I'm packing the last of it in when I lose my grip on the pyjamas and bathrobe. They fall to the floor.

I pick them up and stretch the sleeves apart for refolding. The pyjamas are enormous — big enough, probably, to fit Gord. The bathrobe is the same. I refold them both and place them beside the flight bag. I check a set of drawers across the room, find proper-sized pyjamas, and, on a hook behind the bathroom door, the right-sized bathrobe. I put those next to the bigger ones, and sit down on the bed.

I reopen the pocket on the bag that has the shaving kit and the pills, and check the label on the pills. Only three of the five vials have Jack's name on them. The other two have Gord's. I begin to check around the room. On the night table shelf on the left side of the headboard are two books on forensic medicine and a biography of Michel Foucault, a French writer Gord has been talking about recently.

I do the two-plus-two, and it comes to four. Then I do the subtractions, the multiplications, and the long division on a few dozen loose ends that have been there all along, flapping around inside my head. It's still two plus two equals four. I wander out into the living room, laughing out loud. Jesus H. Christ, you guys. What am I going to find out next? That Junior is an extraterrestrial?

TWENTY

I DROP JACK'S PACKED BAG at the top of the stairs and unlock the office so I can type up the insurance release on his aging IBM Selectric. I've got most of the phrasing in my head: name, address, and so forth. I'll adapt the limited liability clause from the releases we've all signed as players. What that says, basically, is that neither the Mohawk Hockey Club nor the City of Mantua is liable for damages or loss of income resulting from injury, and that a player can't sue the Club or the City for general or punitive damages resulting from his or other players' actions. Of course, if the Coliseum roof falls in during a game and kills us — always a possibility in Mantua — or some other equally gross instance of facility operator incompetence occurs, we have the same rights as anyone else. Our heirs can sue them, and wait until hell freezes over for the courts to rule that we're to blame for everything.

Somewhere along the line I learned to touch type, so putting together the release form doesn't take very long. I use Jack's fax machine to make a couple of copies, slip them into my briefcase, and I'm off to the hospital to deliver the bag and traveling clothes. The entire operation has taken just forty-five minutes.

It takes a few minutes to locate Jack at the hospital. I assumed he'd been sent up to one of the wards the way I was, but Gord has kept him in emergency, probably as a way of keeping him mind-fucked until he's on the plane. Gord isn't pleased to see me with the bag.

"Jesus Murphy, Weaver," he scowls. "I hope Esther didn't let you pack that thing."

"She had a bunch of appointments," I answer. "Who else was there?"

"Anyone but you. You're not supposed to lift anything for two weeks. Are you taking those pills I gave you?"

I've forgotten them at home, but I pat my hip pocket anyway. "Right here," I lie.

"Show me," he says. "You're due for one just about now."

I start fumbling in my pockets. "Uhhmm ..."

"I thought so. Listen. You've got to use those things exactly on schedule, or your chest is going to keep seizing up on you. And if you have another seizure here and I'm not around, you're liable to wake up and find Milgenberger's treated you to a heart transplant."

"Yeah, yeah, I know. And he'll probably just jam it up my ass, right?"

I've made a homosexual allusion, for Christ's sake. Worse than that, Gord picks up on it instantly. The look on my face must have given me away.

It's a ridiculous situation. I go off to pack a bag for a close friend, and when I come back there's about two thousand things I can't tease him and another close friend about anymore. I mean, let's be blunt. I'm surprised to find out that Jack and Gord are gay, but really, it doesn't change anything. They're still my two closest friends. On the other hand, this is a small town, and if Jack and Gord wanted people to know about it they'd have gone public. The really silly thing about it is that just as I've unloaded my biggest secret, I have to put up with theirs. I giggle out loud at the thought.

"I'm glad you're finding life so amusing," Gord says, and strides away, I assume to get me a muscle relaxant. Or some arsenic.

"Anyone talked to Junior yet this morning?" I ask Jack.

"He's upstairs someplace. Milgenberger wants to keep him under observation for a couple of days, and I think it's a good idea."

I pull the insurance release form from my briefcase and drop it in front of him. "How's that look to you?"

A shrewd look crosses his face as he reads it. "It's fine. But listen. I've got an idea for you. Why don't you get Milgenberger to tell Junior he can't play for six weeks unless he's wearing protection. Meanwhile, you go down to Wally's and pick up that mask I've had sitting there for the last two years. We might be able to make a goalie out of Junior yet."

"You've had a mask ready for two years?"

"Sure. I've been waiting for a puck to whack him this hard ever since Blacky Silver crushed his cheekbone three years ago. I've even had Wally paint the goddamned mask in fleshtones, so Junior can pretend it's just part of his face."

"I'll do what I can. But I ain't taking side bets Junior will go for a mask."

"Just talk about how good young Stan was looking," Jack grins. "That might soften him up. But make sure Gord doesn't get wind of this. You know how he is. Oh yeah. One more thing."

"What?"

"Well, I was talking to Old Man Ratsloff last night before the Roosters left. He mentioned that Artie Newman is shacked up with some babe over in West Camelot. You might want to drive down there and see if you can talk him into playing for us the rest of the season. The Old Man said he tried to get Artie to play with the Roosters, but Artie pulled some routine about not wanting to upset his father."

"The lad is deluding himself. Alpo is offended because Artie breathes oxygen, not because he might play for some out-of-town team."

"Go talk to him," he says. "First thing Monday."

Gord returns, tosses me a smaller vial of pills than the first one, and sits on the edge of Jack's bed.

"Time to get ready, pal," he says. "Plane's leaving at one-fifteen."

I tell them I've got to go, wish Jack luck, and ask him, as an afterthought, if he has any more instructions about running the team in his absence. He tells me there's an envelope in his desk drawer at the Coliseum with a list of all the things that need to be taken care of.

"Try not to mess up too bad," he laughs. "Gord will be watching you."

"Take that muscle relaxant before you go," Gord adds.

I open the vial and pop the blue and white capsule into my palm, then into my mouth. "Done," I say. "These aren't going to fuck up my head, are they?"

"No more than usual."

Okay, I deserved that one. "Be serious," I say. "I can drive the car, right?"

Gord pauses to think. "Go ahead," he says. "You should be okay if you don't start popping them like they're candy."

I PARK THE LINCOLN in the usual spot at the Coliseum, and hoof it over to the Alexander Mackenzie Inn through the new Civic Centre complex. "New" isn't the right word for the complex because it isn't really new, and, if we were being precise, the only thing complex about it is whatever motivated City Council to tear down half of the old Centre just because they wanted to get rid of the city's disreputable boxing club. Once they had what they wanted, though, they realized they'd created an eyesore. So they added a few meeting rooms and tatted the whole thing up with cheesy ironwork, series lighting, and walkways made of concrete pavers. Now, if the old folks going to bingo night are senile enough they think they're in Las Vegas.

The ironwork and the lights weren't the worst of it, either. No one told the architect he was building on a land-filled slough, so he gave the walkway contractor normal specs for the foundations. Of course, the contractor cut corners and put down five centimetres of crushed rock instead of the twenty it needed. The whole damned network of walkways turned into an obstacle course when the first spring thaw buckled everything, and a few drunk old-timers tripped on the popped-up pavers and broke their hips. Eventually they'll have to tear up the entire mess and asphalt it like they do everything else, but not until the injury lawsuits are through the courts. And since the frost boils keep popping the pavers, and the Civic Centre walkways are just a lurch out of the direct route between the town's two biggest bars, the lawsuits will probably go on forever.

I get across the pavers without breaking an ankle and arrive at the Alexander Mackenzie coffee bar, just as the courier finishes passing around the text of the Cabinet report. As the Minister mouths platitudes from the wall-mounted television, the room begins to buzz with outrage. The hoped-for harvest cuts are announced pretty much as Wendel predicted, but a special addendum to the report that the Minister isn't going to mention at the press conference, and won't take questions on, designates a huge area for salvage cutting.

Everyone in the room knows what "salvage cutting" means. About thirteen years ago the same designation was given to another area southeast of Mantua, just north of the Bowron Lakes Provincial Park. By the time the salvage operations were over the multinationals had created the largest clearcut on the planet, one that the Forest Service admits is fifty-three square kilometres in size, and which, along with the Great Wall of China, is supposedly one of the two manmade objects visible from outer space with the naked eye.

Gord and I camped out in the clearcut a couple of times several years ago, and it didn't take any rocket science for us to figure out that the clearcut is a lot larger than the one they admit to. Maybe it was the hundred-metre swaths of old timber separating the primary clearcut from the secondary ones that gave it away. Or maybe it was because it looked more barren than the Gobi Desert.

I pull a coffee from the urn by the door, plunk some sugar and cream into it, and sit down at one of the tables near the back of the room. Wendel has moved to the podium, and he's talking about the Bowron clearcut.

"When the Bowron valley was designated for salvage," he says, "they claimed it started with a patch of blowdown at the heart of the valley in the early 1970s. This was followed by a couple of mild winters, which supposedly set off a spruce budworm infestation in the area of the blowdown. Most of the valley was what the Forest Service calls 'over-mature.' In reality, the valley was what a forest ought to be — a full community of plants and animals, dominated, in size and wood volume, by trees that aren't getting any younger, and which, in the next three or four decades may — or may not — die and fall on their own.

"I don't need to remind anyone here of what salvage logging, multinational style, does," he continues, his voice rising to oratory pitch. "They move in massive amounts of equipment, and they flatten everything in the designated area under the pretense that a public and ecological service is being rendered. The Forest Service won't admit this, but when the multinationals 'salvaged' the Bowron valley, they used the bug infection smokescreen to enlarge the cut area as the clearcut grew. Does that surprise anyone? The companies had their equipment on site, the profits were huge, and they owned the government."

One of the academics leaps to his feet to point out that the current government is supposed to be a social democratic one — the kind that isn't supposed to let this sort of thing happen.

Wendel doesn't flinch. "This same government has close ties to the international trade unions, who've become more pro-cut in the last ten years than the multinationals. They'd flatten every forest in the province to keep their membership employed."

A couple of the progressive union guys in the Coalition nod their heads at this, and the academic sits down. Wendel looks around the room. He spots me, but doesn't react. He's got amazing presence for a twenty-year-old, this kid. And just as I'm thinking that he didn't get his presence from me, he rolls on.

"So here's the bottom line. In theory, the government has cut the official harvest of trees. It'll sound great to people watching television down in Vancouver, but we know what they've really done. The newly designated salvage areas will be removed from the 'sustained yield' formula, thus making the sustained yield volume cuts irrelevant but keeping the facade of sustainability in place, and keeping the few Forest Service bureaucrats who haven't been laid off in the government cutbacks smiling. The multinationals will cheerfully accept the cuts, move their equipment into the salvage area, and go crazy like they did in the Bowron. They'll get more trees, and more profits, than they would have under the old formula. A few years will pass, more cuts in the harvest will need to be made to keep the facade in place, and another diseased, over-mature salvage area — read 'old growth forest' — will be discovered, designated, and then decimated."

He's finished. He's about nailed it, and everyone in the room knows it. He asks if anyone has comments or questions, and stands there, calm and collected, to field them.

TWENTY-ONE

THE COALITION HAS THE same problem everyone has these days: it's a lot easier to see what or who's being screwed than to do anything about it. These are people who understand that everyone and everything in Mantua is being humped by the multinationals, and that this isn't going to stop until someone — or something — stops them. Some of the Coalition members, like Wendel, even have a fair idea what changes need to be made.

It isn't that they don't have the courage of their convictions. There are situations in which courage isn't enough. You need imagination, and a willingness to question some much more basic beliefs, the ones we all get drummed into our heads from elementary school on: that in a democracy the government belongs to the people and, ergo, life is supposed to be fair.

I'll tell you what I mean. Just after I came back to Mantua, I assembled some industrial land for a guy named Sid Brickman. He'd pulled together the finances to do something that should have been done around here thirty years ago — he built a finger-joint stud mill.

Finger-jointing is where you take two pieces of scrap wood and glue them together to make a piece of spaghetti otherwise known, non-metrically, as a two-by-four. The result, both in theory and practice, is construction wood superior in strength to an ordinary two-by-four. Even better, the profits are good because you're using wood that's already been milled and rejected, and because the process is relatively labour-intensive it produces jobs and helps out the local economy. In short, it is what every government in the Western hemisphere has been whining about the need for since the gravy started thinning out after the oil crisis in 1973.

Sid got his mill up and running, three shifts and one hundred fifty workers, and it was doing fine until some bureaucrat in the Forestry Department assigned his wood supply contract to InterCon. Sid's mill was soon getting wood he couldn't finger-joint into decent toothpicks, and when he squawked about it, the wood got worse.

Eventually, Sid recognized that InterCon was deliberately trying to put him out of business, and he sued for damages. But the moment the papers were served InterCon cut off his wood supply altogether. And that's where it sat for close to three years, until Sid won his court case. Guess what? The award didn't come close to covering his costs, and the mill, meanwhile, was gathering dust. Right now it's still running at a quarter capacity, because a multinational corporation has ways of ignoring court rulings.

Now, many of the Coalition members would prefer just to hold news conferences like the one they're planning this afternoon, and then go home to their out-of-the-industry jobs feeling morally superior. Reason? Bickering and bitching about corporate malfeasance or government incompetence is safer and easier than sticking your ass into a multibillion-dollar meat grinder. But today, Wendel and a few of the others aren't willing to give up so easily. One of the independent loggers stands up and starts explaining how this is the right time to begin setting up a logging co-operative that will do things differently, even if it has to do it on a demonstration basis. This is the route Wendel wants to take, too. Another group wants to go a different, nastier route — they want to block the highways, sabotage the railways, or do whatever else is needed to keep the sawlogs from leaving town. The rest — a minority, for once — just want to be outraged for a few hours, go to the bar, and then go home and watch television like they usually do. The way things are going, the three factions are probably going to deadlock, meaning that very little is going to get decided. From the frustration in Wendel's face, he sees it too.

I haven't planned to do anything more than watch, but after another fruitless go-around I find myself standing in front of everyone tapping my finger on the table like some schoolmarm. There's about a hundred things I could say that everyone in the room already knows, so I offer the one thing I have that they don't know about. One or two of them — Wendel being the only one I care about — might find it useful.

"I don't know whether you're aware of this," I say, "but I own one hundred acres of fairly decent industrial land down on the flats. If you need a location for your scaling yard, you can have the use of it."

The room goes stony silent for what must be nearly ten seconds. That's how long it takes around here for surprise to percolate down to cynicism. The first response comes from one of the smartassed academics.

"Oh sure," he says. "What's the catch?"

"No catch," I answer. "How about a rental contract for one dollar a year? Plus the co-op pays the taxes on the land if and when it starts making a profit."

Another silence. I catch Wendel's eye and try some telepathy on him. I want him to stay out of this for a moment. He seems to understand, and sinks, watchfully, back in his chair.

The academic is the first one to start flapping his mouth. "Well," he intones, "this is all well and good. But isn't the Forest Service conducting feasibility studies on community scaling yards? Maybe we ought to wait for them to give the go ahead."

I'm tempted to blow the chicken-hearted turd-polisher off, but a glance at Wendel convinces me to circle around him instead. "Maybe we should wait for the Forest Service," I answer. "But maybe we shouldn't. I don't know if you've heard about that photo the Chief Forester has hanging in his office — the one with the line of about thirty haul trucks coming out of the Bowron?"

A rumble crosses the room, and a couple of Coalition members laugh out loud. "I see some of you get my point about what those feasibility studies are going to say. Everybody's known for decades that the industry has the Forest Service in its pocket. That isn't going to change unless we can convince a few more people that having the Forest Service in cahoots with the multi-nationals isn't part of the natural order, and that there's some other routes we can go."

I haven't intended to make a speech, and I'm a little amazed that I'm parroting things I've made fun of Wendel for saying to a bunch of strangers. But the clear approval in Wendel's face tells me to go on.

"I mean, look at the long view. If we know what the words and the pictures really mean, don't we have to make some choices? One of the choices you people have to make is between your anger and your cynicism. The fact that the people who are supposed to be taking care of our resources for everyone aren't doing their jobs ought to make us all angry as hell. But what does knowing that get us, unless we do something about it?"

"So what are you saying?" the academic pipes up, this time with a whiny ping in his voice. "What are you asking us to do?"

"Get up off your behinds and commit to the community scaling yards, for starters. I can't give you technical advice. For that you'll have to find somebody who knows the business end of a chainsaw from his ass. I don't."

After repeating that the offer is a totally serious one, I sit down and sip coffee while the uproar dies down to a calculating buzz. I'll be surprised if they take me up on it, but if they do I'll damned well stand behind it. My speech does flush the chickens out of the underbrush, and the conversation moves on to the practicalities. That's good. It'll help Wendel and his supporters.

Meanwhile, it's time for me to head out. I'm on a roll, so I may as well find James Bathgate's parents this afternoon. Promises are promises, and I'll need to get the kid's insurance release signed so he can be at the practice tomorrow. I repeat once more to the Coalition that my offer is serious, that I'm not about to skip town or run for political office, and that they can appoint whoever they like to carry out the negotiations when and if they're ready to go forward on the deal. I hope I'll be talking to Wendel about it before the day is out. As I leave the coffee bar, he winks at me and mouths a "thank you."

It's a beginning. Even if it ends up costing me a bundle, I'm okay with it.

THERE'S AN UP-TO-DATE PHONEBOOK at a payphone in the lobby, and it lists four Bathgates besides myself. I fish some quarters out of my pocket and start dialing. I draw blanks on the first two, one of them X-rated. The third call gets a woman with a bright, reasonable-sounding voice.

"I'm sorry to bother you," I say, "but I'm trying to locate one or both of James Bathgate's parents."

There's a slight hesitation on the other end of the line. "Yes? I'm his mother. I hope he hasn't gotten himself into trouble."

"Oh, nothing like that," I say, trying to sound reassuring. I explain that I'm from the Mohawks hockey team, and that we'd like her son to be our stickboy, etc. etc.

"Oh, yes," she says, sounding relieved. "James did mention something about it, but I thought he was telling tall tales again."

I go on to talk about the necessity of an insurance release, mentioning that since he's at all the games anyway he's probably safer behind the bench than in the stands. No, I don't tell her that her son's biggest safety hazard is the V8 he's got attached to his mouth — or that I've been the chief threat to his health. She digests the technicalities without difficulty, and asks whether he's expected to travel with the team for away games.

That hadn't crossed my mind, so I have to think quickly. I suggest to her that it can be optional, then correct myself immediately, saying that though the Friday away games will probably keep him up too late he might want to travel with us for some of the Sunday games. I make it clear that I'll abide by whatever she decides is best.

"We've got a practice late tomorrow afternoon we'd like him to be at," I continue. "Is it possible for me to drop out and get you to sign the release before that?"

"That'll be fine," she says. "But I don't know who to expect."

"I'm Andy Bathgate," I say.

There's an audible intake of breath. "When should I expect you?" she asks.

"Let's say somewhere around four this afternoon."

Another hesitation. "Then we'll see you at four."

She's probably going to ask for my autograph. Times like this I wish I was somebody named Joe Fish. On the other hand, that wouldn't help either. Someone would assume I was Country Joe, and want to know where The Fish have gone.

THE ADDRESS LISTED IN the phonebook is in an obscure subdivision far north of town across the Nechalko River, but I have enough time to drop around to Wally's to see whether Jack was kidding about having the goalie mask. If it is there I may as well pick it up and spring it on Junior while he's still in the hospital.

There's no parking spot in front of the store, so I have to double park, put on the blinkers, and hope for the best. "Ah!" Wally says as I breeze through the front doors. "The Great Weaver Bathgate himself, replete with illegally parked civic limousine. What mission of tender mercy brings you to grace our lowly premises this afternoon? No 5030s at Canadian Tire? Can I perhaps sell you a modern hockey stick instead?"

"Give it a break, Wally," I laugh. "Jack claims you've got a goalie mask somewhere around here for Junior. Is that true or was he shitting me?"

"Indeed it is true," Wally replies, sounding not entirely surprised. "Wait here and I'll get it for you."

He disappears into the storeroom, and I hear him shuffling boxes around. "What are you planning to do?" he hollers. "Tease Junior with it?"

"Nothing so crass," I answer. "I'm going to tell him he can't play for six weeks unless he wears it."

"Very cunning. Think it'll work?"

"Probably not. It's Jack's idea, not mine. I take it you heard about yesterday's game."

"I heard," he says as he comes out of the storage room and plants the mask on the counter. "I saw. Quite a moment in the history of local sport."

I pick up the mask and lift it to eye level. It is, as Jack promised, painted in fleshtones. What he didn't say was that the fleshtone would be corpse-quality. Actually, it's worse than that. Some of the flesh appears to have decomposed, while the rest looks like it came from someone who just rammed his car into the side of a gasoline tanker. The total effect is roughly that of Jason *without* his hockey mask. Hard to say whose goofy idea this design is. Somebody has a sense of humour, that's for sure. Probably Wally.

"Beautiful, isn't it?" Wally comments. "And speaking of beauties, your better half was just in here."

"My better half is right where it's been all day," I answer, checking my fly with mock care so he gets the gag.

"Very funny."

"What was Esther doing in here?" I ask.

"Nothing much," he says, then adds, sounding about as mysterious as is possible for someone who resembles the Pillsbury Doughboy, "and none of your business."

I GLANCE ALONG THE street as I come out of the store and see that the meterman is half a block past my car. He turns around just as I open the car door, grins, and waves at me. There's no ticket on the windshield.

TWENTY-TWO

*H*ow does this kid *get to the hockey games?* That's the
pleasantly practical puzzle I sort through as I drive through
the cheesy subdivisions north of Mantua. It doesn't sound like
the boy's father is a hockey fan, and I hadn't exactly gotten the
sense from his mother that she was on top of his comings and
goings enough to be getting him to and from the games.

Out here, he's a long way from town. Maybe there's a neighbour nearby who has regular tickets. Maybe, but the kid never
seems to be with anyone at the games. One thing's for sure. If
anyone is with him, he or she isn't giving him any guidance about
how to behave.

I drop the neighbour transport theory when I find the road
named on the scrap of paper beside me on the seat. There aren't
any close neighbours because the Bathgates live a half kilometre
beyond the last of the subdivisions, at the dead end of a road that,
as I bump the Lincoln along it, isn't much better than a skid road.
But it's been ploughed.

The house is half hidden behind a dense grove of young
spruce and birch trees that appear to have been planted deliberately to shield it from sight. There's power and telephone
lines, and a clearing that doesn't stretch much beyond the

twenty-five-by-fifty-foot rectangle of freshly flooded ice that ends close to the side of the house, and which probably doubles as a vegetable garden during the summer. Aside from that, pretty well everything else is as mother nature would like to have us live: no wrecked cars in the yard, hand-split cedar shingles covering the roof and outer walls, and, at the edge of the cleared area, a half-buried sod-covered bunker with birch saplings sticking from it like porcupine quills. Beyond the bunker is a thicket of half-grown thirty-to-forty-foot lodgepole pines, probably regrowth after a logging cut or forest fire. A murder of crows is calling back and forth to one another, most of them hidden by the boughs, and whiskey jacks are flitting around a birdfeeder atop the bunker.

A place like this is unusual for Mantua, whose citizens — when they're not using their property as a personal dump site — prefer to live in treeless suburbs with lawns that look like they've poured concrete and painted it green. Any way I look at the Bathgate house, it just ain't natural for Mantua: no vinyl siding, no satellite dish, no plastic. The same orderly attention to detail I could see in the landscaping is evident in the house — it's no slapped-together homesteader's shack. I can't see how large it is, but it's sizable. Hmm.

A slim, tall woman opens the door to me just as my fist is descending against it, and I come within a slapstick hair of punching her in the stomach as my introduction.

"That was close," I say, stepping back to reassure her I'm not an axe murderer. "I'm Andy Bathgate."

"Yes," she says, "I recognize you. I'm Claire Bathgate. James's mother. Please come in."

She moves aside and I step past her into a hallway that looks into a spacious living room. The room is sparsely furnished but comfortable looking, with a large olive-drab couch covered in what looks like old velvet, a couple of stuffed chairs of a darker shade, and a big wooden coffee table between the three. There's a large deep red Persian rug covering most of the plank floor, and along the far wall are floor-to-ceiling bookcases that, at a glance, aren't filled with *Reader's Digest* condensations. Aside from several lamps and an airtight stove with a deep wood box to one side of it, that's all. No television, no stereo, and no cereal box bric-a-brac.

I slip off my boots and pull off my coat, which she takes from me and hangs on a hook on the wall behind her.

"Would you like some tea?"

"Please."

"Well, why don't you follow me to the kitchen and we can sign your documents while the water boils."

She turns her back on me without waiting for a reply, and I follow her along a hallway lined with black-and-white photographs. Claire Bathgate is probably in her fifties, and as I watch her move I decide she's gaunt rather than slim. Her step doesn't give away her age. It's sure and athletic, and I'm not quite sure why I think she's over fifty. Her face perhaps, or maybe the careless salt and pepper of her hair. I kind of like the way she looks, actually. She fits with the house.

The kitchen is as casually unusual as the living room. Natural cedar walls and cupboards, a circular oak table, and three chairs. The stove is the biggest thing in the kitchen. It appears to be a wood stove, but much larger than any I've ever seen.

I watch her fill a kettle and slide it atop one of the six stove plates. "It's called an Aga," she says, without looking at me. "Swedish. We do all our cooking on it, and it heats the hot water and keeps most of the house warm."

"Must be a little warm during the summer," I say.

"We don't use it then," she laughs. "There's an outdoor stove out there." She's pointing through the window. "And we're not here very much during the summer."

We make small talk while the kettle heats, mainly about the stove. I get the sense that she's reluctant to talk about herself or young James, and there's no mention at all of the father. She asks for the form, reads it carefully, then signs it without comment and hands it back to me.

By the time the tea is made and properly steeped, I've decided that I like this woman as much as I like her looks. I want to know more about her, her kid, and her husband — if there is one. But she's not giving me any conversational openings on anything but hockey, which she says fascinates the boy.

"I've noticed. How does he get to the games?" I ask. "You're rather a long way out here."

She laughs, and an eyebrow flickers. "Oh, he has his ways of getting around. And don't you worry. If he says he'll be somewhere, he gets there. And he'll be on time."

There's an odd kind of edge to her voice as she says this, as if she's not quite able to take the pleasure from her son's independence she thinks she ought to. We talk more about the boy, and the impression that he's a mixed pleasure for her strengthens. We run out of small talk, and I get up to go.

"I'm sure this will be a good experience for him," she says plaintively. "You'll take care of him, won't you? He thinks the world of you."

"Well," I say, "we do share the Bathgate name, so we have that in common. I'll keep an eye on him." I don't mention any of my previous plans to strangle her son or run him over with my car, and I don't mention that I threatened to make his brains squirt out of his ears just yesterday afternoon.

As I'm passing through the hallway on the way out, my eyes stray to the wall of framed photos. Curious, I stop to look them over. Most are landscapes — a northern lake, two men dwarfed by a wolf fir, a wedding photo I don't examine very carefully, things like that. But toward the top there's a photo of a child in a hockey uniform, an old photo, that arrests my attention. The child, as I stop to examine it, is nine or ten years old, wearing a Montreal Canadiens sweater.

I feel Claire Bathgate's hand on my shoulder. "I should have taken that photograph down," she says simply. "I think you'd better come into the living room and sit down."

TWENTY-THREE

OVER THE NEXT HOUR, Claire Bathgate tells me a tale that makes my head spin. She's my stepmother, my father's second wife, and the boy I'm about to make the stickboy for the Mantua Mohawks is my half brother.

Without meaning to, she confirms some of what my mother told me about my father — and contradicts everything I imagined about what happened after they split up. Yes, my father had a moderately successful truck-logging company, sold it, gave my mother the proceeds, and hit the bottle. But around the time my mother lost track of him, when I was seventeen or so, he began to slowly dig his way out. Claire met him in Camelot, where she was a nurse in the hospital.

She dried him out, fell in love with him — she didn't say which came first — and they homesteaded in one of the valleys to the southeast of the city. My father went back to logging, except this time as a private operator clearing farmland and logging off private woodlots. They stayed in the backwoods for a decade and a half, living a simple life and making a decent living. He'd become something of an expert at small-scale logging, occasionally using horses, and was currently much in demand— outside the country, of course — for some harvest and reforestation innovations he developed along the way.

They'd moved back to Mantua about the time I returned, mainly so James could get a proper education, and, I guess, because my father was getting on in years.

"He must be close to seventy now," I find myself saying to Claire.

"Seventy-one," she says. "Not that you'd know it to look at him."

"He knows I'm here?" I ask. "I mean, that I'm me." I sound stupid, garbled.

"Of course."

"But he never thought to contact me?"

"He's thought about it constantly. But he knew about the trouble you'd had, and he thought you might not want to be reminded about it. And," she says, "he wasn't sure you wanted to hear from him."

"I was convinced he was dead," I said. "I haven't heard hide nor hair of him since I was, let's see — sixteen, I guess."

"I'm sure this is a lot to take in all at once," she says, carefully. "You're going to have to do some thinking about it. You realize that James is your half brother."

"I'm getting my head around it. Shouldn't he be getting home anytime now?"

"We've got some time," she says, then answers my unspoken question without my having to ask it. "He doesn't know. And I don't think he should be told until a few other things are settled. Like whether you want to speak to your father."

This one brings me up short. The thought that I have a living father is one shock. That he's in the same part of the planet I'm in is another. I can't imagine what I'd say to him if he were to walk in the door right now. I'd crawl under the coffee table, probably. The panic it throws me into must be apparent.

"Don't worry," she says. "He's in Denver. He travels quite a lot, these days. He won't be back until Saturday."

She's being incredibly gracious. It must not be any easier for her having me sitting in her living room than it is for me to be here, and I'm at sea trying to figure out how to reciprocate. I stand up.

"Well," I say, "I guess we're just going to have to play this one straight up. I won't mention anything to James, of course. But you can tell my father that I'll be in touch early next week. And it's been extremely nice meeting you."

She hands me my coat as I slip on my boots. "I don't think you have any idea what a relief this is to me," she says, extending her hand. Her eyes are misty.

I take her hand, and, to hell with it, lean forward and kiss her cheek. "Tell James to be at the Coliseum about five tomorrow."

My watch reads four-forty-five as I walk back to the Lincoln. The darkening sky is a deep, transparent purple, and the crows and jays are already silent. In an hour, the sky will be filled with stars. I crank up the engine and let it idle while the heater blows the ice crystals from the windshield.

There's still the possibility that when I get home tonight the locks will have been changed. I don't think that's in the cards, but then again I don't seem to be dealing the cards or deciding what the game is going to be right now. The only other thing left on my list is to visit Junior, and see if I can fit him with a goalie mask. If it sticks to his face and turns him into a horror movie marquee, I won't bat an eye. I pat my inside pocket to make sure I've got the signed insurance release, and flip the Lincoln into gear. The motor guns as the wheels dislodge themselves from the snow, and off I go.

Halfway along the quarter-mile driveway a Ski-Doo bursts out of the trees onto the roadway fifty metres in front of me. The machine swerves as its driver regains control, and heads in my direction spewing a cloud of powdery snow in its wake. It doesn't have lights, and all I can see of the driver is that he — or she — is small. It's fifty metres past me before I realize that it's James.

AS I PULL INTO the parking lot outside the hospital I scan for Esther's truck, hoping she'll be here visiting Jack so she can help me browbeat Junior into agreeing to wear the mask. Then I remember Jack is long gone on the plane. So, no Esther, damn it. I scoop the mask from the seat beside me and walk toward the hospital entrance. At the last moment I remember that afternoon visiting hours are over, and enter through the emergency entrance. I'm practically on a first-name basis with everyone there, and they'll think I'm looking for Gord.

The first nurse I run into tells me that Gord has left, but that Junior is on the fourth floor.

"Not in the psychiatric ward?" I say.

"No," she says, ignoring my attempt at humour. "He's going to be fine. The disorientation was gone by this morning, although he doesn't have much recall of what happened."

I wave the mask at her. "Maybe this'll keep him out of here next time."

She glances at the mask and grimaces. "I hope so. But *that's* perfectly horrible-looking."

"He looked pretty horrible last night after that puck bounced off his noggin."

"Wait till you see him now," she says as she pulls open a curtained stall and disappears inside.

SHE ISN'T KIDDING. JUNIOR, when I find him, is sitting up in bed sporting two giant shiners and a bandage across his forehead that looks big enough to have a baseball stuffed inside it. They've put him in a private room, no doubt as a courtesy to the patients who required peace and quiet last night.

He's a picture of quiet if not peace when I enter, with reading glasses propped on his nose, perusing the latest issue of *Playboy* — open, naturally, to the centrefold.

"Shouldn't you be reading something that'll improve your

mind?" I say, holding the mask behind my back.

"Nice to see you, Weaver," he grins. "I hear you spent last night in here, too."

"Yeah," I said. "They let me out this morning. Nothing wrong with me a few weeks off the ice won't cure. How's tricks?"

Junior lifts the glasses carefully off his nose and sets them down on the side-table. "I'll live. Nice headache, though."

"Gord been around?" I ask.

"He stopped in a couple of times. Took Jack to the airport a couple of hours ago, I think. What brings you to my neck of the woods?"

I sit down on a chair just off the foot of Junior's bed, and manage to keep the mask out of sight. "Good news and bad," I say.

"Give me the good news."

"It isn't much," I say. "You remember that little bugger who comes to all the games and razzes everyone?"

"He razzes you, Weaver," Junior points out.

"Whatever. Anyway, I just made him our new stickboy. Stroke of genius, no?"

"Some stroke," he says. "I know that kid. Dad and I coached him one year in minor hockey. He was a bit of a satellite."

"Say what?"

"You know, one of those kids who's in orbit all the time. His old man is a bit of one, too, I hear. Ran some sort of weirdo hand-held logging operation outside Camelot until a few years ago. When InterCon moved into that area they got his timber licences revoked, or bought him out, or something. InterCon saw him as some sort of threat."

"Anyway," I say, "the kid'll be around the dressing room from now on. Try not to step on him."

Junior rolls his eyes. "Yeah," he answers, "okay. So let's get to the bad news."

"I had a long conversation with Milgenberger this morning, and an even longer one with Jack before he took off."

"Don't beat around the bush," Junior says. "You were talking about me, right?"

"Yeah," I admit. "We've got a small problem."

"Well, you can relax. I'll be fine for the Friday game."

"Afraid not." I slip the mask under the chair and get up to gaze out the window. If I'm going to get Junior to co-operate, I'm going to have to get him thinking that the mask is the only thing that'll save his career.

He bites. "Jesus, Weave. What is it? What did Milgenberger say?"

"He said that whack you got is life threatening. If you get hit on the same spot again, you could be a vegetable."

"Bullshit," Junior explodes. "I'm fine."

"They obviously haven't shown you the X-rays," I say, deliberately keeping a dead tone in my voice. "Apparently your skull nexus disintegrated when that puck hit it."

There's no such thing as a skull nexus, but I'm pretty sure Junior won't know that.

"My skull nexus disintegrated? What the fuck is a skull nexus?"

"It's a small set of bones just above your temple," I say, touching a spot on my head just above the hairline where I can feel a slight ridge, "that keeps the different bones that make up your skull from coming apart. There's one on each side, and they work as lynchpins, sort of." I'm neck deep in the brown stuff here, but it has his rapt attention. "The bones are completely gone on your right side, and they're weakened on other side."

"I thought skulls were made out of solid bone," Junior says, whistling. "Wow."

"That's what I thought, too," I say. "Shows you how little we know. Anyway, Milgenberger says you're through with hockey."

Junior turns white as a sheet. "You gotta be kidding," he says. "I'm too young to quit."

It's time to spring the mask. "There's one thing that can save it." I let the sentence trail off into silence, as if what's on my mind is just too unthinkable to say out loud.

"What is it?" Junior pulls back the covers and starts to climb out of bed. "I don't want to have to quit."

I push him back onto the bed. "Well," I say. "You remember when you got bopped a couple of winters ago up in Okenoke?"

"Yeah," Junior says, suddenly much less casual about his head injuries than ever before in his life — now that his skull nexus has disintegrated. "That was a doozy."

"Well, apparently the beginning of the damage was apparent that time. Milgenberger mentioned it to Jack," I say, "and Jack wrote away to this special clinic in Tulsa Gord knew about" — I reach beneath my chair and pull out the death's-head mask — "and had this built for you."

For a second, it looks as if Junior is about to dive beneath the bed. Then a wily look crosses his face. "You lousy bastard," he says. "You've been stringing me along, haven't you?"

"Not a word, I swear," I tell him. "Cross my heart and hope to die."

"There's nothing wrong with me," Junior snarls. "And I ain't wearing no goalie mask."

"You can't play goal again for the Mohawks without one," I tell him. "The Coliseum's insurance company called this afternoon and threatened to cancel the team's insurance."

I'm blowing more smoke, of course, and this time Junior knows it right away. Given the releases we sign, if he wanted to play with a loaded .45 automatic stuck in his ear, the insurance company wouldn't give a damn unless the Coliseum manager had personally filed off the safety and cocked it for him.

"Screw you," he says. "I can't play goal with a mask, and that's final. I may have to sit out this weekend, but I'll be back the week after. And I won't be wearing any stupid mask."

A voice from the door interrupts him before he can launch the tirade against girly men, poufters, and safety freaks that's coming next. "I think you should stop being a fool, son, and use the mask."

Damned if Don Young, Sr. isn't standing in the doorway. Junior's jaw drops wide open as the old man steps into the room, nods to me, and moves close enough to Junior that he can examine the bandage on his son's forehead. I don't know how long he's been listening to our conversation, but evidently it was long enough.

"I must have had a dozen of these injuries," he says, dryly. "But nobody thought enough of me to get me a mask, and I was too stupid to ask. It's a bloody wonder my brain isn't more scrambled than it is."

Junior is still silent. So, for that matter, am I. The old man makes a fist of his big hand and uses it to tap Junior on the shoulder. "Listen," he says. "You take that mask and you wear it. I don't want to hear any more of this manly man horseshit from you. God gave you few enough brains without you letting the ones you have get turned into Jell-O pudding."

Mission accomplished. I toss the mask into Junior's lap and leave his father to lecture him on the merits of safety and hockey masks.

TWENTY-FOUR

A SMALL JOLT OF relief rattles up my spine when I see Jack's pickup parked in the driveway: Esther hasn't run away to join the circus or been abducted by aliens. So far, so good. When I slip my key into the front door lock and it turns without a hitch, I'm two for two.

It's better than that, actually. She's cooking my favourite dish, shepherd's pie. It's the first time she's ever made it, and I can see she's used my recipe: hamburger, carrots, onions, salt, pepper, and a dollop of ketchup for the sauce, with riced potatoes on top. I've been cooking the dish since I can remember, and there are two tricks to it: never alter the proportions, and don't add any Smarties. No peas, no corn, no ground lamb, no silly spices.

With the news I've got, though, we don't waste time discussing recipes. I start with the visit to James Bathgate's mother. Esther doesn't say much, but I can see she's pleased rather than disturbed. That makes a certain sense: in her way, Esther has been almost as isolated as I've been. She lost her mother to cancer just after Wendel was born, and her father died in a trucking accident a couple of years after that. Since Leo was killed Wendel has been her family, along with Gord and Jack. When I came along I entered a very small circle, and until two days ago I wouldn't have even seen myself as an essential part of it.

Wendel has already told her about the Coalition meeting, and she's a little skeptical about my offer. "Are you really prepared to give up that property for something that may or may not work?" she wants to know.

I tell her I am.

"This is about Wendel, isn't it?" she says.

"Sure," I answer. "He *is* my son, and I've got to start somewhere with him. You know damned well he's not going to buy into any lovey-dovey stuff, so I figure it's got to be something practical. And anyway, it isn't going to cost me my shirt."

"You really think an independent scaling yard has a chance?" It's more a comment than a question.

"Hard to say," I admit. "Probably not, unless a lot of people change their minds about some fairly basic things. But I agree with what they're trying to do. That Equivalent Value idea of his makes sense to me."

"It does to me too, but right now the world's going in the opposite direction."

"Yeah, well, I guess I'm tired of sitting back on my ass watching the big dogs eating the little dogs. All this bullshit about survival of the fittest doesn't do it for me, you know? So I figure I ought to stand behind a few things that do."

"What does it for you, then?"

"Wendel does, when he's not annoying the crap out of me. A few of those people he's been working with are trying to make things better. At least they care about how the things around us get misused. Seems to me that if we're going to run around being impressed by people taking on difficult things, we ought to be more impressed by those kinds of things and not by all these jerks who'll chew off a rat's ass if they think they can make a profit from it."

I'm a little taken aback by my own passion, and Esther sees it. "Well, it's good that you're willing to help. And Wendel was pretty impressed by what you did. He's coming over for dinner, incidentally."

No surprise there. He's as fond of shepherd's pie as I am. He appears at the back door ninety seconds before the dish comes out of the oven.

"Hi, Andy," he says coolly, tossing his mackinaw onto a chair in the dining room. "Thanks for the push this afternoon. Dunno if there's enough testicles out there to take you up on that goofy offer you made, but it was fun watching them squirm."

"Offer's real," I say. "No time limit. It'd be nice if something changes around here."

"Man, am I hungry," he says, smacking his hands together and sitting down. "Let's eat."

OVER THE SHEPHERD'S PIE I relate my efforts to talk Junior into a goalie mask, together with the unexpected punchline Don Sr. provided.

"Now all we need to do is get him to lose twenty-five pounds," Wendel says, "and we're set."

"Set for what?"

"For the tournament."

That's close to the last thing I want to talk about, so I pull first-things-first on him and mention that I'm going to drive down to Camelot tomorrow to see if I can talk Artie Newman into playing for us.

"Good luck with that," Esther says. "But you're two players short, remember? Not one."

"Hey," Wendel interrupts. "I had a thought. How about we pick up Freddy Quaw?"

"*Freddy* Quaw?" Esther asks, just as I'm about to. I must know several dozen Quaws — it's the family name for of the local native band's hereditary chiefs. Esther probably knows at least fifty Quaws, but not, I guess, all of them.

"He any relation to Roddy?" I ask. Roddy Quaw played for the Mohawks a few years back until the effects of a long string of "minor" logging accidents caught up with him. Nice guy, and from what Gord said about him a more than decent player in his day. Now he's running the band council, which recently asked for downtown Mantua as part of their land claim. No one took them very seriously until they started camping on the lawn in front of city hall and it took a federal cabinet minister and a couple million dollars to get them off. Seems the railroad that originally designed the town site didn't file some papers in the right filing tray back at the turn of the century, and there's an outside chance the whole town is aboriginal land. I suppose we could just give the place back to them, but Jesus, I thought we were supposed to *stop* screwing them.

"I think Freddy is Roddy's nephew," Wendel says. "The family sent him to Sault Ste. Marie to play hockey when he was fourteen, but he stoked some referee just before Christmas and they suspended him for the year. He's eighteen this year, so he's eligible for Senior."

"Do we want him if he's just a goon?"

Wendel shrugged. "The couple of times I played against him it looked like he had good skills. You know they try to turn every big kid into a goon in Junior. We could just tell him to play his own game, and see what happens."

"Well, see if you can get him out to the practice tomorrow. It's pretty hard to say how things will go with Artie Newman. He's a long shot. For all I know he's had his head stuck inside a beer keg so long his brain has dissolved."

"You may not be able to tell him from a beer keg by now," Esther says.

"That's entirely possible, too," I admit. "But I figure he's worth a look. Jack's gone for the year, and I can't play for three or four weeks. And we've been under the player limit all year anyway."

I'M ON THE HIGHWAY rolling south to Camelot by nine the next morning. The cold snap that started Saturday night is holding, and the temperatures are hovering just above minus twenty. That's Fahrenheit, incidentally. Like most people around here, I never quite converted to Centigrade when Pierre Trudeau decided it would be entertainingly anti-American if the country went metric.

Whatever the temperature is, it's cold enough to make the snow crisp and tight under the Lincoln's tires, and soon I'm cruising at one hundred thirty-five kph. I'd like to be cruising at eighty to eighty-five miles per hour, but the Lincoln's speedometer doesn't convert. I really don't know how fast one-thirty-five kph is, except that it seems fast enough. I've traveled this route so many times I could drive it in my sleep.

In just over an hour I'm at the outskirts of Camelot, with the stink of sulphur dioxide in my nostrils. The town has just a single pulp mill to Mantua's three, but the Camelot mill's technology — and maybe its location on the north edge of town — makes it smell stinkier.

All I've got is a phone number for Artie Newman. When I phoned the number last night to warn him I was coming, I got a machine telling me gruffly to "leave a message, maybe we'll call you back." Hence, my itinerary this morning has a prior stop at the Camelot Ritz Grill. The easiest way of finding out anything in Camelot is to talk to Lenny Nakamoto, who makes it his business to know everybody and everything that's going on in town. He'll know exactly how to find Artie. The trick is to get him to tell me.

I haven't warned Lenny that I'm coming, but he'll be where he always is in the morning: sitting at the table next to the cash register at the Grill, counting the previous night's bar receipts. He's a man of habit, Lenny Nakamoto. He'll have the book-keeping done by a few minutes before ten, so that he can be the bank's first customer when it opens. From there he'll head back to the Grill for breakfast, which he will luxuriate over until ten-forty-five, when he'll retreat to the bar for its opening at eleven.

I arrive just as he's about to wolf down the first of the four rubbery fried eggs on the plate in front of him. He sees me coming, grins, and motions me to sit down. I slip into the booth across from him, tipping my wrist down to signal the waitress for coffee. It's about the only thing on this menu I can stomach, but I'm not going to insult Lenny by telling him that no one in their right mind would eat in his restaurant. I need his good will.

Let me tell you just one story about the Camelot Ritz Grill. Sane and sober folks don't eat there much, but in Camelot, always a little short on sane and sober, that isn't a problem. The drunks at the Camelot Ritz Hotel bar think the Grill is the best place in the universe, particularly after Lenny boots their asses out of the bar and tells them to sober up.

They stumble down the hallway to the Grill, where they drink a coffee or two — and then order beer by the bottle. It's great for the drunks, who can sober up *and* get drunker without leaving the building.

It hasn't been so great for the Grill's decor. Every few months, things get out of hand and the place gets trashed. Old Man Ratsloff gets around to renovating the place every five years or so, but because he's a cheapskate he never spends enough to make it look decent. The last time the café got trashed he gave the renovation job to JoMo, who'd just bought a router and was into English Tudor and wormwood. He got hold of a bunch of unplaned fir four-by-fours and three-by-sixes, chewed wormy grooves along them with his router, and stained them as dark as he could. Then he slapped them over the old arborite surfaces from the last renovation. To make things worse, JoMo found a couple bolts of purple-and-puke-coloured naugahyde at some liquidation sale in Vancouver and used it to redo the cushions. The place looks like it was decorated by Henry VIII while he was on LSD.

Lenny sees me eyeing the decor while the waitress puts a brown mug of coffee in front of me. "It's not so bad," he shrugs. "Hides the bloodstains. What brings you to our fair city this morning?"

"I need to find Artie Newman."

Lenny's guard goes up. "Why the fuck do you want to find *him*?"

"His old man's real sick," I say. It's true, sort of. Alpo is a sick puppy. "Somebody has to tell Artie."

Lenny peers at me skeptically. "Oh yeah? Why didn't you just phone him?"

"I did. All I got was a machine. Anyway, that isn't the kind of news you should put on an answering machine."

"Sure," he says. "I believe you. Tell me you're not trying to sign him to a hockey contract to replace old Jackie-boy."

I try to keep my face straight, but Lenny reads me anyway. Then, unexpectedly his expression softens, and he reaches for a small black book that's half-hidden under a manila envelope beside him. He flips it open and passes it across the table with his index finger pressed over a written address.

"What do I get for this?" he wants to know.

"It's what you *won't* get."

"Like what won't I get?"

"Well," I say, "you won't get Gord building a nest in your goal crease this Sunday."

He lifts his finger off the address. "Fair enough. You got a pen?"

I hand him my pen. While he's scribbling the address on a napkin, I ask him some questions about Artie Newman.

"He's been in town for a couple of years now," Lenny says, slipping the pen into his shirt pocket. "Shacked up with a woman I heard he's been chasing around since he was about fourteen. She's some kind of woman, too."

"I'm more interested in what kind of shape he's in."

"Well, he's dry, if that's what you mean. I never see him around here. To tell you the truth, the Old Man's been trying to sign him to play with us since he arrived. No deal. But he's been running the Zamboni on the weekends, actually."

"What's he do the rest of the time?"

"I dunno. He and his woman — her name's Elsa, incidentally, and you'd better mind your Ps and Qs around her — they keep pretty much to themselves. I think he's got some sort of U.I. pension, and all he does is work on a couple cars he's got out there. He's a strange duck."

"Think he can play, still?"

"It's strictly a question of whether or not he wants to," Lenny says, scratching his head. "There ain't no physical problem. I seen him skate. I went down to the arena after the bar closed — shit, now, it must have been a month ago — and there's Artie out on the ice by himself, full equipment, with a bucket of pucks. So yeah, he's still got it. But getting him to use it ain't going to be easy."

I finish my coffee while we chat about other things, then pull a couple of loonies from my pocket and tuck them under the saucer. I'm about to slip the napkin with Artie's address into my shirt pocket and vamoose when it occurs to me that Lenny will probably know something about Ron Bathgate.

"What do you know," I ask him, "about a guy named Ron Bathgate?"

Lenny looks up sharply. "Ron Bathgate? He any relation?"

"Distant," I say. It's true, sort of. Until yesterday I thought he was on the other side of eternity.

"Makes sense," Lenny says, with a snigger. "He's a strange potato, that one."

"How so?"

"Well, how many guys do you know who've had the balls to tell InterCon to go screw themselves. Cost him his mill, I heard. People said he must have thought he had some aces up his sleeve that weren't there when whatever game he was playing got hot, but I never believed that."

"Tell me more."

"Oh, Christ, Weaver. I can't recall the details, except that he was into the same sort of ecology nonsense your old lady's kid is.

I'm sure the two of them are pumping it in both your ears these days. Anyway, I heard Bathgate's living up in your neck of the woods now. Why don't you ask him about it yourself?"

I get to my feet. "I guess I'll have to," I say. "Thanks for the address."

"You just keep that walking side of beef out of my crease like you promised."

"Okay. But watch for me when I come off the DL. Just for laughs, of course."

"At your own risk, Tinkerbell," Lenny says without looking up. "Catch you later."

TWENTY-FIVE

THE CAMELOT RIVER JOINS the Fraser just below the bridge over to West Camelot, but it doesn't do it the way the Fraser meets the Nechalko River at Mantua. A few hundred years ago Mantua *was* the two rivers most of the year, and when it wasn't it was a field of washed gravel, dotted by islands of cottonwood crosscut by oxbows and stinking sloughs where the two river streams flooded across one another. Back then, the rivers at Mantua were equal streams, except that Fraser was a muddy brown and Nechalko was clear and blue. Then we dammed the Nechalko and started dumping mountains of shit and debris into it, so that now it's silver-green and half the size it once was.

The way the two rivers behaved was a little like life was around these parts. They ran over one another, sprayed gravel and muck into one another's faces, and didn't apologize for the messes they left behind. I suppose the way they are now, come to think of it, is also about right. One half making the same old mess, and the other half sucking up toxins.

The smaller, sedate Camelot river isn't much like either of Mantua's rivers — or like life. It leaves its orderly cottonwood-lined banks sparkling blue, sidles politely into the murky Fraser, and, within a quarter kilometre, vanishes. I suppose that's how the city of Camelot got its name — its river is an English gentleman, out of place in a land of ass-kicking, over-the-banks, debris-littered rivers and creeks.

Not that anyone in Camelot has ever taken a cue from the river. In all the bad ways, the town is more like Mantua than Mantua itself is: stinkier and with more fights-per-hour in the bars. As many broken beer bottles and wrecked cars litter the banks of the Camelot river as anywhere in Northern B.C.

The address Lenny gave me is on the west side of the Fraser, and as I cross the bridge I realize Artie must be living in the nest of low hills across from the mouth of the Camelot. If anyone in Camelot had any brains it would be the town's choicest real estate, but the area filled up with squatters' shacks forty years ago, and the only improvements since the land got subdivided have been the trailers people haul in to replace the shacks that burn down.

Artie's place isn't difficult to find. It's a rambling shed-like building set at the base of one of the hills. The best thing about the place is the mint late-'50s Mercedes convertible tucked inside a lean-to a few feet from the house. It's a 190 SL from the look of it, a pretty fabulous moment in automotive history.

The house, on the other hand, is somewhat less than mint, and not fabulous at all. It was probably built originally to store heavy equipment, and the conversion to living quarters has been fairly recent and half-baked. Still, the worst thing about it is that it appears to be deserted. I pound hard a couple of times on the most likely entrance, a tall, windowless side door, and while I'm waiting I look around. No empty beer cases — a good sign. Other than that, there's a trail in the snow leading to the lean-to and car, and another that leads into a thicket towards the rear and the hill.

I'm about to go back to the Lincoln when a buzzy speaker I haven't noticed crackles to life above the door. "Up here," a male voice tells me. "Up the hill. Just follow the path."

It takes me some effort to struggle up the snow-packed path with my chest and back both giving me the gears, but at the top I discover another, larger building that wasn't visible from the road. Standing outside its entrance is, I assume, Artie Newman. I introduce myself, and am a little surprised that Artie *isn't* surprised that I'm there. He invites me inside for coffee.

Inside the building are four more elderly Mercedes. One is another 190, this one a sedan rusted as far as those cars do rust, and ravaged for parts. There's also a decent-looking mid-'60s 220 sedan, much more massive than the 190, and a pair of fabulous older models I can't identify. There's also a woman in her late twenties or early thirties, blond and elegant-looking despite the grease-stained mechanic's coveralls she's wearing.

Artie himself looks far more Scandinavian than his father. He's roughly six feet, well-built but fine-featured, and with a thatch of thinning, nearly white-blond hair.

"This is my wife, Elsa," he says. "Andy Bathgate, from the Mohawks."

"Thought we might be seeing you," she says, stepping forward to shake my hand.

"Elsa helps run the bar for Lenny weeknights," Artie says, by way of explanation. "You take cream in your coffee?"

"Black, thanks. I gather you know why I'm here."

"I have an idea," he says, his face suddenly serious. "But I'm not sure I can help you."

I present my case. The further I get into it, the less attractive it sounds, even to me — and the more I want to make it sound attractive. Just on appearance Artie's about two grades above my best hopes for him. He's clearly sober and in shape, and that's very good. And he's no nitwit. The downside is that he's got a life here, and it's hard to see why he'd want to disrupt it to play hockey in a fifth-rate league with a bunch of vicious kids, psycho wannabes, and broken-down veterans like me.

I'm nearly out of things to say when he interrupts. "Okay," he says. "I'll do it."

I'm so startled that I ask him why.

Artie's initial answer is a short laugh and a shrug. He turns his back on me, picks a twelve-inch crescent wrench off the bench next to him, and taps it against a vise.

"Private reasons," he says in a quiet voice. "It's hard to explain."

I look at Elsa, and she silently mouths the word "father."

Right. Chances are he's been sitting here for months — years, maybe — waiting for this invitation. But even if he has, he must know that playing for us will be leaping right into the lion's — or hyena's — mouth. I just hope to hell he can still play some, for his sake as much as for ours. Alpo isn't easy for anyone to please, and the old coot believes he has several thousand reasons to be displeased where Artie's concerned.

I stay for another fifteen minutes, enough time to give Artie — and Elsa, since it's clear as hell you don't talk to one without the other — the basics on practice times and contract arrangements. Artie agrees to drive up to Mantua for tonight's practice. Before I leave, I ask a few questions about the cars.

"I just winch them up and down the hill," Artie says. "They're Elsa's babies. She's the mechanic."

"Why've you got them up here?" I ask her.

"Security," she answers, with a dry chuckle. "Car thieves are lazy."

I file that for future consideration, make sure I shake Elsa's hand before Artie's, and get out of there.

WHEN I ARRIVE BACK at the house, this time it's Esther's truck that's parked in the driveway. I assume that this means Wendel has his Jeep out of the garage, or that they've traded trucks. If the Jeep is fixed it'll be temporary, and probably equipped with brand new queen pins.

As I'm leaving for the Coliseum, Esther pops a small surprise on me. "I may have another player for you."

"If Artie shows up, we may not need one," I say. "Particularly if this Quaw kid of Wendel's can make it through practice without punching the shit out of everyone. Who're you thinking of?"

"Gus Tolenti called me this morning. He's interested."

"What?"

Gus Tolenti is the new psychiatric resident at the hospital. I've met him a couple times at various dos around town, but I wouldn't have tabbed him as someone who'd even be interested in hockey let alone play — or, if so, then maybe once upon a time. He's American, at least my age, bald as a billiard ball, and, well, a bit strange. I think he uses man-tan, and I know for sure he drinks martinis, likes to quote dead pyschiatrists in German after he's got two or three under his belt, and wears white suits under his white hospital smocks. Lord only knows how he landed up in Mantua. Or why.

"What'd you tell him?" I ask.

"I told him there was a practice at five." Then, after a pause, she adds, "Why not?"

She's right: why not? The worst he can do is make a fool of himself. "Did he mention what he plays?"

"I'm assuming it's hockey, silly. What would you like it to be?" Esther lifts my coat from the chair I'd draped it over in the kitchen and holds it open for me.

"We could use a defenceman," I admit.

"I don't think you have to worry, Andy," she says, seeing where my mind is going. "Nobody is going replace you."

"Just so long as you don't," I answer.

BY THE TIME THE players start to appear I'm sitting behind Jack's desk, playing General Manager. Artie is among the first to show, lugging a tattered Islanders equipment bag. I bring him into the office to sign the insurance forms, introduce him to the players already there, and return to the office. I figure the best way to handle his appearance is to make it seem like it's no big deal.

The toughest thing he's going to have to face isn't going to be in the dressing room or on the ice, anyway. It'll be when his father realizes that he's here. That one he'll have to face by himself. Let's hope he doesn't face it from under the wheels of the Zamboni.

I've barely sat down at the desk again when Gus Tolenti shows. Goddamned if he's not wearing a white suit and toting a white bag. I wander out to say hello to him, then try to make some straight-faced introductions. A couple of the younger players, Bobby Bell included, look at him as if he's from Mars, but there's nothing I can do about that. For all I know they're right.

There's a few audible giggles when he opens the equipment bag and everything inside it, including his gloves and skates, is white, too. But the skates aren't figure skates — they're good ones, and well broken in.

"What's with the white duds?" I say, trying to make it sound conversational.

"I played for the medical school team at Harvard," he says. "That's what we wore."

Good enough for me. I've just gotten him into the office to sign the releases when the dressing room goes silent.

With good reason. Wendel and Gord have come in, and they've brought Freddy Quaw. Freddy is a behemoth, as wide as Gord and two or three inches taller. I let Wendel make the introductions, stepping forward only at the end to shake hands myself. "Glad to have you aboard," I say. He looks like the building could land on his head and not hurt him.

Freddy merely grunts for an answer, and tosses his equipment bag onto a nearby bench as if it were as light as a purse. "Let's get on with it," he says.

I glance at Wendel, hoping he'll reassure me that we won't need a half-dozen more new players by the end of Freddy's first practice, but he just grins.

James Bathgate shows up a few minutes before we're ready to

hit the ice, and damned if the little bugger isn't in gear, right down to a Montreal Canadiens sweater. I consider whether to have a little chat with him about arriving earlier, and maybe stuff a gag in his smart mouth as a precautionary measure. I don't.

With barely more than a nod in my direction, and without putting on his skates, he goes directly to the team's equipment locker, flips off the lock I opened when I came in, and gets to work as if he's been doing it for months. He's out of the dressing room before anyone else, and is back for the water bottles and first aid kits by the time the first players are filing into the corridor to the ice. And as far as I can see, he hasn't called anyone an asshole while he's been doing it.

TWENTY-SIX

T HE PRACTICE GOES SMOOTHLY, given that I have three new
   players and one of them is dressed as Frosty the Snowman.
Gord directs the drills from the ice while I stand behind the bench,
puff up my chest a little — too much hurts — and think what I
hope are general manager-type things.

Like evaluating the new and old talent. Sorting out the old
isn't a big job, because once I get past Wendel and maybe Bobby
Bell there isn't much. But Artie Newman is everything I hoped
for, and then some. He's got all the instincts, and, outside of
Wendel, the best speed on the team. He's a little rusty, but the
eye-hand stuff will come back soon enough. Wendel sees what
he's got, and at one point skates past the bench, gives me an
appreciative nod, and says, "You did good, Weaver. I can *play* with
this guy."

Freddy Quaw can play, too. He's fast for a big man, and he
knows what he's doing at both ends of the ice. What surprises
me most is how good he is around the net. In the middle of a
shooting drill, he skates in front of the net and spends five minutes deflecting pucks past poor bewildered Stan.

More important, he doesn't kill anyone during the scrimmage
— not that anyone tries to push him around. Only Gord has the

balls to lay a bodycheck on him, and when he does it's a good, clean hit. Freddy gets to his feet laughing, and tips his stick to him.

Gus Tolenti is a pleasant surprise, too. Despite the goofy get-up, he's for real. Not on conventional terms, but those haven't been working for us anyway. From the bench he appears to be doing everything backassward, banking pucks off the board when there's no apparent reason for it, flipping the puck high in the air on passes so they arrive on the forwards' sticks over their shoulders. He has a number of dipsy-doodle moves I've never seen before, and he's fond, apropos of nothing, of letting fly with them. His antics will probably drive Jack crazy, but they're no skin off my nose so long as they're working.

I try to watch the action with a managerial eye, but I can't keep my eyes off James. He's doing fine, retrieving pucks for the players during the shooting drills and looping soft shots at Stan whenever he sees no one else is ready to go. But generally he keeps out of the way, which is what he's supposed to do. When the scrimmage starts, he retreats to the bench and stays there.

About halfway through practice, Junior shows up. His shiners are looking pretty glorious, and the bandana he's tied around his head to hide the bandage makes him look like a deranged pirate. No matter. His grin as he clambers across the stands to lean against the glass behind the bench convinces me he's not here to assassinate Stan Lagace.

"I hope you don't have any dumb ideas about practising," I say to him.

"Not a one," he replies. "Until Friday, anyway. Gord said I can backup on the weekend."

"If you can get the mask over that puffed-out puss of yours, maybe. I'd like some practice time with you and that mask before I'll let you into a game."

"Yeah, that's what my old man says, too," he answers, hooking his thumb over his shoulder. I look up in the stands and spot

Don Sr. standing along the rails, watching the scrimmage. "Okay by me."

"How come he didn't say something to you about this five years ago?"

Junior looks a little sheepish. "I never asked," he says. "And you know what the old man is like."

"I thought I did. Now I'm not so sure."

"Me neither," he answers. "How's Stan doing? And where'd you get the tyrannosaurus?"

I explain how we came by Freddy Quaw and the two others. By this time Don Sr. has joined us and is listening in.

"Looks like you got the makings of a decent hockey team here, son," the old man says. "Been a long time since we had one of those in Mantua."

As far as I can recall Mantua's never had a decent hockey team, but I'm not about to slander myself and a lot of people I'm fond of by saying so.

HE'S RIGHT, THOUGH. SOMETHING has happened, and the old players — the kids who've played all year, I mean — sense there is both good news and a slight threat in it, and respond by upping their effort.

After the practice Junior shows the autopsy mask around, and that gets some laughs. I watch from the doorway to the office until the office phone rings. It's Esther.

"Practice go okay?" she wants to know.

"Pretty good," I say. "Your pal Tolenti is a player. So are the other two."

"That's not what I mean," she says, impatiently. "Did the little guy show up?"

"Yeah, he did. And he was terrific. Did his work and was more or less invisible, otherwise."

"Hadn't you better see he gets home okay?"

I hadn't thought about it. "I guess so. I'll offer to drive him. I want to know how the hell he gets from place to place anyway."

"Well, this is your chance to find out," she says, then adds, "Don't be pushy about it. I don't have to remind you he doesn't like authority very much."

She does remind me to give uniforms to the three new players for the Friday game, pointing out that a uniform for Freddy Quaw probably isn't going to be a simple matter of pulling a spare out of the closet.

We hang up, and just as I'm putting the receiver back on the hook Gord comes into the office with Freddy Quaw in tow. "Crack the closet," Gord says. "Uniforms."

I toss him the key to the closet, where Jack has at least a dozen numbered jerseys stored, along with a box of leggings, a half-dozen pairs of pants — and about a hundred of the Chief Wahoo crests. Artie and Gus Tolentini crowd into the office behind them.

"Let's see, here," Gord says, looking and sounding a little like Santa Claus at a children's Christmas party. "What do we have?"

"Is there a forty-four?" Gus asks, sounding like a kid at the same Christmas party.

"Size forty-four?" Gord echoes, tossing a pair of sweaters, home and away, over his shoulder to Gus, who scoops them up and disappears back to the dressing room.

"I'm not picky about numbers," Artie says, and is answered by an over-the-shoulder pair of sweaters from Gord with the number 26 on them. Like Gus, Artie retreats to the dressing room with his booty. Inside the closet, Gord is cursing.

"Jesus H. Christ," I hear him grumble. "These blasted things wouldn't fit a midget."

"Look for a number 35," I suggest. "It should be a goalie's jersey."

"It isn't," Gord says, after a pause. "Freddy won't be able to get it over his forearms let alone his shoulders."

Freddy, who's been standing behind Gord with an impassive expression on his kisser, pipes up. "Give me two of each. I'll make do. This has happened before."

"Any special number you want?" Gord asks from inside the closet.

"Makes no difference," Freddy answers. "A number is a number."

Gord sends a flurry of jerseys over his shoulder and Freddy scoops them from the air. "Big pair of pants here, anyway," Gord says as he emerges from the closet and tosses them at Freddy.

Freddy doesn't catch these. He's examining the Chief Wahoo crest on the front of one of the sweaters. "Who's responsible for this stupid-looking thing?" he asks.

"The Chinese Government in Exile," I say, sensing that we may have a problem on our hands. "The real general manager doesn't like them either. Wendel can tell you the story behind it. I've got to check on something."

I skip out of the office, but I'm not just escaping Freddy's questions. James is standing on one of the benches and peering into the office, obviously eager to get on his way.

"Good practice," I say. "You did fine."

He looks at me distrustfully, decides I'm not going to do anything to him, and a grin breaks across his face. "I had fun," he answers. "This is really fun."

"If you need a ride," I begin to say. He cuts me off and for a fleeting second I spot a wildness in his face that looks pretty close to fear. Then he composes himself.

"It's no problem," he says. "I've got a ride. And Mom says I can go with you to Okenoke on Friday."

"We won't get back here until about 2 AM. Does she know that?"

He answers "Sure" so messily that it leaves me without the slightest idea whether she knows anything about it. I make a mental note to call her, and another to check to see how he *really* gets home. "Did you get everything put away?" I ask him.

This time the "Sure" is snappy and clean. I glance over to see what Wendel is up to, thinking maybe I'll have him follow James when he leaves to see if anyone picks him up. Instantly, I understand what at least part of the dressing-room buzz is about: he's sitting on the training table, surrounded by players, and he's talking tournament.

I start over, and am lucky enough to catch Stan's eye. I jerk my head to one side, and he steps away from the group. "Do me a favour," I say. "Follow the kid out and see if anyone picks him up."

Stan lifts his eyebrows. "Didn't realize you were his father."

"I'm not," I reply. "He lives away out of town, and he's a little goofy. I just want to make sure he gets home okay."

Stan gives me a silly salute. "Can do, *Mein Commandante!*"

Back in the office Gord and Freddy are still conferring, now about the politics of naming hockey teams after aboriginal tribes a continent away and then representing them with moronic cartoons figures. It isn't an argument they're having. More like they're agreeing on the general level of idiocy in the world. I listen in for a minute behind Freddy's gigantic shoulders, wondering if Chief Wahoo is going to cost us Freddy's services. But Freddy doesn't go that route. He scoops up two sweaters and says, "Leave this to me." I scuttle out of his path and he's gone before I have time to consider what it is we're leaving to him. Since he may already be part owner of the Coliseum and the rest of Mantua, maybe it doesn't matter.

I close the door behind Freddy and watch Gord refold a couple of the sweaters, give up, and load them helter-skelter. "What do you think?" I ask him.

"Nothing much to think," he answers. "We dress all three, and if they show up, we play them. We can dress seventeen players if we want to, and we haven't had more than fourteen all season. I don't think any of them is going to hurt us out there." A sly grin crosses his face. "Look who they're replacing."

"Very funny. Hey. Did you see Alpo anywhere? He's usually threatening to run us over with the Zamboni by the end of practice."

"Didn't see hide nor hair of him. But I'd bet money he was there somewhere, watching his kid."

"If he was, he's got to be pleasantly surprised."

Gord snorts. "If it was anyone but Alpo, maybe."

"Incidentally, has Wendel talked to you about this loony tournament idea of his?"

Gord straightens noticeably. "I don't think it's a loony idea. It may bring back bad memories for you, but there's nothing basically wrong with a tournament. So try not to rain on the kid's parade too much."

I mumble something noncommittal and paw at a piece of fluff that's gotten itself lodged in my jacket zipper. When I look up, Gord is eyeing me. "Anything else on your mind?"

I tell him about discovering that James Bathgate is my half brother. I half-expect him to tell me he's known about it for years, but he doesn't.

"I'll be damned," he says, then laughs out loud. "We should have known that smart mouth of his had to come from somewhere nearby. You spoken to your father yet?"

"He's out of town right now. Until the weekend."

"That's going to be interesting," Gord says. "On both sides. I've met Claire Bathgate a couple of times. She's a very strong woman. Nice enough, though. Does the kid have any idea?"

"Not according to Claire, no. But the way he'd been burning my butt makes me wonder."

"Well," he says, almost wistfully. "Everyone carries their secrets in their own way. You know better than most people how deep that can go. Time for you to use a little of that wisdom you're always claiming you don't have. Figure out what the discretions are, and try to do the right thing by them."

Gord is staring at me, and it's apparent that there's an implicit request in what he's saying to me. Not the pleading kind, just straight across and straight up. This is about him and Jack, and he wants me to acknowledge it.

"Well, you know," I say, grinning helplessly despite the gravity of the moment, "I can't see a goddamned thing about you that's any different than it was three days ago. Or Jack, for that matter — aside from having only one knee. Have you talked to him?"

"They're doing his knee at eight o'clock tomorrow morning. He's pretty jittery, but okay. Thanks for asking."

I shake my head. There's something wrong with the way Gord said that, too formal or something, as if I were inquiring about a member of a different species or something. And it's important that I not let it get by. "Wait a minute, here. Jack's my fucking friend, too. Just like before. Like always."

I catch the twinkle in his eye before I realize what I've just said. "No," he says. "He's *my* fucking friend, actually. He's just your *friend*."

I give him a playful push — it's like pushing a brick wall — and my chest hurts. "Let's get out of here," I say, "before I need another one of your prescriptions."

Stan enters the dressing room as we leave the office. "Hey, Weaver," he says. "Your little pal ain't as little as he looks."

"What?"

"Well, I followed him out like you asked."

"Uh huh. Who picked him up?"

"That's just it. Nobody did. He's got a Ski-Doo parked out back. And when he went past me there wasn't no adult driving it for him. The little punko was skinning it at about sixty right down the sidewalk."

TWENTY-SEVEN

Okenoke, b.c. is a ninety-kilometre, one-hour road trip from Mantua, across a stretch of post-glacial plateau dotted with small lakes and river valleys cut through by an ice-graded winter road that runs straight as a board from one clearcut valley to the next. I can recall a time — when I was a kid — when it was beautiful, and at this time of year it's possible to forget how little timber is left behind the fifty-metre strips the government makes the companies leave to fool the tourists.

Okenoke itself is another story. It was never beautiful, and now it's a certified shithole, a testament to just how ugly a logging town can get. About thirty-five hundred people live within the city limits, another two- or three thousand more in the surrounding countryside. The hockey games draw a thousand of them most nights.

About the only notable things you can say about Okenoke are that three generations of a family named Silver have played for the Bears, including their current player-coach, Blacky Silver; that the Silver family isn't much like the Ratsloffs of Camelot; and that Okenoke is the only place in the world with a hockey cemetery. Blacky Silver's father donated the cemetery land after the Silvers' logging operations got bought out by the multinationals a decade ago. The old guy was the first to be buried there, and ever since, the Silver family has been scooping hockey-playing stiffs and reinterring them in their cemetery. As the regional coroner, Gord has been a help. He does it, he says, because it gives people in Okenoke a sense of place. Doesn't help the forests or keep the locals from spending their vacation time and money in Thailand, where the Silver family bought a hotel after they sold out, but you can't have everything.

This particular Friday night in Okenoke, though, a few quite notable things happen. One of them is, well, borderline remarkable: the Mantua Mohawks put a trouncing on the Bears nine to two, and there isn't a moment in the entire game when the Bears look capable of beating us. Wendel gets four goals, one shorthanded. I put Artie Newman between Gord and Freddy, and they put up four goals and two assists between them. Artie pots three of the goals unassisted, mainly because the Bears become very distracted trying to avoid his two behemoth wingers. Freddy and Gord don't mind at all. The three of them are so much fun to watch that I forget they're playing on my line, and that there might be a few objections to breaking them up when I return. Screw them. I'll play with Wendel.

The other notables? One is the weather, which begins to warm up Friday morning. By game time the temperature is well into the forties, turning the roads to slush and Okenoke's crowded little arena into a steam bath.

Another notable is Freddy Quaw's uniform, which he's had someone redesign to fit him. He's added a dollop of his own design as well. Chief Wahoo now sits inside a circle of white tape, with a strip of red tape across his face. Freddy doesn't explain the redesign, and no one says anything about it except to laugh. My only comment is that it's an improvement. I won't be surprised if Jack, when he returns, doesn't arrange to have the rest of us do the same thing.

Gus Tolenti doesn't disgrace himself. He even gets into a

fight when the Bears try to tease him about his white skates and gloves. He's in front of their bench when they start in on him, but Gus isn't deterred. "This is hospital issue," he roars as he wades into them. "You'll be seeing more of it after I get through with you."

He doesn't do so well once the fight gets going. He takes on their toughest player, a big winger who worked as a faller and knows his way around. He pulls Gus's sweater over his head and then proceeds to pound him until Freddy grabs him from behind in a bearhug. Freddy's move is more peacemaking than aggression, and the ref doesn't even park him for it. But more than anything Gus does by himself is the effect he seems to have on Pat Horricks, the kid I've paired him with. Pat plays better than I've seen him play outside practice, better than I thought he was capable of. He rushes the puck every chance he gets, and when he does, it doesn't turn into a breakaway for the Bears as usually happens.

James does his job, although I have to tell him to shut up a couple of times when he starts giving the gears to the Bears' players. He takes that well once I point out that he's working now, and that it's my job to stand on top of the bench to scream and yell and point out who's an idiot.

I stuck him with Bobby Bell for the drive up, but on the way home I put him in the back seat of the Lincoln with Wendel, explaining that it's my job to make sure he gets home safely. He doesn't complain, and within ten minutes he's asleep with his head on Wendel's shoulder. Ten minutes later he's in Wendel's lap, snoring.

The sight gives Esther a case of the giggles she can't exactly explain to Wendel, and doesn't need to explain to me. On the whole, it's been one hell of an evening. Partly the easy win, partly that Wendel asked to drive up with Esther and I. And the sight of my son in the back seat of my car with his uncle's head nestled in his lap isn't something I ever expected to see.

We win five to three on Sunday afternoon in Camelot. We beat the Roosters pretty much the same way as we beat the Bears, except that this time Gus keeps his nose clean (and intact) and so does everyone else, including all the Ratsloffs. I don't think the Roosters quite know what to make of us after Freddy knocks Neil Ratsloff cold in the first period. Neil tried to rough him up in the corner, Freddy lashed out an elbow that looked like a six-by-six, and down Neil went without a whimper. After that, it's the cleanest game I've seen in this league for years.

And in between the two games, I talk to my father for the first time in thirty years.

KICK ME FOR IT if you want, but I can't bring myself to call him Saturday morning. I tell myself I don't know when he arrives back, but that's a technicality. Some part of me I don't have any experience arguing with has told me that the next move is his. Hasn't he known I'm around when I didn't know he was? Still, I'm not quite convinced. I keep going to the phone and picking it up, then putting it back on the receiver, like a teenager mustering up the courage to phone for a date.

He calls me. When I get back from grocery shopping with Esther late Saturday morning his voice is on the answering machine, a hesitant, grave tenor that makes me realize I have no private memories of him that haven't been utterly corroded by the contempt my mother heaped on him after they broke up. And I realize another curious thing: ever since I've learned that he's here in Mantua and still alive, I've held back from imagining him.

"Andy?" the voice on the machine says. It is a voice absolutely without authority, neither quite asking a question or demanding my attention. "This is your father. I arrived back this morning on the plane, and Claire tells me you'd like to see me."

There is an excruciatingly long pause before he continues. "I can't tell you how happy this makes me. And that you seem to have taken James under your wing. Can you call me when you get a moment, so we can set up a time where we can meet face to face?"

Click. For a moment I stand looking out the window, with Bozo nuzzling my hand and Fang tugging at my pantleg. When I turn around to face Esther, there are tears rolling down my cheeks.

Esther guides me into the living room and sits me down. Next thing I know, she's pressing a cup of tea into my hand. But the tears just keep coming, without anything else, no blubbering, not even the familiar constricted throat. Just these strange tears.

I sit there for fifteen minutes, until Bozo remembers that tears are deliciously salty and begins to slobber all over my face. As abruptly as they took me, they're gone. I push Bozo gently away, not quite sure if I'm grateful for the intervention, pick up the phone, and dial the number from memory. As I listen to the telephone's *drrrrrup*, I realize that the number I've just dialed is the only thing in my head. The rest is blank — I have no plan whatever, not even for the formalities on which to coast into this thing. I'm hoping I won't start blubbering over the phone, that's all.

Claire Bathgate answers, which throws me because, well, I'm not sure who — or what — to ask for. Do I ask for "father," or do I take possession and ask for "my" father? Or is it a stranger named "Ron Bathgate"? All of them, I guess. What did I call him while I was a kid? *Dad*. But that was nearly thirty years ago, and I haven't used the word since.

In those seconds between Claire's "Hello" and my reply, I go through a virtual lifetime. I see a tableau of my father from a childhood I thought I'd forgotten — looking up at him backlit through a haze of sunlight, a tall, potentially terrible figure who somehow wasn't ever terrible or frightening but rather a soft-voiced warmth with a thick halo of dark hair and large rough hands resting on my shoulders. I recall a view of him from the back window of a car — was it a taxi? — as my mother and I left him.

I hear my voice ask this question: "Can I speak to my father, please?" Before I speak to him, it is done, over. I've taken possession of him, reclaimed him from the long absence.

His first words confirm the claim. He repeats the words he used on the answering machine: "Andy? This is your father."

For an excruciating moment, no words will come. Then they stutter from my lips: "I know. Yes. It *is* you." Absurdly, I find myself closer to laughter than to tears. I stop myself, try to compose the tangle of feelings, and succeed so far that I can deliver a single coherent sentence. "I'd like to come out there and see you."

"Yes," he answers. "I'd like that very much. Will you bring your wife and son? I'd like to meet them, too."

"Sure, yes." There's no way to explain the complexities of the situation to him right now, and no reason to. Esther will come with me, but Wendel is off on his own — plowing his way through the slushy streets on his way, as is James by a different route, to the hockey practice I'm going to skip. "An hour?"

"That'll be just fine. I'm looking forward to it."

THE THREE HOURS THAT follow are exhilarating, excruciating, illuminating, disappointing. Big words, small events. We shake hands, we embrace, we sit down in chairs, we talk. But the big moment — the true, real one, is the first one, on the telephone. Everything that follows is aftermath, the settling in. I guess that shouldn't surprise me. The big moments in life never turn out to be dramatic or long. They're so quick and unexpected that most of the time we miss them and we're left with the rest of what our lives are made up of. But if we're lucky enough to catch and appreciate those moments of real life, everything that follows is bigger and wider and richer than it was before. But not, I think, any easier to explain or to live.

What I'm saying is that after an hour or so of conversation, Claire and Esther are in the kitchen talking up a storm and on the verge of friendship, and my father and I are in the living room talking — and close to arguing — about the wisdom of letting my half brother operate an illegal snowmobile on city streets.

I'm getting the distinct impression that my father's attitudes are borderline survivalist, and that he has more in common with Wendel than he has with me. I'm also getting bits and pieces of a very complicated life story from him — cryptic details of the breakup with my mother from his point of view, the alcoholic years, the depth of his gratitude to — and affection for — Claire, the way they've brought up James.

There is no carelessness or neglect there. My father's survivalism — if that's what it is — is carefully thought out, but it isn't fanatical. James has been brought up to take care of himself, and to understand the machines and tools he uses. My father has planned the trail by which he comes to and from town, he's gone over it with him on foot, even cleared and leveled stretches of the trail to make it safe. James uses the Ski-Doo in the winter, and in other seasons a dirtbike.

My father isn't, of course, aware that James has been bringing the Ski-Doo right into town. He's supposed to park it in a rented shed near the bridge, and to use the bus system from there. My father hasn't accounted for how goofy an independent fourteen-year-old can be, maybe because he missed that part of my growing up. We agree that both of us will talk to James about it, and that, between the four of us, we'll make sure he keeps the Ski-Doo off the streets.

Will we tell James that I'm his half brother? Yes. When? We set a date for it: Tuesday, after the hockey practice. Esther and I will drive out, and we'll do it together.

Explaining the way my life has gone to my father and Claire is harder than listening to them relate their story. Mostly, and graciously, Esther tells it for me. She leaves out the details of the bus accident, which I'll explain to my father some other time. I'm pretty sure he knows the story, since everyone else seems to. Questions will be asked, answers given. A life stretches out in front of me now, different than I could have imagined ten days ago, much more complicated but infinitely better.

TWENTY-EIGHT

HOCKEY IS EASY WHEN you've just won three games in a row after a semi-permanent losing streak. Even the practices. They're fun: fundamentals go out the window, and with them goes the nastiness that losing breeds. In the scrimmages you find yourself stunting like the hockey stars you secretly hoped you were, rediscovering the joy of play. That's what the Mohawks do, and that's what I'd be doing — if I weren't on the DL.

That's all I am now that Jack is back: an old guy on the DL. I've been relieved of the general manager's duties, and of Fang, who spent half his time with Esther and I hanging from my pantleg and the rest pestering Bozo and chewing on the furniture. We weren't exactly unhappy to see him go, even if we did offer to keep him until Jack is mobile.

He didn't take us up on the offer. Maybe it was the look on my face, or maybe it was the chewed-up legs of the coffee table. "Gord's around for a few weeks," he said. "He can walk the little thug until I'm back to normal."

Jack's in fine form, meanwhile, crabby and cheerful at the same time, glad to be home despite the cast and crutches he'll have to put up with for the next two months. Gord says the operation was a success, as far as it can be, and Jack's way of dealing with it is a predictable mix of "one day at a time" and "anyone who makes a cripple joke gets a crutch across the side of the head." Okay by me. He's pleased at what I managed to add to the team, and I'm glad to be rid of the problems, Fang included.

But five minutes into Jack's first practice James hasn't yet appeared, and that is a problem. I let it go ten more minutes, then begin to fret seriously. When another fifteen tick by and he still hasn't showed, I retreat to the dressing room to call Claire Bathgate.

She picks up the phone on the first ring. "No," she says, "He left soon enough to get there on time. In fact, he should have been a few minutes early. But the weather, you know ..."

The way her voice trails off triggers my alarm bell. We're thinking the same thing: the thaw could have made the back-woods trail James uses to get to town treacherous, particularly after last week's heavy snowfall.

"Listen," I say, still stumbling over the awkward nomenclature. "Is Ron ... is my father around?"

Her voice is instantly terse and decisive. "Yes," she says. "I'll have him head down the trail."

"Okay," I answer. "Tell him I'll pick up the trail from my end. I'm leaving in about two seconds."

We hang up, and I phone Esther to explain what's happened. She's as quick on the uptake as Claire. "I'll meet you at the bridge," she says before I'm halfway through my explanation.

"Bring my snowshoes, will you?"

"I'll bring all your gear."

THE DARKNESS IS OMINOUS beneath the bridge when I pull into the lot where I think James has been parking the Ski-Doo — when he's been parking it. On the way I follow the route he'd be most likely to use if he brought the Ski-Doo across the bridge, but it's only a precaution. I'm pretty certain he isn't a complete idiot.

With the thaw most of the streets in town are bare, and the bridge itself is dry and completely clear of snow.

By the time Esther's pickup skids to a halt beside the Lincoln, I've located both the empty parking shed where he should have been storing the Ski-Doo and the trail he uses. This isn't hard, despite the time of day. Once out of the car and in the open, the darkness isn't complete. We're just on the far side of a full moon, and the overcast of the last few days has lifted even though the temperature is well above freezing. James, I detect, has been up the trail in the last few hours but not back down.

The pickup hasn't come to a complete stop before Bozo leaps out of the back and is by my side. She doesn't give me her usual slobbery greeting, and there's none of the usual elated fumbling around. She's alert and composed, ready to work. I'll be glad of her company and her tracking skills. I just hope I don't need the skills.

Esther has brought everything else: snowshoe gear, a light pack, an eighteen-inch Maglite flashlight, and a boy's axe. I pass on the wool pants — too warm — but pull off my leather jacket for the wool shirt, which is lighter and breathes. She sets my snowshoes while I remove my galoshes and lace up the leather-tops, and she straps on one snowshoe more quickly than I can put on the other.

"I put your cell phone in the pack," she says, handing it to me with the flashlight and the boy's axe. "Go."

Go we do, but the going isn't easy, even for Bozo. The thaw is in its fifth day, and the snow is wet and heavy. With each step it slips up into the snowshoe thongs, slowing me. Worse, off the trail it's rotten and treacherous, forcing me to stay carefully atop the narrow track of the snowmobile so I won't topple into some barely disguised snag-filled hole.

If I slip from the trail it's a piss-off, a delay, at most a minor injury. But James is on a machine that weighs nearly half a ton. I can suppress what lies beneath that thought, but I can't elude it.

By the time Bozo and I are over the first rise, I'm showing myself technicolour movies of James lying trapped under the toppled Ski-Doo, chilled, wet, and injured. I hope to hell he was wearing a helmet.

I have to push myself to get any pace, and that makes my tender chest muscles complain bitterly. Screw them, I think. Screw everything. My legs begin to pump in synch with my heartbeat, the familiar rhythm of the trail fueled by adrenaline.

A kilometre in, the trail converges with a back road I recognize as leading to an abandoned machinery dump. The dump, if it's the one I'm thinking of, is an old gravel quarry cut into a steep hillside, and filled to bursting with obsolete logging equipment no one has been willing to take the trouble — and expense — of recycling legally. The dump also has a certain notoriety around town. A couple of years ago some clowns with M-16s thought it would be funny if they shot up the dump, and one of them caught a ricochet above the ear and had to be flown to Vancouver to have it dug out. My theory at the time was that the ricochet had hit him in a non-vital part of his body. And since he survived, and is back in town minus his M-16 and a few parts of his brain but still drinking beer and driving his pickup, I guess I was right.

On this day I'm glad for the road, and never mind what it leads to. Someone ploughed it a couple of snowfalls back, and the Ski-Doo's trail follows the shallow grooves made by some fairly recent visitor to the dump. For several hundred metres, the going is swifter. Just before I reach the dump the Ski-Doo trail diverges again, wandering uphill along the dump's steep edge. I stop to catch my breath before heading uphill, remove the flashlight from the pack, and play the beam along the edge and across the dump's expanse. There are signs of recent activity in the dump, and they aren't very pretty. The snow is dotted with shiny, dark green lumps — garbage bags. Someone, or something, has been at them, because the snow around a number of them is littered with debris. But when I play the Maglite's powerful beam along the upper rim of the slope, there are no signs of the Ski-Doo having gone over the edge. That's a small relief.

Bozo, meanwhile, is perfectly still, sniffing the air. When I motion her forward she hesitates, then begins to paw her way slowly up the slope — not like her.

We're about halfway up the rise when I spot the Ski-Doo close to the crest and apparently abandoned. I push myself harder, playing the beam across the base of the trees near the top of the hill for signs of James.

We're no more than fifty metres from the snowmobile when Bozo stops in her tracks and backs into me, growling. I spot James at the same instant. He's huddled in the branches of a scrawny pine tree, about midway up, with his back to me.

A jumble of recognitions hammer me. First, James is okay, or at least alive and hale enough to have made it into a tree. Second, he's likely been treed by a moose or, worse, a bear. Third, a moose ought to be visible from where we're standing, so it must be a bear. Fourth, this is the end of February, and even with a thaw, a bear ought to be at den. Fifth, this bear is a dumpsite bear, probably denning inside the wrecked logging equipment stashed in the dumpsite.

If a bear has James treed, Bozo and I are already too close. I get just a split-second to consider that and no time at all to study the options before I hear a throaty cough. A good-sized black bear clears the top of the hill on a dead run. It's headed straight for us, and that reduces my options to just one: run for it. There's a spruce tree three or four metres away, about the same size as the tree James is in, and it has a solid-looking branch about three metres above the top of the snow that I might be able to make. I drop the axe and flashlight, punch hard with my left snowshoe at the edge of the snowmobile trail, take a long, lighter step with my right leg, and launch myself at the branch. But the rotten crust collapses the moment I step off the trail, the fingers of my left hand graze the branch, and I land in the snow.

I brace myself for the impact without looking up, but it doesn't come. Instead, there's a thud and a snarl, and a mass of black fur plunges into the snowbank not more than a metre away from me. It's the bear, and it's Bozo.

If I'm lucky, she's bought me enough time for a second attempt at the tree. I struggle to get erect and recognize my luck — at least I landed horizontal, not head-first. While Bozo and the bear disentangle themselves for round two, I throw myself at the tree trunk, get lucky, and clamp my arms and legs around it. The snowshoes are still attached to my feet, but they don't matter. I couldn't do this normally, but nothing about this situation is going to reward normality. I snatch at the low branch with my left hand, throw my body upward, and as my right hand catches the limb I pole vault myself upwards, out of the bear's reach.

It's a damned good thing, too. A third try wasn't in the cards. Bozo is no match for the bear once the surprise is gone. As I'm twisting my body so I can see what's happening to her, I see the bear land a blow that sends her spinning over the edge of the slope.

No longer distracted, the bear turns its attention back to its original quarry: me. It might have been able to drag me from my still-precarious perch were it not for yet another a bit of luck. As it crosses the snowmobile track, it loses its balance and crashes head-first into the unpacked snow, halting momentarily. This gives me just enough time to claw my way farther into the branches. I don't have the time to kick off the snowshoes. They're awkward, but I'm not performing these gymnastics for the points, I'm just trying to get my ass out of harm's way. The real leverage is coming from my thighs and arms — and from the adrenaline that got me into the tree in the first place. My cracked sternum doesn't count.

It's a bigger bear than I first thought, almost certainly a male, although it's hard to tell for sure in the poor light. What I can see is that it is drooling foam from both corners of its jaws. I don't need Klieg lights to hear what language it's speaking. This is a very pissed-off animal we're dealing with.

The bear's size is a help: the bigger the bear, the less likely it is to climb a tree. This one's rage makes it try, but the weight of it simply pulls down the branch I used to lever myself and snaps it off. Every instinct I have, meanwhile, is telling me to climb higher, but I'm aware that if I do it could be fatal. If I climb too high, *my* weight will become the issue.

That it's winter helps me, too. If this little party were taking place in the summer, the bear might have already toppled the tree and be chewing on my butt. But in these conditions my tree's roots are encased in ice, and the snow pack is firmly cradling more than a metre of its trunk. Still, if I get too high the bear will be able to snap the trunk and bring me down.

Now that I'm clear of his range, the bear settles at the base of the spruce and begins, noisily but without much enthusiasm, to tear out the tree's roots. I'm safe from that, but it's small consolation. James is up one tree, me up another, Bozo lying somewhere below the crest of the slope injured — or worse, injured *and* trying to figure out a way to take another run at the bear. Or, goddamn the fucking bear, dead. I unstrap one snowshoe, pull it off, and, leaning down, bounce it off the bear's broad skull.

More stupidity. The bear whirls about and cuffs the snowshoe into the darkness. The second shoe I pull up into the branches beside me. If the motherfucker does manage to climb into the tree, it'll be my only weapon.

"James," I holler across the darkness. "You okay?"

I hear Bozo bark, and then a quavery voice from the tree at the top of the hill answers. "I'm okay so far. Who is it?"

"It's Andy. Don't come out of that tree."

"You think I'm nuts?"

That tells me his mouth is okay, at least. "Just stay there," I tell him. "Your father is coming from the other direction. Try to keep an eye out for him. If you see him coming, warn him."

"Okay. Now what?"

I don't have an answer, nor anything that remotely resembles a plan. This is a bear that shouldn't be where it is, or when. Whatever kind of den it had built down in that boneyard of abandoned machinery must have collapsed under the weight of the melting snow, and that's what woke it up. But a normal bear would simply redig the den and go back to sleep. So, this bear is seriously screwed up to begin with. Hard to say what it'll do next.

The bear seems to have some ideas about that. It leaves off trying to push my tree over and goes to the flashlight, which I dropped — still on — in the middle of the snowmobile trail. I see the bear, in silhouette, paw at the light. His head dips, there is an audible crunch, and the flashlight goes out.

For a very brief moment, silence reigns. I can't see the bear through the branches, and I can't see the tree James is in until I snap off several small twigs and let them fall. Even then, it's my ears that tell me where the bear is and what he's up to. The sonofabitch has gone back to the tree James is in, and he's having another go at pushing that one down. About the only good thing about the situation is that Bozo hasn't reappeared. And depending on how badly she's hurt, even that may not be for the good.

"Andy," I hear James's voice calling. "He's coming up after me!"

Shit. "Try crawling up higher."

"I can't," James yells. "I'm stuck."

The next sound is confusing. It's a distinct thud, followed by a bloodcurdling yowl that, if I didn't understand the range of sounds a bear can make, I'd have thought was human. I hear James's voice yell "Dad," then my name, and I'm out of the tree and scrambling in the snow for the axe, which I was lucky enough to drop next to the trail.

The racket from the hilltop is eerie, but I'm dead certain about what's happening: my father arrived as the bear was climbing into the tree after James, and he did what he had to — he attacked it with whatever he was carrying. Judging from the yowl, he's done some damage.

I won't ever know how long it takes me to cross the fifty metres between my tree and the one James is in. Faster than I'm capable of — and not fast enough. But I know that the bear is mauling my father, and maybe James as well.

Ten metres away, I can see I'm partly right: the bear is straddling my father, tearing at his arms and elbows, snapping at his face. Without breaking stride I turn the axe backward and aim a crossing blow at the bear's shoulder with the blunt edge. I'm hoping to distract it, and if I'm lucky break its shoulder blade. I can't use the sharp end or swing downward at it because my father is underneath, and the bear can move faster than either of us.

Once again, I get lucky. The axe head slams hard into the bear's right shoulder, and as it turns to confront me I twist the axe head over my left shoulder, turning the cutting blade and using my own momentum to position my body. I plant my left leg and propel the axe downward from the left side with every ounce of my strength at the arc of the bear's neck where the vertebrae are most vulnerable.

My aim is close, but not perfect. I feel a sickening thud as the axe head bites into and through the flesh of the bear's shoulder, and then the axe is gone and the bear with it, spinning sideways, and I see the spade my father used for his attack, a long-handled one, the handle still held across his chest as a defence, but before I can do or say or think anything else I'm knocked flying, it's the bear and he's on me, grunting and salivating so close to my face I can feel the hot, foul breath on my cheeks, and something else, drool or blood across my throat, spilling on my chest, and then another solid thud I feel in my own body, and the bear shrieks and is gone again, rolling sideways through the snow, and I'm gazing at my father's blood-drenched face.

I scramble to my feet, looking for the axe so I can fend off the next attack, but it's over. The bear is writhing and coughing in the snow, the spade lodged squarely in its spine at mid-back. One of my cheeks is stinging, but I'm not sure if the blood on my wool shirt is mine or the bear's. Somehow, that seems the least concern. There are slashes on both sides of my father's face, and a deeper gash on his neck that runs down inside his shredded wool shirt. Judging from the blood that was spurting onto me when the bear had me, not all the blood he's dripping is his own. But that's what I hope, not what I know.

TWENTY-NINE

RON BATHGATE LEANS BACK against the tree, and with his back propped against it slides to the ground. "You okay?" I ask, stupidly. The momentary eye contact told me he isn't.

He turns to watch James as he climbs down from the tree. "I think so," he answers when James is down, as if what we've just been through is nothing more serious than having walked across an icy street. "What about you?"

I play the game. "Some scratches, that's all. I think the bear had a better shot at you."

He nods, then lifts his left arm as James approaches. The boy is wild eyed, but apparently unhurt.

"Is there a first aid kit on that Ski-Doo?" I ask him. "And a flashlight? The bear got mine."

"In my pack," Ron interjects, waving his arm in the direction he came from. He motions to James, who is now kneeling beside him, his own terror replaced by anxiety about his father. "Get it for me, will you, son? Just up the trail there."

"I've got a cell phone in my pack," I say. "I'll call an ambulance."

My father shakes his head. "Don't need an ambulance. I'm fine." I note that he's not using his right arm for anything.

I squat in the snow before him and grasp his upheld forearm.

The jacket sleeve is torn and bloody, but that's all. When I reach for his right arm, he flinches. The sleeves are shredded, and the contusions there are deep enough that I can see exposed bone just below his right elbow.

"Let's cut the crap," I say to him under my breath. "You're not okay." I look up at James, who is now standing stock still, watching us. "James," I say, "Move your tail. You get the flashlight and first aid kit, I'll get the phone. My dog's down there somewhere, too. The bear took a round out of her when she tried to keep it away from me. I'd better have a look to see how badly she's hurt. Can you do first aid?"

"I can do some," he answers, and scurries up the trail to find the pack without explaining how much he can do.

I wade off through the snow, skirting the dying bear. When I reach the edge of the bank I call Bozo. She barks back a wan reply. She's alive, at least. I struggle back to the trail, following it to the spot where my first encounter with the bear took place. There I find my pack, and the snowshoes. I put them back on.

Bozo is fifteen feet down the embankment, lying on her side in the snow. I call her name, and in the faint light I can see her tail wagging. There's a break in the bank's edge below me where she can climb back up, if she's capable of moving at all. If she isn't, I'm in big trouble.

"Bozo," I call, making my voice authoritative even though I don't feel it. "Get your butt up here, you cowardly bugger."

She whimpers, but gets to her feet and follows me to the opening in the bank. "Come," I say. She does, but doesn't make it on the first try. The trail of blood spots are visible against the snow behind her even in this light, and she's favouring her right rear leg. Gamely, she tries again, and this time I'm ready. I drop down on my stomach, grab her by the collar, and wrench her toward me. It's enough, and a second later she's lying on top of me, licking my face. "Good dog," I tell her. "Not a coward at all."

A quick inspection of her haunch reveals a bloody patch about five or six inches in diameter where the bear's claws got her, and three or four more smaller gashes. She's badly bruised, and there's likely tendon damage, but at least her leg and hip don't seem to be broken.

She follows me back up the hill and settles down a few feet up the trail, giving the now-still hulk of the bear a wide berth. James already has the first aid kit out and is expertly encasing a large surgical pad with a roll of gauze binding around his father's forearm.

"We'd better put a tourniquet on that one," I suggest. Without a word, he scurries over to the Ski-Doo and returns with a length of thin rope and a flashlight. While he applies the tourniquet I check my father's upper torso and head. There's a gash in his scalp just above the hairline that's bleeding profusely, and a neck wound that looks deep, but along which the blood is already coagulating. I staunch the scalp wound and fashion a makeshift bandage to hold it there.

James gently pushes me aside, and I defer. He refits the head bandage, hands his father a gauze pad, tells him to hold it against his neck, and orders me to sit down. I do, and he applies a gauze pad to my cheek and deftly tapes it into place with a strip across my forehead and another beneath my nose.

While he's doing this, I retrieve the cell phone from my pack and tap in 911. I'm able to calm myself sufficiently to inform the emergency operator that there's been a bear mauling, and get her to dispatch an ambulance to meet us in the parking lot beneath the north end of the Nechalko bridge. Then I call Esther.

She's as clipped and efficient as the emergency operator, not even asking which of us is injured. "I'll be waiting," she says.

I'm lightheaded, but I fight it off. Too many things still to be done. I ask James if the bear went after the Ski-Doo.

"I don't think so," he answers, but doesn't move.

"See if you can crank it up," I tell him. "Scat."

While he restarts the Ski-Doo, I play the flashlight across the bear. The animal is still alive, spread-eagled in the snow with the hilt of the spade protruding from its back, its deranged blood pumping out in the dirty snow. When the flashlight beam reaches its head, its eyes flicker. It snorts, convulses, and is still. Dead, I hope.

The beam reveals a few other things. The bear's hindquarters are a mass of running sores, and when I step closer for a look I see that the lesions run the length of its spine and continue to its neck. Presumably the chest and belly are similar, but I'm not about to check. The mystery of what it was doing awake in midwinter suddenly isn't quite so mysterious. This character is no relation to Smokey the Bear. He may look like the bear from hell, but he's a local product, all the way. Hard to say exactly how or why he got to this condition except to point to the garbage strewn around the dump, but it's a question somebody better find the specific answers to.

I glance back at Ron Bathgate — my father. He hasn't said a word since I brought the dog back, and it occurs to me that he might be slipping into shock, if he hasn't already. Behind me, where James has been jockeying the Ski-Doo into position, I hear the engine stall. Great, I think. An injured man and dog. But again, we're in luck. The ignition spins once, a second time — then the machine kicks to life.

"Can you stand?" I ask Ron.

He nods, braces himself against the tree to rise, and falls back. "Maybe not," he says.

"No matter," I say, manoeuvring myself beside him and slipping his less-damaged arm over my shoulder. "James," I yell. "Get the packs!"

"Screw the packs," he yells back. "Let's get out of here."

I retrieve both packs and stack them beside a tree, spearing my snowshoes tip up next to them as a marker. Then I lift my father to his feet, trying to keep us from toppling into the depression behind the tree. A searing bolt of pain ploughs through my sternum, but I hold my balance, and we stagger across the snow past the bear to the Ski-Doo.

James is standing beside the machine, ready to go. "What now?" he asks.

"We'll have to load the dog onto this thing, too. You drive," I say. "Help me put Dad between us and I'll hold him and the dog on. For Christ's sake keep it on the trail."

He's looking at me quizzically. "*Dad*? You called him Dad." It isn't so much an accusation as a statement.

"He's my father, too," I say flatly, and turn around to call the dog over.

"Don't you want to drive?" he asks, as if the two things are connected.

"No," I answer. "It's your machine. You drive it." One confession is enough. I've never been on one of these things in my life, and I couldn't drive it if all four of our lives depended on it.

We settle both Ron and Bozo onto the seats. It's crowded, and if we hit a good bump I'm going to go flying. Bozo hasn't ever been near a Ski-Doo, but she allows me to position her awkwardly across my lap behind my father.

"Ready?" James calls out from the front.

"Let's go," I answer.

As we pull away an instinct tells me to turn around. It's a good instinct: the bear isn't dead. It is facing us, standing, its front paws outstretched as if to embrace us, its open jaws a bizarre collage of foam and blood and teeth. I've got nothing to stop it with this time, except a feeble beam of artificial light.

"Go!" I holler at James. "Go!"

As the snowmobile lurches forward, the bear collapses snout first into the fouled snow, defeated by its useless hindquarters and the spade lodged in its spine. For a split second I'm unsure if the roaring in my ears is the bear or the snowmobile, and we're out of sight before I'm convinced one way or the other.

I'M ABLE TO STAY on the back of the Ski-Doo even though James drives like a maniac, but I'm beyond exhaustion by the time we arrive back under the bridge. A couple of times Ron Bathgate turns to say something to me, but the din from the Ski-Doo is too great for me to pick it up. And a couple of times I catch him starting to slump to one side, but with my steadying hand on his shoulder he keeps it together. Esther is waiting when we get there, and so is the ambulance.

I let the ambulance attendants pull Ron from the Ski-Doo, and as I stand to hug Esther a still-deeper weariness settles on me. She holds me for a moment, then moves away to go to James, who is watching the attendants settle his father on a portable sled. She lays her hand on his shoulder.

"Are you okay?" she asks him.

He half-turns to her, keeping his eyes on the sled. "He got it, not me. And" — he jerks his head in my direction — "him. Check him."

She lets James go and does what he suggests, running her hands over my chest and neck, and touching the bandage on my face. "You're going in the ambulance, too," she says. It isn't a request.

"Did you call Claire?" I ask.

"Oh yes," she answers. "Wendel's on his way up there right now. They'll meet us at the hospital. I'll take James with me." She speaks the last sentence loud enough for James to hear.

I've damned near forgotten about Bozo, who is sitting on her haunches next to the ambulance. The attendants lift my father gently into the back, and with what feels like the last of my strength I lift the dog into the ambulance and crawl in behind her. James reluctantly closes the door.

"What's that dog doing in here?" the ambulance driver snaps at me.

"That dog just saved my fucking life, you asshole, and she's hurt." My tone tells him he'll have to throw me out if he wants to toss my dog. "She's going to the hospital with the rest of us."

The second attendant, who I recognize as one of the linesmen who works the Junior B games and has done some of ours, helps me out. "Let him take the dog," he tells his companion. "It won't hurt anybody. But" — he turns his attention to me — "there's nobody there who'll treat her. She's your problem."

The first attendant is bending over my father. "Shock?" I ask him.

"Looks like it," the linesman answers for him. "He's lucky you could administer decent first aid, or he would have lost a lot more blood than he did."

I don't set him straight about who did the first aid because I've got other fish to fry. The cell phone is still tucked in the pocket of my wool shirt. I pull it out, open it, and tap in Gord's pager number. I listen to the message and answer it with the number of the cell phone. For once, my photographic memory for telephone numbers isn't just cluttering up my brain.

We haven't gotten much beyond the bridge when the cell phone jangles with Gord's return call. "What's up, chum?" he asks.

I explain what's happened, and, without my having to ask, he picks up on what I want. "You want me to play veterinarian, right?"

"Something like that."

"Okay. I'll be there a few minutes after you arrive. Keep Bozo in the ambulance for the time being, will you? I'll want to check you and your father out first."

I relate a few more details about the bear, including my worry that it might have been rabid, and then hang up as the ambulance is pulling into the hospital's emergency entrance.

THIRTY

WHEN THE ATTENDANTS OPEN the ambulance doors about all I've got left is a headful of telephone numbers and Gord's instruction to leave Bozo in the ambulance. I don't have to explain why I want her left there — the linesman has caught the drift of my brief conversation with Gord, and probably realized who I was talking to. I sit still, holding Bozo in my lap, while a couple of young guys in white coats pull my father out and wheel him inside. When they come back with another gurney for me, I crawl onto it without a word and close my eyes.

Esther and James barge in through the front entrance, trailing several protesting nurses, just as I'm being wheeled into the cubicle next to my father's. The emergency intern and a nurse are already working on him, cutting away the jacket and shirt from his upper body so they can see what the damage is.

Esther unbuttons my wool shirt after retrieving the cell phone, and soon has me stripped to the waist. My injuries aren't any worse than I thought, except for a bruise that's blossoming across my right biceps and back where the bear crashed into me just before my father planted the spade in its spine.

"That's going to feel nice by tomorrow," she says without flinching. "I'm going to get something to clean you up with."

She disappears and is replaced by Gord's looming bulk. "You just don't seem to be able to stay out of trouble lately," he says. "Dunno what's going on with you." He isn't smiling.

"The dog," I answer plaintively. "Esther can take care of me for the time being."

"Sternum okay?"

I can't quite repress a grimace. "Sure. Speak of it in the plural, and you'll get the idea."

He nods, eyeballs the cuts, then probes my chest firmly enough to invoke a groan. When he's satisfied that my estimate of the damage is accurate, he turns on his heels and disappears the way he came.

The intern leans back from working on my father. "If you don't stop this crap we're going to have to assign a permanent bed to you," he says.

"He's promised to go straight after this one," Esther interjects, as she returns with a stainless steel washbasin and a box of gauze pads. "I hope I'm not going to compromise your insurance with this."

"Be my guest. We're understaffed tonight. And anyway, insurance is overrated."

I tune out while Esther goes to work. She seems to understand that most of the blood on me isn't mine. It occurs to me that we're lucky, both my father and I. If just one of those last two shots we took at the bear had missed their mark, it could be chewing on our guts right now.

Not a very nice thought, I tell myself as I watch Gord thunder in through the steel doors with Bozo. He's carrying her, and she almost looks like a poodle in his big arms. He sets her down on the gurney I was brought in on, and tells her to stay. She whimpers a greeting to me and I see her tail wag briefly, as if she's thinking of jumping back into my lap, but she stays where she's told to.

"Good dog," I tell her.

"Seriously injured dog," Gord corrects me as he manipulates Bozo's hindquarters with his fingers. "She got herself clubbed pretty good out there. You'd better tell me *exactly* what happened."

I give him and Esther the long version. By the time I'm halfway through, everyone else is listening, too.

"You're goddamned lucky," Gord says. "All four of you."

Esther turns her attention to James, who's been nodding assent to my version of the story while I was recounting it.

"What happened before Andy and your dad arrived?" she asks him.

"I dunno," he says. "I was coming into town, like I was supposed to, for the practice, and I ran into that bear."

"You hit it with the Ski-Doo?"

"Yeah, sort of. Not head on or anything. But it knocked the Ski-Doo off the trail and stalled it."

"And you got up that tree. Smart thinking."

"Didn't feel very smart while I was waiting for someone to come," he answers. "But that's what Dad told me to do a long time ago if something like this ever happened, so that's what I did."

Ron Bathgate speaks for the first time. "Good boy, son," he says. "You did the right thing. Just be thankful that Andy here realized you weren't at the practice and acted as quickly as he did."

James gives me a quick glance. "Oh yeah," he says. "My *brother*."

I can't quite read his expression.

Gord, meanwhile, has disappeared again. When he returns, he's carrying a tray of fully loaded syringes.

"What's that for?" I ask him, sullenly. "Something to calm us down?"

"Damned near everything but." He lifts a syringe from the tray and inspects it. "Let's see what I've got here: rabies, tetanus, a couple million units of ampicillin. Hmm ... I think I'll do the dog first while you two bare your behinds for me."

I start to giggle despite the situation, but Gord glares at me: no jokes about that, even here.

A nurse pulls the curtain between the two beds shut, and moves into my father's cubicle to help him prepare. Esther gets a hospital sheet from somewhere and tosses it in my lap. "Do you need help?"

"Don't think so." I answer.

I have to call her in a moment later. Baring my backside is a production I can't quite handle.

THE NEXT HOURS AREN'T exactly the picture of clarity. I know what you're thinking — I've spent so much time that way lately someone ought to install fog lights on me. But this fog isn't my doing, and it's accountable, it turns out, to the bear. I don't get the worst of it, either.

A few minutes after Gord gives the three of us our shots, and just as Wendel shows up with Claire, Ron Bathgate's throat swells up and he goes into convulsions. If he were anywhere but in a hospital emergency ward he'd be dead, and even now it's close. Gord and the intern recognize that he's having an immune system reaction, and inject him with adrenaline and antihistamine. Just as they get him breathing again and on a respirator, Bozo has pretty much the same reaction. Before I can get a bead on any of it, so do I.

We get the same treatment as Ron does, but without the oxygen. I don't need it, and it's hard fitting an oxygen facemask over a dog's drooling snout. But my temperature shoots up, and it stays there until the antibiotics kick in.

I wake up hours later staring at my dog, who's been left on the gurney next to my bed. She's strapped down now, snoring loudly with her swollen tongue lolling on the metal surface of the gurney like a dead salamander.

My body temperature has gone back to something like normal, but it's left me lightheaded and feeling more than slightly giddy. I'd have preferred to have woken up to Esther's face, but Bozo's will do. She's alive and breathing, and that's enough. Esther's there, too, talking to Gord.

"How's Bozo," I croak.

"She's got a crack in her hip," Gord answers, without getting up. "It'll heal on its own, but you'll have to make her take things pretty easy for a month or so. Given your condition, that won't be hard. How do you feel?"

"Strange," I answer. "How long was I out?"

Esther gets to her feet. "Long enough. You had a reaction to something."

"So I gather. Man, do I feel odd. Like I've been reborn."

Gord laughs. "You got mauled by a bear, not the Lord."

"No, not reborn *that* way," I answer. "Just cleared out, sort of."

"You're joining Scientology? I knew I shouldn't have given you that sedative."

"Stop making me laugh, you idiot. It hurts. And I'm feeling clear headed, not empty headed."

Esther is standing over me with the light above her.

"Will you marry me?" I say to her. I'm feeling *utterly* clear headed, suddenly, about that.

It's her turn to laugh. "Make an honest woman out of me, you mean."

"You're already an honest woman. This is serious. Where is everybody?"

"Claire's here somewhere, asleep I think. Wendel took James to our place. He'll sleep there overnight because Claire wanted to stay near your father. And Jack was hobbling around here for a while, but he went home."

"Listen," I say to her. "I'm serious about this. I want you to marry me. I want my cards on the table, my eggs in your basket, whatever. I'm here for good, you know? This is my home."

Gord hoots in the background.

"No, I mean, *you're* my home."

"Sensible," she says, after a moment of thought. "Yes. Of course, I'll marry you. But you have to be standing on your own two feet. I'm getting sick of these deathbed scenes of yours. I don't want them to become a habit."

PART THREE

THIRTY-ONE

S EVEN WEEKS LATER, THINGS are back to normal around here — although normal isn't what it used to be. I'm just about to suit up for my first practice since the run-in with the bear when Esther sticks her head inside the dressing room door.

"I need about five of you guys out here," she says. "Not including you, Andy."

The seven or eight of us who don't have our skates on yet troop to the door, Wendel among them. She motions them down the hallway and steps inside.

I put one of my skates on, stand up, and then sit down to lace it up. She sits down beside me. She's holding something behind her back.

"What you got there, sweetheart?" I ask.

She hands me a new helmet, a bulky white Bauer.

Jack's making smart remarks before I can even get the damned thing on. "What's he supposed to do with that? Go deep sea diving?"

"Maybe," Esther answers. "He looks like a pinhead with the old one, and it isn't safe."

"Well, better get him a flak jacket. His head's so full of rocks you could whack him across the side of the head with a sledgehammer and not hurt anything."

Esther doesn't miss a beat. "Try the helmet on, Andy," she says. "I'll get you the flak jacket later."

I don't get the chance to argue because the helmet isn't all she's brought. Her bearers are returning from safari carrying large cardboard boxes. Wendel rips into the box he's carrying, and pulls out a pair of forest green hockey pants. "Cool," he says. "Let's see the jerseys."

Our new uniforms have arrived just in time for the tournament.

A FEW THINGS HAVE happened.

One of them is that the Mantua Mohawks are no more. No, we didn't disband. For the first time in decades there hasn't been a reason to. We didn't lose a single game while I was on the DL. We've made second place, six points behind the Roosters with two games left, one in Okenoke and the other in Wilson Lake. But a week ago some yahoos broke into the Wilson Lake arena and started a fire in the concession booth. The fire spread, turning the arena's north side into a write-off, including the ice-making equipment. The facility is out for the year, and there's talk of tearing it down and starting from scratch.

That touched off a whole set of consequences. The Stingers were in last place, and with their arena gone, an arson investigation underway, and charges pending against the coach's son for being one of the yahoos, the team decided it wanted to opt out of the playoffs. Jack and I drove down to Camelot for a league meeting, and we all agreed to cancel the playoffs. We wanted to play but Wilson Lake didn't, Blacky Silver from Okenoke agreed with them, and Old Man Ratsloff said he didn't care one way or the other. It wasn't like he'd gone yellow. More like he'd made a decision about where the Roosters would have a better shot at beating us — in a five-game playoff in a dead league or in a possible one-gamer in a tournament.

The Mantua Memorial Tournament has grown up from Wendel and Esther's Saturday night pipe dream. Co-sponsored by Wally Weimer's Northern Sports and the Native Band, it's going to be four days of hockey, fun, and mayhem starting Thursday night March 29th and ending Sunday afternoon April Fools' Day. Twelve teams are coming in from as far off as Saskatchewan and Idaho. One of them is the Chilliwack Lions.

Once we made the decision to go ahead with a tournament, getting teams to play was easy: a half-dozen phone calls, and five days later we were turning them away. I guess Senior tournaments are like the Senior leagues: more players and teams left than leagues and tournaments.

Teams kept calling in weeks after, and some of the teams that wanted in got pretty damned strange with their offers. Jack got bribes, threats, and a couple of propositions he won't talk about. The strangest one was from a team of musicians from Vancouver, who offered to play music wherever we wanted if we'd let them into the tournament — sort of like a tournament orchestra. I think Jack was tempted by that one. They sounded like fun.

It helped that we made the economics attractive. Entry fee of five hundred dollars a team, tournament prize of ten thousand dollars, with five thousand for placing second, twenty-five hundred for third. We got a big chunk of the prize money from the Native Band, who I think put it up as much to tweak Garvin Snell's nose as anything else. Snell unwittingly set himself up for the tweaking. He got his nose up around the middle of his forehead the first moment he got wind that a tournament was in the offing, and after Jack approached him for financial support it went higher yet.

When Wally surprised us by kicking in three grand without being asked, it was clear that the tournament was going to fly. City Hall might want to ignore it but they weren't going to stop it from happening. Gord and Jack coughed up a cheque each for one thousand dollars, and I gave Esther my cheque for the same amount. I'm allowed to change my mind, aren't I?

There was one other complication that made everyone happy by the time it was worked out. The Native Band made their support conditional on us changing the name of the team: no more Chief Wahoo on the jerseys, no more Mohawks. Only a moron would have missed that one winging its way toward us. It was coming from within the team anyway, with Jack being encouraged by Freddy Quaw's creative defacing of Chief Wahoo.

Mucking around with Chief Wahoo was contagious. By the time we were five games into the winning streak, nearly everyone had been messing with him. Most just imitated what Freddy'd done, but a couple of guys, no doubt egged on by Gus Tolenti, whited Wahoo out completely. Bobby Bell got a black pen and extended the chief's nose so it reached around to the back of the sweater, and Junior used the same pen to blacken half of Wahoo's teeth. Anyway, last week we held a team meeting after Jack and I came back from cancelling the playoffs, and we made it official. The Mantua Mohawks are dead, long live the Mantua Lumbermen.

That's when I discovered what Esther was doing at Wally's the day I picked up Junior's mask: she'd been ordering new uniforms for the team. She saw it coming before anyone. She'd ordered the uniforms without crests, but when she talked to the Native Band about sponsoring the tournament and caught wind that they weren't very happy with the Wahoo crests, she got Freddy to design a new one with the only name that made sense. It's a beaut, like the new uniforms: green on white, with "Lumbermen" on an ascending diagonal over a healthy but slightly squat spruce tree.

In an ideal universe I suppose we'd have all sat down around a table and voted on the new name and uniforms — in which case the uniforms would have arrived around the year 2050. Sometimes you have to cut across a few people's lawns to get where you have to go. I'm glad Esther had the sense to do it for us even if it cost her four grand.

What else? Well, as you can see, Jack is back, smart mouthed as ever. His playing days are over, and even now that the heavy cast is off his knee his idea of rehab is high-speed gymnastics on his crutches and a lot of hop skip and jump manoeuvres when he loses track of where the crutches are. He's aware of what I discovered when I packed that bag for him, but without us having to come right out and talk about it we let each other know nothing's changed. Anyway, what was there to say about what's really just another secret that's breaking down, outliving its usefulness. While we were co-coaching we amused ourselves with some cheesy jokes about limp-wrist shots and come-from-behind victories that nobody else except maybe Gus and Gord could make heads or tails of. Nothing new there, either. About the only change is that he and Gord are uncles to a slightly larger family than they had before. They don't seem unhappy about the New World Order.

Bozo is back to normal, or almost. The vet says she'll likely end up with some arthritis when she's older, but the hip has mended fine, the wounds are closed, and her immune system seems to have relaxed. Come summer, she's going to have company. Esther and Claire are cooking up a scheme to start breeding dogs, and Esther has ordered a pair of pedigree Newfoundland pups from a breeder north of Edmonton.

THERE WERE JUST TWO objections to the new uniforms when Esther showed us the colour scheme and the crest design. Gus wanted to know if "Lumbermen" shouldn't maybe be "Lumberpersons." That got him guffaws and some advice about what would happen to his "lumberpersons" if they showed their prissy cans at the bars.

"C'mon Gus," Jack said when the laughter died back enough for anyone to be heard. "Tell us what you really want the team to be called."

"How about *The Mantua Seedlings*."

"We're a little old for that, aren't we?" I asked.

"Speak for yourself, white-hair."

The only other criticism was mine. I wanted to know if maybe the ascending diagonal on the crest shouldn't have been descending, given the state of the industry. That got me a wise-ass grin from Wendel, and more laughs from the others.

Now that the new duds are here, I have to say that Wally did a fabulous job putting them together. The jerseys are named and numbered without mistakes, and the materials are first class. We're going to be so pretty when we hit the ice in these duds people are going to swoon.

Yeah, sure, we're still a Senior hockey team from a league that might not see another season. But in our different ways, we all feel like we've earned the right to be gorgeous and good for a few weeks. Me, Jack, Gord, Junior, and one or two others for having hung in as long as we have, some of the others for having played as well as they have in the last while.

For Artie, for instance, it's been pure pleasure, and you can see it written all over him. Never mind that Alpo still hasn't acknowledged him, or that his wife probably isn't pleased that her husband is spending so much of his time in Mantua. He's a player, and there's no one in the league outside of Wendel who's better. Alpo is dead wrong about his son. He's no piss-tank washout, no traitor to his family and ethnic heritage. Artie Newman has grown up, and he's a better man than his father. Alpo gets smaller each day he refuses to see it.

Artie wasn't the only one who grew in my estimation over those seven weeks. Junior is finally earning his status as starting goalie. For a guy thirty pounds overweight, he's always had surprising reflexes. But with everyone in the league shooting for his head, all anyone saw of his reflexes was how good he was at ducking pucks, falling on his face, and avoiding stitches and sutures. I mostly saw the puck hitting the twine behind him. I missed the talent he'd used up keeping it from hitting him in the face.

The mask made him utterly fearless. For a few games, he seemed to want to stop as many shots with the mask as with the stick or blocker. I don't think he'd ever had so much fun in his entire life. But once the shooters around the league realized he wasn't ducking they stopped head-hunting, and the real test of his skills took over. Junior passed that, screeching with derision as a shot from the blueline bounced harmless off his chest and into his glove, howling with glee as he sprawled along the goal crease to kick a deflection into the stands. The crease became his hunting preserve, and he laid the lumber to anyone who got too comfortable inside it.

He makes mistakes, sure. He got caught wandering from the crease a couple of times, and the first brawl with the Roosters he stormed down the ice to dance with Lenny and got thrashed.

But it's true what they say: winning works. A whole generation of lousy Mohawks got dragged up to the level that Wendel and Artie play at. Dickie Pollard, who'd gotten onto the team a few years back because he was Bobby Bell's best friend, and had spent as much time sitting on the bench as Jack could manage, suddenly turned into our best defenceman. Winning helped his confidence, but what helped more was a conversation between five or six of us after Dickie had left one of the practices. Jack and I were talking about how to improve our still-porous defense for the tournament, and it didn't take long for Dickie's chronically rotten play to come up.

"Dickie's hopeless," I said, "but what can we do? He won't hit anybody, and every time someone comes near him he gives away the puck."

"It isn't him," Wendel interrupted. "Haven't you ever noticed that he's pretty decent in practice and when we're on the road?"

"So what if he's Bobby Orr in practice?" I snorted. "He turns into a gerbil when there's anything on the line."

"Well, next time he's on the ice, check out the old bag sitting just above the penalty box."

"Oh yeah. I've seen her," I said. "That woman's really something. Didn't they toss her out of the Coliseum last year for whacking JoMo Ratsloff with her purse while he was in the penalty box?"

"That's the one," Wendel said. "Dickie's mother. She's been riding him ever since he was in Peewee. He can't play when she's around. He takes one look at her and his spine goes Jell-O."

"Nothing we can do about that," Jack said. "We can't exactly ban her from the games."

Freddy, who'd been listening in on the conversation, had a suggestion. "We could have somebody sit next to her and have them point out the error of her ways next time she gets out of hand."

"Like who?" Jack asked. "Jack the Ripper?"

"How about my sister?"

"Who's your sister?"

"Frieda Lane."

"Frieda Lane is your sister?" I said. "Holy shit. That's really something."

What it is is really funny. Every bureaucrat in North Central B.C. is terrified of Frieda Lane. Frieda has a law degree, and she's been the motor behind the Band's attempt to reclaim downtown Mantua. She's supposed to have a mean streak a mile wide, but the several times I've run into her she's been decent enough. If genetics run true, she'll have the right sense of humour for what we need.

"Why don't you talk to her?" someone suggested.

Freddy laughed. "Consider it done."

It got done. I don't know what Frieda said to the old bag, but it must have been good. Dickie's mother stopped showing up for the games, and Dickie's play improved, night to blinding bloody sunlight.

BUT ALL THE NEWS isn't good. We might not get to wear our beautiful uniforms next year. A four-team Senior league can cruise along out of sheer habit, but a league with just three teams is too small to survive. Personally, I can't see any way there'll be a functioning arena in Wilson Lake by next fall. And anyway, for leagues like the NSHL, the writing has been on the wall for a long time. Senior hockey is in trouble just about everywhere. It's mostly television, I guess. It kills local local sports like it does everything else.

Back in the glory days, when the leagues were the main action in town and the players really were semi-pros, the community got them good jobs and other perks to stay around for. That's why the Penticton Vees or the Trail Smoke Eaters could win the World Championships and not have their players ripped off by the NHL. They were better players and better teams than we've got now, and the towns they came from loved them better. Those days are long, long gone, and they aren't about to come back. Not even if the Mantua Lumbermen play their games in the most beautiful uniforms in hockey history.

Garvin Snell, meanwhile, is a man in touch with his time, even if he spends most of his energy licking its boots. A Major Junior franchise in Victoria is up for grabs, and, not more than a week after the Native Band helped us bully him into giving the permits for the tournament, Snell phoned Jack to say he was putting together a consortium to transfer the Victoria Junior A team up here. He also told Jack that he'll be calling for proposals to build a five-thousand-seat arena in Mantua, in which case the Mohawks should starting looking around for new digs. Hard to say whether or not he's just yanking our chain. If he's serious, the corporate sponsors will line up to support him. Maybe I'll support him, too. Maybe our time is over and we ought to pack it in.

Maybe, maybe. But not quite yet. There's the Mantua Memorial Tournament in a few days, and the Mantua Lumbermen, the beautiful green-and-white Lumbermen, will get one last shot at winning the Mantua Cup.

THIRTY-TWO

I'D BET MONEY THE Enola Gay would still be revving its engines on the runway and the scientists would still be in the labs scratching their heads if building the A-bomb had been as complicated as delivering a double knockout hockey tournament draw. An exaggeration? Maybe. But one part of the Bomb builders' job was dead easy. They weren't trying to be fair to everyone.

Okay, bad joke all round. But I swear, making a double knockout hockey tournament look — and be — fair to everyone involved is A-bomb-level complicated. First, the double knockout part isn't optional. No team deserves to travel five hundred miles, pay a five-hundred-dollar entry fee, and then get sent home after a single game. Second, you have to set up the draw so the weak teams feel like they've really had a shot. That's not as easy as it sounds, because while you're stroking the weakies you can't let the good teams beat each other's brains out in the first games, either. The fans have rights, too.

The tournament object, naturally, is to get the two best teams into the final. But you can't get them there by screwing around with the rest. Still not convinced about how complicated this is? Remember that you're dealing with muscular men, and occasionally they show up with small brains. Their managers and coaches, this being the modern age, have learned to whine about their rights with the best of them.

In the end, Jack came up with a draw that was fair enough that no one could challenge it, and which let nature take its course as far as that's possible: we're placing teams in the draw according to when they arrive in town. That may not sound like Darwin's version of natural selection, but the parallels are there. Jack realized, things being what they are, that the teams that come for non-hockey reasons — like wanting to have a major piss-up or wanting to see our particular backwater of the wide world — will tend to arrive early. A few of the serious, well-organized teams will show up early as well, so their players will have time to eat, catch some sleep, and generally unwind from traveling. The late-arriving teams will be the goofs — and the teams that have the least distance to travel. Since he knew that group would probably include the Roosters and Okenoke, one good team and another fairly decent team, it would mean the late draws have a decent mix as well.

Into that we have to fold another set of complications. For the first two rounds, we have to use two arenas. Mantua has four artificial ice surfaces, but only two have any spectator seating. The Memorial Coliseum can put roughly twenty-five hundred bums on boards, but the rink north of town we've rented can only sit about two hundred fifty people on the benches above the dressing rooms, with another fifty or so standing around behind the glass on the far side. We have to get the best games — and the best draws — into the Coliseum.

Then there's the time frame. With the first games starting at seven and running in four-hour slots, the third set of games might start as late as three am. Commerce being what it is, we have to set ourselves in the first or second game at the Coliseum. That will mean a slight advantage to us, but only morons would object.

THE TOURNAMENT DRAW SHAPES up as we hope. The Battleford Raiders drive in late Wednesday afternoon, and go straight to the bar for a piss-up right after they register and before they check into the Columbia, which is Mantua's version of Piss-Tank Central. All they'll have to do is stagger upstairs when the bar closes.

I'm not around when they arrive, but when I glance over their roster an hour or so later I recognize a few guys I played against in the Alberta leagues. If they're halfway sober by the time the tournament starts, they'll do fairly well.

The Creston Cougars and Idaho Saints pull up in front of the Coliseum while I'm looking over the Raiders' roster. As the Cougars roll off their bus, it's evident they don't need to go to any bar. If you closed your eyes when the bus doors swung open you'd have sworn they were climbing out of the back end of a beer truck. And as if to prove that no one had been holding them captive, they stumble back onto the bus as soon as they're registered and head to the bar. Like the Raiders, they're staying at the Columbia.

The Idaho Saints file off their bus looking like Mormon missionaries, all of them scrawny and decked out in white shirts, skinny dark ties, and Superman haircuts. When their coach called in weeks before none of us had heard of the team, and we had no idea how they got wind of us. Their coach begged his way into the tournament, claiming his team has been playing tournaments all over North America for seven years, and that they're highly competitive. Jack let them in because they were the only American team to enter.

They turn out to be students from a Bible college outside Missoula, mostly teenagers from the look of them. I've seen their kind before. They've come to praise the Lord, perform acts of missionary-type piety, and, more or less incidentally, play hockey. Why they're called the *Idaho* Saints eludes me. Missoula is in Montana. The Lord acts in mysterious ways.

Jack and I have a quick conference in which we decide to let the Cougars register second so they'll play the Raiders in the first round. Jack then signs up the Saints and places us fourth in the draw. That way, the missionaries will get at least one game in before they're butchered. It isn't exactly ethical but it is, definitely, the Christian thing to do.

LATE THE FOLLOWING MORNING, the Fort St. John Drillers, Terrace Flyers, and Chilliwack Lions show up. All three teams seem serious about the tournament, at least judging from their arrival times and states of sobriety. I have my most careful look at the Chilliwack team — big surprise. They aren't calling themselves the Christian Lions anymore, but I have a feeling they're still sponsored by car dealers, and there's likely to be some devout Christians on the bus.

I felt a small bump when I heard the Lions had arrived, and another when Esther mentioned that their manager said they were coming to defend the Cup. They even came up with the old Mantua Cup from somewhere — dug out of somebody's closet or rescued from a police evidence archive — and considerately sent it along two weeks before so we could have it fixed up.

As they step off the bus, I realize I'm looking at them not as hockey players but as survivors. Even though I know better, I'm looking for *specific* survivors. A dozen total strangers, young, beefy ones who all look like they know how to play hockey, file off the bus before I find the one I'm looking for.

When he appears, he's more than I'm expecting: a dead ringer for Mikey Davidson. Same height, build, colouring, probably the same age as Mikey was. The same sweetness in his eyes, even. Startled, I call out the family name. He looks up.

"Do I know you?" he asks, eyeing me as he walks toward me.

"You're related to Michael Davidson, aren't you?"

The boy shrugs. "Everyone called him 'Mikey' I heard," he says in a matter-of-fact way. "He was my uncle, father's brother. Died a long time ago, in that bus accident, I think. You probably know more about him than I do."

"I knew him," I admit.

"You play with him or against him?" he asks, getting interested.

"With," I answer. We are veering toward some dangerous ground. "Some, anyway."

"I heard those were pretty great Lions teams, back then. Won this tournament the last two times, didn't they?"

"They did," I say.

"So who are you?" he asks.

"Andy Bathgate."

He says nothing for a moment. Then his eyes narrow. "You're Andy Bathgate?"

"No, no," I say. "Not the famous one."

"I didn't mean that one. I meant Andy Bathgate. Billy Menzies."

I freeze. How does this kid know this? As far as I know, there's still a warrant out for my arrest as Billy Menzies. And how come he doesn't come after me for being the one who killed his uncle?

The kid sees that I'm startled. "Everyone knows that story in Chilliwack. People have been wondering for years why you haven't shown up."

"I haven't shown up because I killed four people. Who told you Andy Bathgate was Billy Menzies?"

He stares at me for a moment. "Christ," he says. "You don't know, do you?"

"Know what?"

"Those charges were dropped a year after you disappeared. The coach was driving the bus when it hit that semi-trailer. The bastard let you take the rap, and it only came out when he got drunk one night and confessed the whole thing. Couldn't stand the guilt, I guess. He did four years for it. No one ever told you?"

"I never checked."

"Hey, I gotta find my gear," he says. "Maybe we'll talk later."

"Sounds good to me," I say, forcing a laugh. "Maybe I'll see you on the ice."

"You coaching one of the teams?"

"I still play," I say. "For the Lumbermen. Host team."

"Stay cool, man," he snaps back, pleased that he's gotten to me. "Are all the Lumbermen OAPs like you?"

"You'll find out when you play us."

In his mind, he'd just recited an ancient piece of local history — but it's a lot more than that to me. I wander back inside the Coliseum, stunned, and run into Jack.

"Jesus, Weaver," he says. "You're white as a sheet. You okay?"

"I think so. I just need to go for a walk."

I HEAD OUT THE back door of the arena, and a few moments later I'm sitting halfway up the hill behind it. Screw the weather, and screw the raven that's sitting above me in one of the trees, telling me to get off his turf. Some things I've been puzzled by for a long time are slipping into new perspective. The first is that a lot of people seem to know what happened to Billy Menzies, and haven't been judgmental about it. Esther's remark when this all broke open, for instance, about "the poor bastard" suddenly makes sense. I thought she was forgiving me out of some unfathomable generosity, along with Gord and whoever else knew who I was — my father and stepmother, probably. And all this time, they've assumed that I knew the real story, too. I didn't check my version against theirs.

A FEW MINUTES AFTER climbing down off the hill I run into Blacky Silver from Okenoke in the Coliseum lobby. He's come in looking for Jack, and unintentionally screws up our draw strategy. I tell him where to register, and as a courtesy explain how the draw works. I let him know that Chilliwack is the seventh team to register, and that if he registers now they'll play them at the Coliseum at eleven PM.

"They look any good?" he wants to know.

"One of the better teams, I suspect."

"Good," he grins. "Where are you guys in the draw?"

"In the first draw, playing a bunch of teenage missionaries from Idaho. It seemed like the decent thing to do for them. They'll get one game before they're slaughtered."

"Better you than the Roosters," he agrees, and heads toward the registration counter Jack has set up outside our dressing room. It occurs to me that he's brought the Bears into the tournament out of loyalty and tradition, not because he thinks they have any chance of winning. Blacky's no dummy, so maybe he's recognized that these games might be the last the Bears will ever play. Whatever his motives, he's unmoved about playing a hot team in the first draw. Maybe he wants to go out quick and clean.

The other teams drift in as the afternoon progresses, and they pretty much confirm Jack's theory: the Hinton Locomotives drive in from Northern Alberta in a snazzy silver bus that turns out to be another mobile brewery. The Grande Prairie Huskies, who arrive a few minutes later, and the Fort St. John Drillers are from the same league; they're more or less sober when they pull in, but they're a little green around the gills from the rickety school bus that's had them sucking exhaust fumes for four hundred fifty kilometres, and they seem pretty eager to hit the bar and flush out the carbon monoxide. The Roosters begin to appear in their fleet of Camaros around three, but Old Man Ratsloff doesn't show until nearly four. The last team to register is the Burns Lake Cowboys, from just one hundred fifty miles west. They were in and out of the NSHL until a few years ago, and from the look of them they've entered the tournament strictly for a lark. They appear in a fleet of four rented minivans, via the minor miracle of drunk driving.

By showing up last the Cowboys have drawn the Roosters for the three AM Coliseum game. They aren't happy about this, but their manager isn't sober enough to raise a coherent objection. Cowboys is what they call themselves, but it'll be more like cows in a slaughterhouse.

I hang around the Coliseum running errands for Esther and Jack most of the afternoon. Around four, Gord shows up and Jack sends the two of us off to the Columbia Hotel to deliver the first draw to the Battleford and Creston teams, and to make sure they know where they're playing. Since both teams are staying at the Columbia — which hints that they're dedicated drunks coached by idiots — we're really there to roust them. The clerk at the hotel desk rings both coach's rooms, gets no response from either, and suggests the obvious. We head for the bar.

It's the Columbia's usual weekday crowd: bikers, unemployed loggers, and the small portion of the business community that still isn't convinced that eating croissants and drinking decaf cappuccino will make HQ executive asses taste sweeter when they have to kiss them. About half the Creston players are sitting over on one side with their coach, gulping down glasses of beer, watching the strippers, and wolfing down hamburgers. I don't see any Raiders in the bar, but their coach is sitting in a corner nursing a glass of Pepsi and poring through what look like computer printouts.

I walk over to his table while Gord sits down with the Cougars. "Hi," I say. "I'm Andy Bathgate."

He looks up at me, then nods. "Sure you are," he deadpans. "And I'm Punch Imlach."

A smartass. I drop the sheet with the draw on it, pull up a chair, and sit down anyway. "Don't see any of your players around."

He's not as dumb as the Creston coach. "They're upstairs," he says, "putting their heads together after last night. I figured they'd play better if they got the partying out of their systems before the games start."

"Makes sense to me. You clear about where your first game is, and when?"

He names the arena and time without looking at the draw sheet. "Somebody gave us a map when we checked in," he says. "We'll make it there okay. Who're we playing?"

"First come, first play, so you draw your pals over there." I point to the table of Creston players. "The big guy is just giving them the lowdown."

"He might have to stand a few of them up," the Raider coach laughs. "And then carry them out to the bus. They've been loading up pretty good."

I glance over at Gord, who is tapping his finger on the Creston coach's chest, no doubt explaining that it's time to get his players out of the bar and up to the arena. As I watch, Freddy Quaw wanders in and stands behind Gord like a giant exclamation mark.

"I think they're getting the word on that, too," I tell the Raider coach. "Should be a pretty easy opening draw for you guys."

He straightens in his chair. "I'm Joe Pisconti," he says, offering me his hand.

I reach over and grasp it. "Most people call me Weaver. But the last name really is Bathgate."

"Oh, right," he says, brightening for the first time. "A couple of my guys played with you years back. They were wondering if you'd show up. Nice to make your acquaintance. You coaching the Mantua team now?"

There's no malice in his voice, so I play it straight. "I'm still playing. Must be the climate around here. Works as a preservative."

"Pulp mills," he grins. "Don't they use some of those same chemicals to cure bacon?"

I grin back without answering. Across the room, with a tableful of beer glasses between them, I've spotted a pair of what look like uniformed bus drivers. One of them is the driver I glimpsed behind the wheel of the Chilliwack bus while they were unloading a few hours ago.

"Listen," I say to Joe Pisconti. "I'll catch you later. Got a small matter to take care of."

"Sure thing."

I amble over to the Creston table just as Gord concludes his lecture. He stands up and rolls his eyes. "These guys are three sheets," he grumbles. "Let's get out of here."

"Just a sec," I answer. "I need you to back me on something here. You too, Fred. Come with me. And look convincing."

They follow me over the bus driver's table and stand behind me as I sit down. The Chilliwack bus driver glances dully at me and reaches for his beer glass. I put my hand on top of it and lean forward.

"Let me make this very clear and simple for you," I say. "If I catch you within ten yards of another alcoholic beverage in the next few days, I'm personally going to rip off your scrotum and pull it over your head."

The man's eyes widen momentarily, then harden. "Oh yeah?" he sneers. "So who appointed you to the police commission? Who are you, anyway?"

"Never mind who I am," I say. "Have a close look at my two friends here."

He looks up at Gord and Freddy, who have their arms crossed and are glowering at him. "What about them?" he squeaks.

"Think about what they're going to do to you after I'm through."

"Geez, man," he whines. "Cut me some slack here. I'm just having a few beers."

"No slack," I answer. "No drinking until you've got that bus back to Chilliwack."

"You're serious?"

"Oh, I'm serious. Believe it. You stay dry this weekend. Now get the hell out of here, and stay out."

Both drivers scurry out, and Gord and Freddy sit down at their table while I glue myself back together. Gord understands what I just did, but Freddy is in the dark. "What's with you old guys, anyway?" he wants to know.

"Nothing you need to know about," Gord answers. "Weaver's just making sure history doesn't repeat itself."

Freddy looks up at the ceiling momentarily, and then he taps one of his big fingers on his forehead. "Oh, right. I heard what happened after that last tournament. What's that got to do with Weaver?"

"He was there," Gord says. "And he has a thing about drunk bus drivers."

Freddy is silent for a moment, still trying to fathom my weird behavior, but then he remembers why he's in the bar. "Oh yeah. Jack wants both of you over at the Coliseum."

"How come?" Gord asks.

"Well, a thirteenth team has shown up."

"What?"

"Yeah, no shit. A bunch of rock musicians from Vancouver called the D.O.A. Murder Squad, or something. In a great big rock tour bus with about two hundred colours painted on it. They're really something," he adds. "Wendel's down there with them."

"Didn't some team with a name like that try to enter the tournament?" Gord asks me.

"Yeah, I think so," I answer. "They called in about two weeks after everyone else, and Jack kind of blew them off."

THE D.O.A. MURDER SQUAD bus is parked in front of the Coliseum when we get there, and Freddy has underplayed the paint job. There's four hundred colours, from the look of it. But the Murder Squad itself isn't a joke. They're all musicians, sure, but if size is anything to go by they'd make a better showing than the Idaho Saints will, even if you pumped the Saints up with a couple gallons of steroids.

It takes us a while to sort out the story. D.O.A., in case you're not familiar with the term, means *Dead On Arrival*, but this particular D.O.A. is the name of a hardcore band famous enough that even I've heard of them. Seems they sponsor a team in the Vancouver Rec Leagues. A couple of the D.O.A. band members occasionally play on the team, too, although it isn't clear if they're here now.

Jack has already told them they can't play in the tournament, and they're being amazingly amiable about it. As far as they're concerned the whole trip is a lark, and they're prepared to watch a few games, hang out in the several bars that feature bands, play a few guest sets, and bite the heads off a few hundred weasels.

The only difficulty Jack's having is that Wendel has lost his mind over them. He's a D.O.A. fan, and he's acting like a nine-year-old at his first rock concert, wanting Jack to kick the Saints out of the tournament so the Murder Squad can play. Jack isn't having any of it, naturally, but he does pick up on Wendel's enthusiasm enough to friendly up with them, suggesting a couple of hotels the musicians might want to stay in (and wreck). He also offers them free passes for the games. "They should," he whispers to me, "liven things up."

I have to collar Wendel and drag him inside the Coliseum when it's time to prepare for the game.

THIRTY-THREE

IT'S A FEW MINUTES before seven PM when I step onto the ice
for the warm-up to the tournament's first game, us against
the Idaho Saints. The Coliseum is nearly full, and, for a few
minutes, rumbling with confusion: where are the Mohawks?
Once the crowd realizes that it's us in the green uniforms the
rumble changes to cheers, and when the cheers build it's clear
they like us, and maybe the uniforms and the name change even
more.

When the game starts at seven on the dot, Jack sends me out
to take the opening face-off. I'm not about to get a swelled head
over this even though my father and stepmother are at the game,
standing behind our bench with Esther and cheering louder than
anyone. The honour is ceremonial, because I'm no longer on the
team's first line. Over the weeks I've been out, first line honours
have evolved to Artie, Gord, and Freddy, with Wendel double-
shifting the second and third lines, playing with whoever Jack
throws out with him. Wendel will get his share of goals even if his
linemates are a pair of fence posts.

In this game I'll draw third line work centering Wendel and
hope I'll be more use to him than a fence post. But mostly I'm
going to sit. I haven't played full contact in nearly two months —

not that the Saints look interested in contact — and I don't have a clue what I've got. It might be nothing.

If I don't have anything, a game like this is the best I could ask for. When I watched the Saints come off their bus I suspected they wouldn't be able to beat us even if we were playing with broomsticks and wearing gumboots, and when Wendel scores while I'm trying to get off the ice my suspicion is confirmed. I've even got an assist to prove it. By the end of the first period the score is eight-nothing, and we haven't even been trying.

The crowd loves it, and none of us are exactly suicidal about playing a laugher. Except Gus. He takes the incompetence of his American compatriots personally. Just over ten minutes in, he scores a goal by flipping the puck high in the air, retrieving it himself inside the Saints blueline, and plunking it behind their goalie — but he doesn't celebrate. Instead, he skates past the Saints' bench and stops to jaw at their coach. I lean over the boards to catch what he's saying. The Saints' coach, it seems, had his players going door to door all day trying to convert the local heathens, and Gus is chewing him out for it.

"These sorry fucking specimens of yours are supposed to play hockey," he says loud enough for our bench to hear. "And you've had them out all day trying to bust these fine heathen folk around here with your silly Oral Roberts crap about sin and damnation. You think anyone around here cares about damnation? We're all fucking damned. Why else would we be living here?"

The coach doesn't have an answer, so Gus goes on to explain, in graphic detail, what's going to happen to his team if they keep playing hockey in the missionary position. To hear Gus talk, you'd have thought he was born in Mantua.

Larry Godin is refereeing, and he lets Gus blather on a while before threatening him with a delay-of-game penalty. Gus won't listen. He goes into another rant about arrogant Americans screwing Canada out of its birthright, which Godin decides is too far off the topic. Up goes Godin's arm, and when Gus *still* won't give it up, he lays a misconduct on him. Gus storms off to the dressing room to chill out, and I can hear him cursing all the way. After he's gone, though, the Saints take a little more interest in hockey, and we don't score on them for nearly five minutes.

During the intermission Jack gives us a little inspirational speech of his own — aimed mostly at Gus, who's still mumbling about missionaries and other disgraces to the US Constitution. Jack is being more practical. He just tells us he doesn't want us getting chicken blood on our new uniforms, and although he can't quite bring himself to say it out loud, he makes it clear he doesn't want any cruelty.

"This is going to be a long tournament, and not all of us are as young as we used to be," he concludes, tapping his cast and pointing at Gus, Gord, and me. "There's more than one team in this tournament capable of cleaning our clocks, so let's save the tough stuff for when it's needed."

His point is made, sort of, and we coast through the second and third periods as if it's a practice. For me it's exactly what I need. I play three or four shifts each period, just enough to test my timing and my sternum. Four assists tell me that my timing is at least in synch with Wendel's, and when, early in the third period, I have to dive over a Saint defenceman when he trips over his own skates, I hit the boards hard enough to give me the health clearance I want.

The "sort of" is Gus, who's still annoyed. He doesn't lecture the Saints again, but early in the third he can't keep himself from slamming one of their defencemen against the boards from behind. It's the only serious hit in the entire game, and it's so flagrant Godin tosses him.

The final score is fourteen to one, and it's over by nine-thirty. We rag the puck through most of the third period, and it would have been easy to shut them out. But as the third period begins I hear Jack lean over and tell Bobby Bell to let them score one so Junior's head will still fit inside his mask when the serious games start. Bobby isn't too subtle about it, either. He picks up the puck in the corner during one of the few times the Saints manage to get it inside our zone, sees one of them standing about ten feet in front of Junior, and lays it right on his stick. The kid looks surprised, but he knows what to do.

WENDEL, JAMES, AND I join the rest of the family in the stands to watch the Bears play Chilliwack. Well, I watch, anyway. Esther and Claire are swishing back and forth in the shorthand they've developed, alternately discussing dinner on Sunday — now a weekly event — and talking about the pair of breeding New-foundlands that're coming in a couple of weeks. Wendel, who is trying hard to hide how eager he is to get to the bar where several members of the Murder Squad are playing sets, is chatting up my father about some complication in the non-profit society they incorporated last week to enable the community scaling yard. They're pretty much birds of a feather, at least when it comes to politics and trees, which they agree are one and the same. I guess I shouldn't be surprised. Wendel had to inherit that super-serious side from somewhere, and he didn't get it from me or his mother. I can't get a word in edgewise with either conversation.

At least I have James to watch the game with — or I do until Gord stops by. He just happens to have the autopsy results on the bear, and I lose James to that in two seconds. I listen distract-edly as Gord relates the details, which aren't pleasant. The animal's tissue was so riddled with PCBs it should have been glowing in the dark. Someone — chances are we'll never know who — unloaded enough transformer oil in that equipment dump to contaminate it for a couple of hundred years.

I lean over to interrupt. "Fabulous. That means Mantua's now got it's very own Love Canal."

Gord doesn't blink. "Depends on how far into the water table the PCBs have penetrated," he says. "They'll be running tests out there most of next summer."

I tune them out, all of them, and try to watch the game, which is very good hockey but not much of a contest. The Bears, to a man, play as hard as I've seen in a couple of years, but they're outclassed and outgunned. The Lions are younger, faster, and better skilled.

During the intermission Wendel takes off for the bar, and Gord leaves with Jack to catch some sleep. They're going to need whatever sleep they can get, since they're more or less running the tournament.

James and I watch the second period with my father, whose new interest in hockey is more family loyalty than passion for the game, while Esther and Claire stroll around the Coliseum concourse arm-in-arm, talking up a storm. It's a curious organism, this family that's settled around me.

The easiest relationship to settle was the one with James, which is the one I would have predicted would be the hardest. But ever since I've gotten the taste for dealing the cards off the top of the deck whenever I see they're not marked, things like this are easier. With him, I simply told the truth.

About a week after the mauling, I sat him down and told him I didn't know I'd had a brother, and that I thought my father was dead. I left a few hesitations and blank spaces in the explanation for what I *don't* know, and for a couple of discretions he doesn't need to trouble himself with. He didn't need to live with what I thought I did all those years ago, or with what his father did fifteen years before he was born, so I skipped the part about the bus accident, and I didn't say I spent twenty-five years thinking my father was wandering around drunk or living in a detox. Being a kid with no discretion at all, he asked about my mother, and why she and Dad broke up, and I answered that I really wasn't sure except that they didn't get along. Like I said, there are some secrets that don't need to be revealed. My mother's grievances against his father aren't his responsibility.

He took it pretty well. He'd had a few days to think things over, and I got the impression he'd already forgiven me short and long: short for walking into the bear and getting myself treed, and long for, well, existing.

For sure, he took it differently than Wendel did when Esther finally told him I was his genetic father. Wendel exploded with laughter, yelled "Give me a break," and stomped out of the house. We didn't see him for three days, and when he arrived for dinner unannounced on the fourth day he didn't say a word about it. Still hasn't, either.

ESTHER AND I LEAVE after the second period, with the score five to one. I hear later that it ends that way, but if the puck hadn't been acting like it was playing for the Bears all night, the score might have been eighteen to one.

THIRTY-FOUR

T HE OTHER GAMES IN the first draw go roughly as expected, too. The Raiders thump Creston twelve to three. In the late games the Fort St. John team mows down the Terrace Flyers six-one, and, in the dead of the night, Hinton gets by Grande Prairie five to four and the Roosters put the boots to the poor Burns Lake team thirteen to four.

Despite the first-night partying, everybody makes it to our game against Hinton none too worse for wear except Stan Lagace, who Gord had to roust along with the Burns Lake Cowboys when he drove over to their motel at seven AM to make sure they'd show for their game. He found Stan passed out in the front seat of his car outside the Cowboy units. One of his cousins, it seems, is the Cowboys' goalie, and the two of them made a night of it.

Wendel and Freddy must have had a particularly good time at the bar, because all through the warm-up they've got a bad case of the giggles.

The Hinton Locomotives aren't the Idaho Saints, and we come off the ice after the first period tied at one, and sucking air because their defencemen are lining up along the blueline and thumping us when we try to carry the puck in. They aren't much on offence

— the goal they get is a looping fifty-footer that Junior boots — but they play decent hockey. I take a regular shift.

In the dressing room Jack tells us to dump-and-chase for the second to loosen up the blueline barricade. It works, and the score is five-one after another twenty minutes. I pick up two of the goals, without anyone laying a finger on me. Both times Wendel dumps the puck in, turns on the jets, and has it behind their net before they know what's hit them. He puts the puck on my stick as I'm arriving in the high slot, and I hit the upper right corner, stickside, both times. Speed isn't everything.

We've already heard that the Lions have taken the Raiders, but during the second-period intermission we get a surprising score from the other arena. It isn't that Creston has beaten the Cowboys in the eight AM game. It's that, early in the second period of the Okenoke/Saints game, the Saints are ahead three-one. It doesn't make any sense to me, but for some reason Wendel and Freddy think it's hilarious. And somehow, they don't seem to surprised.

"What the hell is going on up there?" I ask Wendel.

The question sends both of them into hysterics. "Don't ask," Wendel answers once he gets control of himself. "Really. You don't want to know."

When Jack tells me he wants me to cool my heels so I'll have something for the next game, I spend most of the period wondering what it is and why Wendel thinks it's so funny. Either the Bears found Jesus or they all decided to play the game with one arm tied behind their backs.

We cruise through the third, not taking chances and letting Junior get some business. Gus is the only one who won't let up, buzzing around the ice like a Tasmanian devil, getting successive penalties for boarding, slashing, and roughing.

Halfway through the period the Hinton captain, a big, amiable centre I played against years ago after he'd washed out of Junior A, skates by our bench and stops to chat.

"Hey, Weaver," he says, not very seriously. "Put a leash on your pit bull before I have to whack him over the head with something."

"We don't control him," I answer. "He's on remote from a ship in outer space."

"Well, bench the sucker, then."

"We don't want him on the bench when he gets like this," Bobby Bell says. "He chews on things."

The Hinton captain skates away, laughing. Nice guy, but just after the next face-off he decks Gus with a hip check in the neutral zone, and Gus hobbles off the ice cursing.

"Someone get that sonofabitch," he demands, slumping down on the bench beside me and rubbing his knee. "That was a deliberate attempt to injure."

Jack steps in behind him and pats him on the shoulder. "It was an attempt to educate," he says. "If he'd been trying to hurt you, you'd be lying face down on the ice right now."

Gus turns to complain more, sees that it isn't going to work, and relaxes. "Is this great hockey or what?" he asks no one in particular. "I *love* this game."

I give him a nudge. "Are you sure you're really a psychiatrist?"

He gives me a look that half-convinces me he's been giving himself electroshock treatments. He answers in his best Bronx accent. "I'm from New Yawk City. We're all escapees from the loony bin."

"Just like around here, then."

He shrugs. I'm not sure whether or not he's kidding.

WE WIN GUS'S GREAT hockey game six to three, which is no surprise. The surprise, ten minutes after the game ends, is when Wendel gets off the phone and tells us that the Idaho Saints have defeated Okenoke by the same score.

"Okay," I ask Wendel. "You want to tell me what you know about all this?"

"Know?" he answers, trying to appear puzzled, but losing it mid sentence. "What is it exactly that I'm supposed to know?"

"Well, what you two are finding so funny about the Bears losing to those goofy missionaries."

"Geez," he says. "You got us all wrong, here. Did somebody pass a regulation about not looking happy when we win?"

"No, but you didn't start the heavy chortling until you heard the other score. Don't give me the gears."

He motions me over to a corner where one of the visiting teams has stashed their equipment and plunks himself down on top of an equipment bag. "The Saints," he says, "uh, didn't make it to their game."

This makes sense. "Someone did. Who?"

"The Murder Squad," he answers.

I don't really want to know how this was engineered because I'm pretty sure Wendel was riding in the locomotive. I need to know just one thing.

"You want to tell me what became of our missionary brethren?"

"They're up at Ward's Lake, I think. In the community hall." Ward's Lake is a small fishing resort about sixty kilometres north of town.

"You *think* that's where they are? Where's their bus?"

"Oh," he says, "Their bus is at the other arena. Where it's supposed to be. The missionaries were, er, transported out to Ward's Lake and left in the hall. To hold prayer meetings. They were supplied with refreshments, and stuff."

Oh, oh. "Refreshments" is local code for grain alcohol, which, if you're not expecting it, can be successfully mixed with anything: Coke, ginger ale, lemonade, probably even hot chocolate. It's used around these parts for wedding stags or other occasions where you need someone drunk enough that you can paint them up and chain them to parking meters, truck bumpers, the front doors of City Hall, and any other location that'll make them look silly when they wake up.

"What else?"

"That's about it. Freddy told them a religious group up there wanted to meet with them for a midnight prayer jamboree. We dropped them off with the refreshments and told them we were off to pick up the group they were to meet with."

"You planning to retrieve them or anything?"

"Didn't think about that," he admits, his grin suddenly sheepish. "We just wanted to get the Murder Squad a game, that's all. I mean, they *did* drive all this way."

It's the first time in a long while I've seen Wendel without a contingency plan, and the first time he's *ever* acted like a goofy kid.

"I'll try to straighten things out with them. We'll probably have to refund their entry fee, and it's hard to say what the Bears will do when they find out they've been mugged by a bunch of pansy rock n' roll musicians."

"They know," Wendel says. "That was Blacky I was talking to on the blower. The Murder Squad wore their own jerseys for the third period. The Bears don't mind. It was a better game than they were expecting, and it isn't as if they're strangers to losing."

The Saints could make a major stink about this, but something tells me they won't. They'll get another game if they want it, and they can go home and tell their pastor they won a hockey game, which is something I'm pretty sure they haven't been able to do before unless they snuck into a Bantam tournament. That's confirmed half an hour later when the coach of the Saints shows up looking sheepish rather than righteous. I think he's decided that Mantua is too full of agents of the devil for his boys, and he just wants to get them out of town and back home. He doesn't even want a refund of the entry fee.

I get Gord on his cell phone, explain what's happened, and tell him to get Wendel to talk to the Murder Squad about continuing to play in place of the Saints. I don't think they'll have a problem with that.

THIRTY-FIVE

I'M BACK AT THE Coliseum to find that the Drillers have sent the hopeless Cowboys to the bar for good, and that the Roosters, in surprisingly good shape after whacking the Cowboys at three AM, have won their game.

Jack and Gord are standing at the entrance when I pull the Lincoln into my regular spot by the door. They're talking animatedly with someone wearing a black and grey jacket that looks like it belongs to the Hinton Locomotives. I've already let them know about the deal I've made with the Saints, and when I join them they're trying to sell it to the Locomotives' coach. He isn't too happy to hear his team will have to face a gang of crazy rock n' roll musicians who can play hockey instead of the skinny Bible-slappers they'd been expecting.

I've done enough negotiating with morons for one day, so I hang back and listen until it's clear that Gord and Jack are going to make their argument. Then I pull Gord aside while Jack finishes.

"Good news," he tells me. "We don't play until noon tomorrow."

I'd already figured this out, more or less, from listening in on their conversation. "Good thing. I'm a little wiped out. Anything else going on?"

Gord shrugs. "I talked to Blacky Silver. He was pretty decent about the game with the Murder Squad. I think he's already gone home, and so have most of the rest of the Bears."

"I don't think their hearts were really in this one."

"Yeah," Gord agrees. "Kind of a sorry situation, really. Good chance we'll never see a lot of those guys on the ice again. Oh. Before you disappear into Esther's lap for the evening, I want you to do a little pub crawl with me."

"Clear the chilluns out of the bar?"

"Something like that. Your kid is on his way to the Columbia. Those yo-yo musicians have really got him wound up."

It's my turn to shrug. "Wendel's pretty sensible about drinking. Did Esther get James home okay?"

"They hung around to watch part of the Roosters game, and then your dad picked him up, I think."

"I'd better call her and let her know I'll be late, and get her to call Claire about tomorrow's game. She's expecting me about now." I look over to Jack and see he's concluding negotiations. He's smiling, so things have come out as he wanted them to. I duck out and go to one of the payphones to call Esther. Maybe I'll collect Wendel from the bar and bring him home for a decent meal.

I'm thinking like a parent all around.

THE THREE OF US head to the Columbia. On the way over Jack seems preoccupied, even a little worried.

"Something bothering you, chum?" I ask.

"Something Mayfield said while I was browbeating him into accepting the game with the Murder Squad," he says after a moment's thought.

"What'd he say?"

"It was something one of his players overheard in the Columbia. About Wendel."

"Somebody probably shagged them with a story that he's rocket-boosted or something."

"No," Jack says. "This wasn't about the tournament. It was about your community scaling yard. Apparently there was some sort of union-industry pow-wow a couple of nights ago to try and stop it."

"What did you expect? If it flies, the yard's a major bucket of piss in their lap. But how did Wendel come into it?"

Gord interrupts. "I think you'd better pay attention to this. Some of those U.I. fallers who hang out down at the Columbia have decided Wendel's right up there with Karl Marx as the head of the Communist Menace."

"That's idiotic. There isn't a Communist Menace anymore."

"Well, half of them haven't ever read a newspaper, and the other half won't ever believe the commies are gone so long as there's even a Liberal party. They feel a threat to their pickup payments and start seeing commies in the woodpile. It's bred into them."

"Anyway," Jack continues, "A bunch of them were supposed go drinking in the Columbia tonight, and who knows what they'll do if Wendel shows up."

The parking lot behind the Columbia is full when we pull in, about half rusty pickups and the other half Harleys. The bar is packed to the rafters as we enter, and I notice a couple of bikers removing the stripper poles from the stage. No Wendel, so far.

I stop one of the waiters. "You seen Wendel Simons around here?"

"Not bloody likely," he answers, jerking his thumb in the direction of three or four crowded tables of beefy guys near the entrance. "And I hope he doesn't show up."

"What's happening on the stage?" Gord wants to know.

"Some guys from Vancouver are coming in to do an acoustic set. Real famous, I heard. Okay by me." He points to the back of the bar. "You'll probably want to take those boys with you when you go."

It's Bobby Bell and Dickie Pollard with somebody else who's face down on the table. It's no great deduction figuring out it's Stan.

I point them out to Gord, and he rumbles off to perform the roust. Meanwhile I've got to think fast. I'm betting big money Wendel is going to show up with the Murder Squad, and that's guaranteed trouble.

"You thinking what I'm thinking?" Jack wants to know.

"That Wendel is going to appear any second?"

He nods. "Let's just hope Freddy's with him. This could be ugly. We don't have a lot of friends in this bar."

I glance around the room. He's right, but I'm not frantic with regret about that, and neither is my liver. There's no time for any other regrets, because a roar goes up as five burly musicians enter through the front, each packing a guitar, trailed by an entourage led by Wendel. Freddy isn't with them, damn it.

Wendel isn't three steps inside before I hear a rumble from the yahoos by the door, and the scraping of chairs being pushed out of the way.

For a split second I experience the same sinking sensation I felt when I saw that bear coming over the hill toward me — another obligation to respond to, lousy tools to work with, and no time to think.

I calculate the trajectory of the loggers and block the path of their leader about midway across the floor. I'm staring into a set of bloodshot blue eyes without anything to say to them but "Stop." So I raise my arms in front of him and say it three times, loud as I can.

The leader recognizes me. "Get out of the fucking way, Bathgate," he says. "We don't have any beef with you."

"Wrong," I say. "I know what you're up to here."

"You don't know jack shit about nothing," someone behind the leader shouts.

"Wait a minute here," I answer, loud enough for all of them to hear. "I know I'm supplying the land for that scaling yard that's got you all wired up. And the kid you're planning to pound on happens to be my son."

"Okay, fine," a voice calls out. "We'll bust your ass too, fucker."

"Is that so?" I hear Gord say from behind me. "I'm this man's personal physician, so I guess you'll have to dance with me and my nurses here." I glance behind me and take in four of them counting Stan, who cancels himself out when he staggers backward and lands in the lap of a biker who's turned in his chair to watch the festivities. Wendel is on the stage helping the musicians set up, oblivious.

I turn back to the leader, and we make eye contact. If a brawl is in the offing, my best bet is to make him think I'm unafraid and wait for him to make the first move — and hope to hell he telegraphs it with his eyes. I keep my hands up in front of me, close to my body, partly because if I touch him he's going to drive me, and partly because it puts me in the best position to hit him first — and partly because I'm scared shitless and don't want to move.

I've been here before, but not for about ten years. Still, you never forget what a real fight is like. Not like the action movies, which make it look like the fighters are dancing acrobats, not animals out to wound one another. Hockey isn't much help here because when you're fighting on the ice your skates keep you from getting much leverage on a punch. A real fight is an ugly, graceless thing: a human fist slamming into flesh and bone makes the kind of sound you hear in butcher shops, not the canned whip-cracks they lay onto movie soundtracks. I don't want to hit another human being ever again, but ...

"Leave Simons alone," a menacing voice I don't recognize intones from behind me.

When I turn around to look there are fifteen or twenty bikers standing behind Gord, and some are big enough that he doesn't block the view.

"This isn't about you," the leader of the loggers says, sounding less sure of himself.

"Sure it is," one of the bikers answers. "The kid's okay. You want at him, you gotta take us first."

"He's a fucking commie," screams someone just behind the leader. "He wants to screw us out of our jobs."

The big biker is contemptuous. "Gimme a break. If you assholes were working you wouldn't be in here. You think Inter-Con's going to give you a job for whacking this guy, you're even stupider than you look. They're not giving anybody jobs anymore."

"Anyway, fuck you," another biker chimes in. "We wanna see Simons play in the tournament."

One of the loggers steps forward, but his aggression is gone. "If Simons and those other commies get what they want, we'll all end up tied to a team of horses, trying to cut down trees with a pair of scissors with one hand and holding a shovel in the other to scoop up the horse shit."

It's such a great line I laugh out loud. "Well, better that than parking your sorry asses in a permanent welfare lineup," one of the bikers snaps back. "Simons and his friends make more sense than those InterCon flacks who've been fucking with your heads — or the Forest Service. Or the IW-fucking-A."

If a brawl was going to happen, the crack about the union would have been the flash point. But the loggers are cowed. One of them yells out that the bikers wouldn't know what value-added industry looked like if it walked up and bit them on the ass, and what ensues is, I swear to God, a *technical* argument. When we collar Wendel they're still at it, flinging around ideas like Sustained Yield and Equivalent Community Value like they were born with them in their mouths. It's not quite the rebirth of civilization, but it's better than sitting in front of a television set listening to why we're going to get screwed no matter which way we turn, and a damned sight better than me and Wendel getting killed for our so-called communist ideas.

THIRTY-SIX

BEFORE WE LEAVE THE bar, Gord and I let the musicians know they've got a game at eleven o'clock. I know these guys are supposed to be a bunch of brick-headed drug addicts, but they're also amazingly organized. After a two-second conference one of them skips the set to round up the rest of the team, and the other four prepare to play the set they've promised. Wendel, who still isn't fully aware of how close he came to getting his skull bashed in, decides to hang around. I'd have preferred him to come with me, but with all the bikers around to keep things civil he can do what he likes. They'll no doubt escort him and the musicians to the Coliseum for the game, and anyway, by that time the loggers will be too shitfaced to punch their way out of a green garbage bag. Or maybe they'll go to the game. Anything's possible.

We send off Bobby and Dickie to scour the other bars — and to park Stan somewhere where he won't be stepped on — while I drop off Gord and Jack at the Coliseum before heading up Cranberry Ridge.

Esther has ordered Chinese food, and it arrives just as I'm getting out of the shower. I haven't eaten since breakfast, which means Bozo will get about half her normal ration of chow mein. Jack has parked Fang with us for the tournament, and Bozo's too occupied with the little pest to care that I'm taking food out of her mouth. In fact, she parks herself beneath my chair and dozes off while I'm eating, hoping I'll keep Fang off her for a few minutes.

"What's wrong with her?"

Esther laughs. "She's exhausted from walking around the house with that silly little mutt hanging from her collar. I love the little monkey but I'm glad we don't own him."

I look down and see Fang chewing on one of Bozo's ears. Reaching down, I push him away. He growls at me possessively.

When I look up again, Esther is eyeing me with a calculating expression on her face. "How tired are you?" she wants to know.

"Surprisingly alert. You want to go down there and watch those musicians play hockey, don't you?"

"I wouldn't mind. I've been hearing so much about them I've gotten curious."

"About which parts?"

"Don't be silly," she says, giggling like a teenager. "I'm old enough to be their mother. Besides, I want to watch them play hockey, not go partying with them afterward."

I'm as curious as she is, so we watch the local news on television. — Most of it feeds from the networks, including the sports, which is ninety percent NHL video and financial reportage on this year's baseball spring training holdouts and ten percent about the tournament. It's lazy and depressing coverage, but it's what you'd expect from a small station owned by a conglomerate. And I'm in too good a mood to be depressed about anything short of all-out nuclear war.

THE BLOCK OF SEATS reserved for the tournament players are good ones, right behind the visitor's bench. I spot one or two players from the tournament teams, but most are filled with Wendel's new biker friends. Considering that it's close to midnight and the game is being played between two out-of-town teams, it's a big crowd — and a noisy one. Then I remember that one of the teams on the ice has made themselves into local heroes by playing music in every bar in the city the last two days.

Esther and I locate a couple of empty seats three rows above the players' bench, and settle in to watch. I have to admit that the Murder Squad are a pretty fabulous looking bunch in their white-on-black LA Kings-based uniforms with a huge skull and crossbones for a crest.

"Look at that, Andy," she says. "Every damned one of them is using the number 13."

It is funny, but I don't get to enjoy the joke for long. Seconds later the puck flies into the crowd and Mayfield, whose team is occupying the visitors' bench for the game, spots me in the crowd and motions me and the ref over for a conference. Neither Jack or Gord are at the game, so he decides to appoint me commissioner in charge of complaints. He doesn't think the number 13 gag is funny in the least.

"Look at these assholes, Bathgate," he shouts. "They're all wearing the same number. It constitutes an unfair advantage. Isn't there some rule about this?"

"What's the advantage?" I ask. "You don't know these guys from breakfast anyway."

He keeps on whining that it's unfair, that his players can't tell who's who. He's right, sort of, but there's nothing I can do about it.

"Okay," I say, finally. "You want me to have them pin pieces of paper on their backs telling you what they like in bed or what instrument they play or something? Make a real request here."

Mayfield glares at me sullenly. "Well, do something."

Esther is close enough to hear most of this, and she's rolling around in her seat laughing.

"Look," I tell him. "The big ones are the guitarists, the skinny ones are probably drummers, and they're all perverts. Is that good enough? Now play your game and stop whining at me."

Mayfield shakes his head in disgust and turns back to the ref. "Forget the whole thing," he says to no one in particular.

When I sit down, Esther is still laughing.

"What's so funny?" I ask.

She chokes out an answer. "Men," she says. "You get around a rulebook and it turns you into ninnies."

We leave at the end of the second period with the score tied four-four. The Murder Squad are the bigger and slightly better of the two teams, but they keep taking stupid penalties — more for what look like practical jokes than for anything nasty, and it costs them. On two of the ensuing power plays, the Drillers score.

Before I leave, I give Wendel and five or six other players who're sitting with him strict instructions not to go drinking after the game. I don't have much faith that they'll pay any attention to me — least of all Stan, even though he's sitting there with the same bucket he kept between his knees through this afternoon's game. He looks at me bleary-eyed and wants to know who appointed me his father.

"You just do what you're told or I'll turn you in to the cops," I tell him. "You and your girlfriend there. You asked her to marry you yet?"

Stan starts to say something, then either forgets what it is or thinks better of it. It's my job to tell them what they ought to do, but I suppose it's their job to ignore me. I just hope we don't have to play the Murder Squad next if they win this game.

But when we go home and I fall asleep instantly, I don't have nightmares about playing the Murder Squad, nor do I dream about pissed-off loggers or bears dripping PCBs from their jaws. I dream about cruising through centre ice with the puck on my stick. On my left side, darting toward the blueline, is Mikey Davidson.

ESTHER AND I ARE back at the Coliseum by noon, coming in just as the game between Chilliwack and the Roosters is ending, which the Lions win four to two. Of course the Murder Squad won their game last night, and of course we're playing them this afternoon. In the three AM game the Drillers got a team that wasn't quite as easy as the Cowboys, but they beat them five to two anyway. That leaves six teams in the tournament: we're undefeated, and so is Chilliwack, while the Saints/Murder Squad, the Drillers, the Battleford Raiders, and the Roosters are two-and-one.

The Roosters are using our dressing room, and there's something almost sweet about the exchanges between our players and the Ratsloffs as they troop in. Those of us who arrived early enough to watch the last part of the game talk about good plays they'd seen the Roosters make. Even Junior gets in on it, consoling Lenny Nakamoto even though he's scared silly of him. The rest of us imply, casually but somehow sincerely, that the Roosters lost the game because of bad bounces and bad luck, not because they were playing against a better team.

It's true and not true. The Lions were the better team and everyone knows it. But the Roosters weren't outclassed. Between two teams like this, a couple of pucks bouncing one way or another can always change the results. Anyway, we're extending a courtesy to them, not undermining the whole of human reality, and the Roosters return the courtesy through their body English as they move amongst us, subtly trying not to infect us with their bad luck.

It's weird, and sort of impressive. These men aren't quite the Ratsloffs who've been pounding on us all these years, but that isn't what impresses me. It's a reminder that for all the competitive crap and violence in the world — and in this hockey league over the years — decency is kind of, what's the word? Ubiquitous.

One thing's for sure. This tournament is more civilized than the ones I played here twenty years ago. The boozing is less frantic, the games more skillful and less nasty. Or maybe what I'm mistaking for a small advance in civilization is the shortening of my own self-centred radius. Until everyone's gone home, and we get the damage reports from the hotels and motels they're staying in, the jury's out on all of it.

On us, meanwhile — the Lumbermen and the NSHL — judge, jury, and executioner have come in. While we're suiting up, Don Young, Sr. crashes the dressing room waving the Saturday paper. On the lower half of page one, it has the announcement of an agreement to move Victoria's Major Junior franchise to Mantua for next season.

"Lemme see that," Bobby Bell says, grabbing the newspaper.

Nearly everyone, including the remaining Roosters, crowds around him to read over his shoulder, but I don't need to. Neither do Jack or Gord. Jack catches my eye and shrugs: Snell's timing is impeccable. It's about what you'd expect from a guy who has his nose stuck that deep in the crack of the corporate sector's ass. They've probably promised to install a gin pipeline to his office at City Hall.

Bobby, meanwhile, has finished reading, and tosses the newspaper in the air. "Someone ought to fit Snell with a pair of D9 treads for ankle bracelets and see if he can swim across the river to InterCon's office."

It's an interesting suggestion. Bobby looks at the three of us for confirmation, and the lights come on. "You knew this was going to happen, didn't you?" he says.

"There were rumours," Gord confirms. "We were hoping it might be the year after next."

"So," Dickie wants to know, "what does this mean for us?"

"Put two and two together," Freddy answers for us. "You can handle that."

"Never mind that silly shit," Jack tells them, then spends ten minutes explaining the density and extent of the shit for them without commenting on its lousy odour. "Anyway," he concludes, "a lot of things can happen before next fall. We've got a game to play in fifteen minutes, so let's concentrate on that. These musicians aren't going to be pushovers."

That isn't all Jack has to say. He continues with a rah-rah speech while we finish getting ready, one that's so good it even has me convinced that the tournament is the centre of the universe. As I'm heading out to the ice, he stops me. "You take it easy out there," he warns. "We may have to play a second game before the day's out."

I'VE UNDERESTIMATED WENDEL. FROM the first face-off he's flying, and I let myself be swept up in his turbulence like a piper cub in the jetstream of an F-18. I play more with that than I play against the Murder Squad, letting it create open ice for me, and for my right winger, Lanny Becker, even though he's too dumb to see it.

But there's a problem. By mid period it's apparent we've got just one defenceman with a full deck. That's Gus, whose deck isn't exactly the standard one to begin with. Bobby Bell, Dickie, and Gus's partner Pat Horricks are still wrecked from last night, or dazzled by the Murder Squad's fame, or, most likely, both. Whatever it is, they're running around in our end whenever the Murder Squad is on the attack, and they're hanging back when we're in their zone. We're going to have to win this one with our forwards.

Artie is on his game, and he scores one goal and sets Freddy up for another without Freddy really catching on until it's too late to do anything but put it in the net. Not that Freddy appears to be under the weather. He's up to something all his own. He's teasing one of the Murder Squad's defencemen, a scrawny little guy I assume must be one of the drummers. It's definitely teasing, but to the crowd it looks like Freddy is trying to kill him. At least five times he lines the drummer up and crunches him against the boards. Only we can see how careful Freddy is. He keeps his elbows down, and makes sure the drummer is right against the boards when he hits him so that the boards absorb the force, not the drummer. It isn't long before it gets to the little guy. After the fifth or sixth hit, he loses it and jumps Freddy from behind. What Freddy does next gets both benches laughing: he skates around the ice with the little drummer draped around his shoulders. Eventually the linesman drags the drummer off and escorts him to the penalty box.

I go out with Wendel and Gord for the powerplay, win the face-off, and push the puck to Gord, who drills it around the boards behind the Murder Squad's net. Wendel picks it up on his wing and carries it behind the net, drawing three players with him. He stops on a dime, ties all three of them up, and throws the puck into the slot as I arrive there to put it away. Two shifts later, I intercept a clearing pass in exactly the same spot and find myself with another clear lane to the net, and I ring it in off the inside crossbar.

We go into the dressing room ahead five-four, with Junior cursing a blue streak at the lousy protection he's getting. Number 13 scores all four of the Murder Squad's goals. None of our defencemen have any answers, except maybe Gus, who's played his sanest and cleanest period in weeks. We're ahead, and no one is too worried that we'll lose this game.

Artie scores another beautiful goal early in the second, and after that the game slows down and our defencemen clean up their act a little. Jack has two forwards staying back and keeping the Murder Squad from getting anything together between the bluelines. The game isn't penalty-free, but there's no malice on either side, and no one loses his mind except the little drummer boy, who Freddy keeps crunching against the boards like he was trying to turn him into an accordion.

He's picked the right guy to torment. The drummer is evidently their designated goon, crazy as it sounds, and he goons it up on every shift they let him out for — which isn't too many once they catch on to what Freddy's game is. I'm having trouble figuring out how the Murder Squad makes decisions. There's no coach behind the bench, and no one else seems to be in charge.

I give the problem to James, but he can't solve it either, except to detect that about every three shifts they end up with seven players on the ice. What the hell. I already knew democracy is a flawed system, and with a two-goal advantage we can live with a few political transgressions.

Between the second and third periods, Stan begs Jack to let him play a few minutes. He's pretty green around the gills from the last two days, but after Wendel and Freddy score on successive shifts to give us a ten-to-six lead around the ten-minute mark, Jack puts him on the ice. Stan lets in two goals and drops his cookies into the back of the net after each one, but putting him in is the right thing, except maybe for Alpo and the cleanup crews.

I leave the dressing room without bothering anyone with more of my parental advice, and Esther drives me home, stashes me in bed, and joins me. I doze off in her arms and sleep like a baby while the Raiders turf the Drillers from the tournament nine to one. That's the score Jack gives me when he calls at seven PM to tell me I'm supposed to be on the ice in exactly one hour to play the Roosters.

"Brilliant," I answer. "I take it you've set us up for two games in eight hours to prove that we're manly men."

"I did it because so far we've had the best draw in the tournament," he snaps. "And because if I didn't we'd be making the Raiders play consecutive games."

I apologize, hang up, and drag my sleep-sodden bones out of bed and away from Esther's warmth.

THIRTY-SEVEN

I'M LAST ONTO THE ice for the pre-game warm-up, but not because I'm late getting to the Coliseum. On the drive down, the all-too-familiar tightness in my lower back tells me I'm closer to forty-five than twenty-five. I listen, and stay in the dressing room to stretch the muscles.

Through most of this tournament I've been first man on the ice, or near to it. And no, I'm not a born-again keener. The pre-game skate has been my chance to size up the skaters on the opposite side of centre. But that's hardly necessary here. I've seen the Roosters so often in the last seven years I practically know their dick sizes.

The good news is that most us don't appear to have gone to the bars after the game with the Murder Squad the way I thought they would. Gord tells me a few took naps, and the rest hung around the Coliseum to watch the game between Battleford and the Drillers.

The exception is Stan, who slipped his collar and trotted after his heroes. As he suits up, it's plain to me he's still pissed out of his lips. When he veers into a doorjamb on the way out for the warm-up and nearly knocks himself cold, everyone else gets it too. It's funny, but if anything happens to Junior during the game we're in trouble.

I'm not alone in the dressing room while I stretch. Gus stays behind, but he isn't there to keep me company. He clears the equipment from a corner of the room, parks his noggin on an old seat cushion he's found, lifts himself into a headstand against the wall — skates and all — and begins to moo like a pregnant cow.

He holds both the posture and the mooing for close to three minutes. When he comes down, his face — and his bald head — most resembles a huge beet. He shakes himself like a dog, lets fly with a blood-curdling scream, then picks up his gloves and stick and heads for the passageway to the ice.

"Stress management," he stops to explain on his way by. "Learned it from some Tibetans while I was in medical school."

"Sure thing," I answer. He's gone by the time I realize why he was doing it. He's petrified of the Roosters.

GUS HAS HIS FEARS under control by opening face-off. Through the first period he's a model of concentration, determined, efficient, and deathly silent. He unloads the puck quickly each time he gets it, quickly but accurately, and without a trace of panic. Few Roosters get close enough to try to whack him, and when one of the twins goes out of his way to throw an elbow, he telegraphs it and Gus is long gone when the elbow arrives.

The Roosters are game, but it's our game they're playing, not theirs. From the first whistle they're back on their heels, reacting. Jack is sending the wingers deep to pressure their defencemen, who respond by trying to move the puck through centre. About four minutes into the game Artie picks off a pass just inside their blueline, dekes Lenny, and scores. JoMo is playing pretty sedately while Artie's line is on the ice, and so is the big cousin they've flown in from Medicine Hat for the tournament. But when my line is on, both of them are beating the crap out of Lanny, and they're doing the same to the third line even while Wendel's double-shifting.

It makes no difference, and it isn't a defence against motion. Chris McBride scores a rare goal for us with a wrist shot on a puck he intercepts in the slot, and Freddy, seconds before the buzzer, puts both the puck and JoMo past Lenny in a goalmouth scramble.

Through the second Jack reverses tactics, sending the centres deep and holding the wingers back so they can obstruct the neutral zone. I take a regular shift as I did in the first period, but this is much harder work. I spend much of the period behind the Roosters' net dodging their attempts to splatter me on the boards. I'm a little battered as the period winds down, but I've managed to put the puck onto Wendel's stick often enough that he scores twice.

Artie scores his second goal of the game on an end-to-end rush that begins behind our net, circles theirs twice, and has everyone's jaw down around their knees by the time the puck plunks down behind Lenny. It's the prettiest goal I've seen in a long time, and as Artie skates to the bench I see Alpo standing on top of the Zamboni jumping up and down and screeching his brains out.

I lean over to Artie after he settles on the bench and point at the Zamboni. "Didn't think I'd ever see that," I say.

Artie grins. "Yeah," he agrees. "It's kind of weird, ain't it. The old guy's come around. Elsa and I have been staying with him the last couple of weekends. He's still the same miserable old shithead he's always been. But he's my miserable old shithead."

WE GO BACK TO the dressing room up six-one. The game is closer than the score, but it's ours now, and Jack's main strategy for the rest of it is to head off a brawl. He stops short of suggesting we give up a couple of goals — and thus put the Roosters back in the game — but I can tell it's in the back of his mind.

Personally, I don't see a brawl happening. If they can't win the tournament, the Roosters would prefer to see us win, and I figure there's enough functioning brain cells on their bench to put the brakes on their other instincts for once. Then I remember that a couple of months ago these same Roosters came within a hair of burning Okenoke, and wonder if I'm kidding myself.

If a brawl starts, it won't be Gus who starts it. As Jack finishes his pep talk, Gus gets to his feet and bangs his stick loudly against one of the lockers.

"Listen up, you guys," he says. "Be cool out there. I've never won anything in my life, and I goddamned well want us to win this game and this tournament. Anyone who starts goofing around out there is going to find me in their face. So keep your lips buttoned and don't take chances." For a moment he looks as if he's finished, but he's not. "If you see any of those animals trying to injure Artie or Wendel or the Old Guy here" — he points his stick at me — "feel free to take their heads off right around the kneecaps."

On our way back to the ice for the third, I tap him on the shoulder.

"Thanks for the compliment, asshole. You really know how to tune up a guy's ego."

He grins but doesn't turn his head. "No slur intended," he answers. "If you want your ego returned to its original inflated condition, come see me in my office next week. This is hockey, not therapy."

THE ONLY ONE ON the bench who doesn't heed Gus's advice is James. He starts in on JoMo with his sharp, high-pitched needle the moment the period starts, and jabs it into him mercilessly whenever he's on the ice. JoMo ignores him for a while, but when James rams it in up to the hilt after JoMo carries the puck over our blueline offside, JoMo skates over and flicks the puck toward him.

I lunge across the bench at it, but I'm too far away. Stan, who's had his bucket between his legs through the first two periods and has looked as if he's in a coma, calmly reaches across and picks the puck from the air an inch in front of James's face.

JoMo doesn't get away with the stunt, either. Freddy decks him before he can take two steps, cracking the face shield he's been wearing since Gord broke his nose. I look over to the Roosters' bench and see Old Man Ratsloff yanking players back off the ice. The ref sends both of them to the penalty box, JoMo for unsportsmanlike conduct and Freddy for roughing, and the moment passes.

I motion James over. "Stuff a cork in it," I say. "You heard what Gus said."

James does what he's told, at least until the Roosters score a couple of quick goals. When they let JoMo out of the penalty box I notice Old Man Ratsloff chewing him out, and JoMo doesn't make it out on the ice for the rest of the game.

The final score is seven to three, and we clamber over the boards to shake hands with the Roosters. Even the one year we made it to the league finals nothing like this happened. But tonight things are different. There's respect between these two teams now, and a certain amount of regret — although no one is willing to own up to the latter.

"Next year," Neil Ratsloff says to me as we're shaking hands.

"For sure," I answer. "Come on up this summer and I'll take you fishing." I don't have the slightest idea where that one came from, and from the look on his face, neither does Neil.

"You serious about that?" he asks.

"Offer's genuine. Just don't push me out of the boat, that's all."

"Well," he says, "I might just take you up on it." He skates away with a dumbfounded smile on his face.

I DON'T RECOGNIZE HOW dog-tired I am until we're in the dressing room, and I can't seem to muster the energy to take my skates off.

So I sit there, gazing happily around the room like I'm senile, until Esther appears and takes charge.

"You're coming with me," she says. "For a back massage and a good night's sleep."

There's no point arguing with her, although I'm tempted to when I catch Wendel mimicking her behind her back, the smart-ass. She's probably right, anyway. I may have felt like a twenty-five-year-old this morning, but I'm feeling my age now, and then some. We could have two games tomorrow, possibly three, if the Lions win tonight. Given that they've already beaten the Raiders back in the opening round, odds are they'll win this one. That'll leave two undefeated teams, and in a double knockout tournament, that means a best-of-three final.

THERE'S AN UNSEASONABLY WARM breeze blowing across Cranberry Ridge when we arrive home. The same breeze has been blowing for three days now, and it's melted the last of the snow in town and much of what's left up where we are. But until this moment I haven't acknowledged that there's been any world beyond the tournament, and so I've missed three sunny spring days the breezes have brought with them. Spring is still a month off, but whatever this is, it isn't winter.

"I think," I say to Esther as I'm unlocking the front door, "I'll take the dogs out for a ramble."

"Mind if I join you?"

I don't mind, and the dogs don't either. Bozo has already gotten used to walking with Claire and Esther, who have taken to long Saturday walks so they can discuss their schemes without my father and I teasing them. Fang, of course, is being himself: boing, boing, boing. I pull both pairs of gumboots from the closet along with the replaced Maglite, and off the four of us go.

The cycle of the moon is close to full, but the orb is still low in the sky, leaving the skies to the stars and the hydrocarbon haze from downtown. The faint band of the Milky Way over us reminds us, if we want the perspective, that an infinity of hockey tournaments are being played out there, together with an infinity of everything else.

The dogs range ahead of us, Bozo leading sedately with her still-tender hip, Fang bounding around her like a spotted yo-yo. Esther and I walk beside the ribbon of unmelted snow from my winter snowshoe trail, silent as the dogs but holding hands, drinking in the familiar redolence of mud and last fall's fermenting poplar leaves. It's one of those annual perfumes that life smears across your sensorium around here, and it took me a long time to decipher the message. Life, it suggests, doesn't start anew each year. It percolates and composts everything that came before, and out of *that* comes the rebirth.

"Andy, where are the dogs?" As always, Esther is in the real world.

I play the Maglite's powerful beam across the landscape until it finds them at the edge of a thicket of Russian willow. They're motionless — Bozo with her nose to the earth, Fang alert, one paw lifted from the ground. Curious, I widen the flashlight's sweep and find a pair of coyotes not more than forty metres from them, equally alert. The coyotes seem uncertain, and it's hard to say what they think they're on to. Their noses are telling them that it's domesticated dogs, but their eyes are telling them they've got a black bear hanging out with a rabbit or a rat.

Startled, I flick off the beam. Now that I know they're there, I have enough light to follow them without the beam. Or so I think. I'm expecting the coyotes to slink off now that they know we've seen them, but either they're habituated to human presence or hunger is making them bold. For a brief moment I lose sight of them, and when I flick on the Maglite it's just in time to see them closing in on the dogs. Before Bozo senses they're around, the lead coyote darts past her and picks up Fang by the scruff of his neck and disappears into the willow thicket.

There's an outburst of snarls and yelps, followed by a high-pitched scream of pain. Fang trots out of the thicket and into the beam of the Maglite with his eyes glowing red and his mouth clogged with coyote fur. A Jack Russell terrier, the coyote has learned, is no bunny rabbit. Bozo lopes over to greet him, and then follows him as he canters proudly to us to be congratulated.

It happened too quickly for either of us to be frightened for Fang's safety, and he's unharmed except for a small cut at the back of his neck where the coyote picked him up. He'll need a rabies shot as a precaution, and probably something stronger to deflate his canine ego.

We walk on for another half kilometre before turning back, and this time the dogs, at Esther's insistence, stay closer to us. It's a good thing. The long winter is giving up its gruesome treasures, and not all are as pleasant as the perfume of mud and poplar leaves. Fang finds a dead badger by the trail, and is just about to roll himself in its decaying gore when Esther grabs him. She has to carry him half the way home before he forgets about the badger and tries to lick her face.

We're almost at the door when the coyotes start howling, no doubt telling and retelling the legend of the terrible spotted rabbit that looked like a rat, hung out with a bear, and fought like a wolverine.

They're still telling the story as sleep closes in on me, joined by a raven as their colour commentator, and my alpha waves tune in on the conversation and ride it.

THIRTY-EIGHT

T HE TELEPHONE IS JANGLING, and I reach across Esther to pick
up the receiver.

"What is it now?" I demand irritably. I'm pretty sure it isn't the
Queen calling at this hour, so I don't care who I snap at.

It's Jack, and he's all business.

"How's the backside this fine morning?"

"Gord's my doctor. You're supposed to be my accountant. And
I can answer a phone, so it must be okay." I check the window,
and he's telling the truth about it being a fine morning. "Your dog
tangled with a couple of coyotes last night."

"I hope the coyotes are okay," he answers, unconcerned. "Listen. I'd like you down here in about an hour."

I check my watch. It's already ten. "How'd it go last night?"

"Chilliwack won."

"Oh, shit. So we have to play them at least twice today?"

"Well, maybe not. I got a call from them this morning suggesting we might want to make it a single game, winner take all."

Esther's awake, staring at me with her eyebrows lifted. "Jack?"
she asks softly.

I nod, and lean over to kiss her. She grimaces and turns away.
"Your breath smells like you ate that dead badger from last night."

"I did," I answer. "Snuck out after you were asleep."

Jack interrupts me. "Pay attention," he hollers in my ear. "Are you still in bed?"

I confess that I am. "Get your butt out of there and meet us in the Alexander Mackenzie at eleven," he says, and hangs up before I can whine.

I'M FIFTEEN MINUTES LATE, and never mind why. I've got Esther's cell phone in my coat pocket so I can call her with the game times.

A single-game final would be a piece of luck, if we can swing it. I'm not sure why Jack didn't just say yes to the offer, because it's to our advantage. The Lions are younger than we are, and probably better conditioned. If we end up playing three games, they'll toast us.

When I wander into the coffee bar and see most of my teammates there, I understand why he didn't accept the offer outright. Jack's a democrat at heart, and he wants everybody there for a team decision. I sit down, order coffee, and listen.

Typically, the younger players would like the whole set of games. They want to win the tournament, but they also want to play as much hockey as they can. It's a tougher decision than I thought. Gus makes the point that given Snell's announcement yesterday these may be our last games as a team, and maybe we should play as many as we can.

Gord answers that one. "I don't believe we should think that way," he says. "And if we want the team to have a fighting chance next year, we ought to do our damnedest to make it hard for Snell to boot our asses out of the Coliseum. If we win this tournament," he adds, "it'll make him think twice. So which way do we have the best chance?"

It's almost a rhetorical question, and he emphasizes this by lifting his left knee onto the table — or rather by trying to, and failing. I can see from Wendel's expression that he's rounding the corner on this one.

"What do you say, Weaver?" he asks.

"I'll play as many games as we need to," I say, and leave the sentence hanging.

Wendel finishes it for me. "But you think we'd have a better shot in a one-game final."

"I didn't say that."

Wendel persists. "But you're thinking it."

"Okay."

"Good enough for me," he says.

Jack sees a couple of the Lions enter, including their coach, and he motions them over. "We clear on this?" he asks us.

It's unanimous, and I breathe a sigh of relief. Wendel sits down beside me. "So," he says, teasing, "my poppa's a putz, is he?" Before I can answer, he drops it. "Where's Mom?"

"She'll come down for the game. As soon as I phone her and let her know when it starts."

I watch as the Chilliwack coach sits down a few tables away to yak with Jack and Gord. I haven't had a close look at him until now, and I realize he's Neil DeBerk's younger brother Dave. He must be in his late thirties now, but the last time I saw him he was a nasty kid playing Junior B hockey and trying to hang around with his older brother and his friends. Me, in other words.

Wendel and I talk for a few minutes, and when he decides to head over to the Coliseum I join Jack and the Chilliwack contingent. I'm introduced, and listen quietly as the deal for a one-game final is settled. Their motive, it turns out, is simple expedience: most of their players have to be at work on Monday morning, and a three-game final might not get them home in time.

With the deal concluded, Dave DeBerk turns his attention to me. "Don't I know you from someplace?" he asks.

I shrug, feeling suddenly weary again.

"Just a move you made — the way you used the big guy as your screen in the second period against Camelot. The only other guy I ever saw do it that way used to play with my older brother before he died in an accident years back. Mind you, this kid had a different set of wheels on him. One hell of a player, but messed up."

Gord gives me a cutting look, then stares out the window. And there it is again, one of those strands that has been dangling down the middle of my life for two decades, now resolved in my favour, even though I didn't stop what happened and will never completely forgive myself. So do I reach out here and pull this one in with the others in front of this man? It won't help Dave DeBerk to know that a man who watched his brother die is sitting across from him or that until two days ago I thought I was guilty of killing him. Esther knows. Gord knows. My father knows. Someday I'll tell my brother and my son the story, but not this year.

So no. I'll remain a stranger to DeBerk. To reveal myself would be imposing my own need for symmetry, and, like most private needs, it'd be cruel and selfish. It's enough that I'm freed of it. It's taken years for those families to heal from the losses of their brothers and sons. If I stepped out of my place in their scar tissue, all I'd do is tear open the old wounds. A totally symmetrical life is a life without others in it, and a life without kindness or real love. A real life has loose ends.

So the four of us, Dave DeBerk, me, and my two closest friends sit around making the smallest of small talk, until it's time to get ready to play hockey. Almost as if the past had never been.

ON THE WAY OUT I punch the digits of our number into the cell phone and let Esther know we're playing at one-thirty. "It's one game," I add.

"Well, that's a relief," she says. "What was the meeting about, then?"

"Jack did the right thing. He let all of us decide." I feel a childish need to see her. "Can you come down to the dressing room before the game? I want ..."

I can't quite explain what I want.

She cuts me off. "I'll see you about one," she says.

BY THE TIME SHE arrives, I'm suited up and the need is gone, swallowed up by the dressing room's intensity, by the sheer crazy normality of what we're trying to do — win a stupid hockey game in a stupid tournament at the far end of a kind of hockey that's as doomed as the dinosaurs. She comes into the dressing room, sits down beside me, and talks to Gord about some social event next week. More normality. When it's time to go she tells me to be careful on the ice, and I give her a peck on the cheek. Then she pats my new helmet and I stomp away from her down the hallway as if I'm really going someplace important.

As I line up for my first face-off, I realize that I don't much care if we win this game — at least, not for myself. It isn't that I'm tired. I'm not. In every other sense, I'm ready to play. It's just that I'm more interested in playing in the game than in winning it.

By halfway thorough the first period, I've learned something else: we may not win. The Lions are the best team we've faced. Man for man they're faster than we are, they're younger, and they bang hard enough in the first few minutes to let us know that they want this game as badly as we do.

Their best two players are forwards, and one of them is Paul Davidson, Mikey's nephew. He has everything you can ask for — speed, puck sense, and an unpredictability you can't buy. He makes me wonder why he isn't in the NHL, because his skills are close to Wendel's. The other good one is the centre on his line. He's a tall, rawboned kid who doesn't have great wheels, but he's powerful and intelligent. Their defencemen are smaller than ours, but more mobile. We come off the ice after twenty minutes huffing and puffing, without either team scoring a goal.

A couple of minutes into the second, I catch Paul Davidson carrying the puck along our blueline with his head down. He's looking for his centre, who's snaking in along the far boards and heading for the net, and he's completely vulnerable. I have a split second to decide: I can hit him with a clean check, and quite likely put him out of the game. Or I can dodge him and let him get by me to make the pass, in which case they'll likely score. I do neither. He sees me at the last second, and as his head comes up I step to one side. As he's going by me, off balance, I bring my shoulder down and clip him with it so that he loses his balance and the puck, and slides along the ice toward the far boards.

The ref sees a trip that isn't there, and whistles me to the penalty box. It's a bad call, but he isn't about to reverse it because I whine, so I skate over to the open door and step in. Davidson skates past the box, spins around, and stops.

"Thanks," he says. "You could have creamed me there."

"You're welcome," I answer back. "Keep your head up if you want to keep it on your shoulders. Next time I won't be so nice."

He nods, and skates away. Nice kid, which probably explains why he didn't make it to the NHL.

Thirty seconds later the nice kid crosses the blueline, catches Gus on his heels, puts the puck between his legs and picks it up behind him, and flips it past Junior. It's the first time in the tournament we've been behind.

Jack doesn't say much during the intermission, except to instruct Gord and Freddy to crash the net more so Artie can get some skating room, and to tell Wendel to use his speed to the outside more. He knows rah-rahs aren't going to help us, and if we get too wired up they're likely to screw up our heads. This is a game that'll be settled by skill and by the breaks, not with any Knute Rockne nonsense.

As we're gathering our equipment to head back to the ice to finish it, I bang my stick against a locker. "Okay, you guys. Let's win this one for the Gimp."

James is standing behind me. "Oh yeah?" he wants to know. "Which one of you guys is the Gimp?"

I see Stan, who's fully sober for the first time in a couple of days, scratching his head. "Isn't it supposed to be 'The Gipper' we win it for? And what the hell is a gipper, anyway?"

Everyone hits the ice laughing.

WE HAVEN'T HAD THE tempo of this game down, maybe because it's too tight and tense to have a tempo. But as the period reaches the five-minute mark Jack shortens the lines, and we begin to pick it up. Maybe it's Gord and Freddy crashing the net, but the Chilliwack defencemen begin to back in, and the openings appear, small at first, then larger. Artie ties it eight minutes in with a high stickside wrist shot the goalie doesn't see because he's got five hundred and fifty pounds' worth of green monsters obstructing his view.

On my next shift I lose another face-off, but Paul Davidson gets careless and banks the puck off the boards toward our zone — and right to Gus a step inside our blueline. I see the play in the same instant Gus does, and so does Wendel, who heads down right side. Gus steps over our blueline, hits me with the pass at theirs, and I'm behind their forwards with just a single defenceman to beat. I know where Wendel is going to be without having to look, and I know he's in the clear because I hear the defenceman who's in position move for me and I can feel the other one chopping at my forearms with his stick.

I put the puck on my left skate, reach back, and yank the defenceman's stick out of his grip. Then, before he can wrap his arms around me, I flip the puck to Wendel with my forehand. In one move he puts it in the short side, and we're ahead two to one.

The Lions start running around in their own zone, and we pour it on. With five minutes left we're up four-one. Gord scores both goals without touching the puck with his stick. Artie, I swear, deliberately banks both shots off his behind.

"Christ," I say to Gord when there's just a couple of minutes left and Jack sends out the third line, "we're about to win a hockey tournament for this crummy town."

He gives me his best meathead grin. "Yeah. Life can really surprise a guy sometimes, can't it?"

Maybe it's because I may never play a serious game of hockey again in my life, but I want back onto the ice. I want to be out there when it ends.

Jack sees the two of us talking, and, for the last minute, puts us on the ice together with Wendel on the right side. We get ourselves crossed up and the Lions score a second goal, but that doesn't matter.

Nor does it matter that I lose my last face-off. Wendel picks up the puck behind our net, flies down the ice without anyone touching him, and gets the goal back. I don't make it as far as centre ice before he puts it in the net, but that doesn't matter either. I'm cruising, watching my son, watching the sun set.

THE FINAL BUZZER SOUNDS, and it's over. Mantua has won its own tournament for the first time, and I'm going to have my photograph in the lobby a third time — even if it's only for a couple of years until the new arena is built, and the Memorial Coliseum is torn down, and the photographs land up in somebody's basement, and what we did continues to exist only in the diminishing republic of human memory. Screw all that. This moment belongs to us, and we skate around the ice like we've won the Stanley Cup.

Is it bittersweet? Not at all. Jack set up the referees to select the tournament all-stars, but he hasn't thought to get anyone to present the tournament trophy. He wasn't about to let that shithead Snell take the honour — or more likely, being an habitual pessimist, he thought he'd be presenting it to someone else. While Larry Godin calls the tournament all-stars down — most of them are already on the ice — Jack spots Greg Friesen, the manager of the television station, and scrambles over to talk him into making the presentation. It's an out-of-measure payment for the lousy coverage his station gave us, but at least he's wearing a suit and can speak an English sentence or two without garbling it.

The refs have selected Wendel, Artie, and a big right winger from the Raiders to the first team, together with a slick youngster from Hinton and one of the guitarists from the Murder Squad on defence. The Chilliwack goalie, whose name I never do get a bead on, is the first team goalie.

Junior is the second team goalie, JoMo Ratsloff makes second team defence — there was probably a death threat involved — and Gus is the other defenceman. Paul Davidson is the second team left wing together with his centre, and Freddy is the right winger.

They aren't bad choices, not far from mine, except maybe I'd have put Dickie Pollard on instead of Gus or JoMo. Gus'll look better in the photo, so I guess that's okay. Jack's already taken care of the important thing. This time the photographs are going to be black and white, so the future can't turn us lime green.

Friesen gives a short speech to the rapidly thinning crowd and hands over the trophy, which Gus promptly grabs out of Gord's hands and won't give it back, skating around the ice with it and performing credible imitations of Serge Savard's spin-o-rama move whenever anyone tries to take it from him. And eventually, because we can't stay out on the ice and be heroes forever, we skate over to the gate and, one by one, leave the ice.

Someone pops the corks on a couple of bottles of cheap champagne and sprays them around, but the television crew has already packed it up and, without them around, no one is very interested in acting like jackasses. It occurs to me that if we could get rid of all the television cameras in the world there'd be a lot fewer jackasses to put up with.

A few guys shower — mostly those who've had the champagne squirted over their heads. Others don't, including me. Esther comes in after a discreet interval, smiling. It's really her I want more than a shower. I'm already in my street clothes, bundling my equipment into my locker. I plunk the helmet she bought me on a hook inside, close the door, and reach for her hand. "Let's go home, babe. I'm about done with this."

"No you're not," she says. "Your father and Claire are outside. They're taking us out for dinner."

"What about Wendel?"

"Him, too, of course. Gord is invited, and Jack, if he's got the time."

She's right. I'm not done, and we're not done. Spring is coming, I've got a family to take me out to dinner, and there are things to do, things to be. They're going to be new things, different, and difficult, some of them. Maybe the only thing I'm done with is hockey.

Who am I kidding? Maybe I'll coach a Midget team next fall, maybe teach them — and their parents — not to be jerks. There's a challenge, if ever I've seen one.

Hard to say what the rest of us will do. Go on living, I guess. I catch Wendel's eye as I'm pondering this. He grins back, but says nothing. Wendel could do anything from here. Go back and play in the NHL, or stay here and work the claims he's staked, grow old, and maybe drop a tree on his head someday if there are any left big enough to give him more than a slight headache. But whatever he does, he'll do it with his family around him.

Christ, it's got me biting my lip thinking about all this stuff. Yeah, I can now imagine a future, and I can imagine it without getting frightened or sentimental. Let the liars tell their lies, let the fools pump up their megaproject paradise. In the end, every damned one of them will collapse, not because the ground beneath us is unstable the way Cranberry Ridge is, but because the future is here, among the things we can renew and rethink and rescue from the rubble and waste we've already made. Let the young play their games. That's their right, their job, and their burden. I've got the rest of a life to work on.

THIRTY-NINE

THAT'S THE STORY OF the last Mantua Cup tournament and the story of my life, as much of it as I know. Other people might tell it differently, I guess, but that would make it another story, someone else's. There's just one more thing I want to add.

The wedding will be in May. The only thing we haven't figured out is what James and Wendel are going to be doing during the ceremony. I keep teasing Wendel that he ought to be the ring bearer, wear a velvet suit with short pants. I know James would like to be the best man, but that job has to go to Gord because he is, you'll agree, *the best man*. The others — there will be lots of them — will be ushers, I guess, and ush people. And there will be a hush over everything and everyone as I slip the ring onto Esther's slim, strong fingers, because the world, for once, will be as it ought to be, and as it is.